FIT
for a
KING

P. Sharee

Life Changing Books in conjunction with Power Play Media Published by Life Changing Books P.O. Box 423 Brandywine, MD 20613

Library of Congress Cataloging-in-Publication Data;
www.lifechangingbooks.net

13 Digit: 9781943174003

Twitter: www.twitter.com/lcbooks
Facebook: Life Changing Books/lcbooks
Instagram: Lcbooks
Pinterest: Life Changing Books

ACKNOWLEDGMENTS

I'll keep this short and sweet; you kinda have to when your circle is small. I want to thank God for blessing me with such a wonderful opportunity to pursue my dreams! Thanks to my loving mother who has always kept it "real" in every sense of the word. Mama, you truly are fierce and my best friend. I couldn't have asked for a better person to raise me! Thank you to my father who I know is resting in heaven and smiling down on his baby girl and who encouraged me to always do my best.

To all my family and loved ones who supported me through this incredible journey, you know who you are. Thanks to my brother Robert and my sister Ericka; I love you and thanks for stepping up when I needed you the most! Desie, thank you for believing in me and holding my hand through it all, love you. Thanks to my good friend Iesha for encouraging me to submit my work for the first time and listening to all my crazy ideas during the revision process. You're the best and an excellent test reader!

To my honorary sisters, my favorite cousins and fellow 'Wolf Pac" members Uniqka and Latrice, thank you for believing in me and supporting Team P. Sharee! Calvin a.k.a. "My Fave", thank you for letting me bounce ideas off of you and just being in my corner every step of the way, love you! To my loving grandmothers Faye and Margaret, you are two of the strongest and kindest women I know, thank you for being you.

A special thanks to LCB and my amazing publisher, Azarel, for taking a chance on me, for believing in my project and me as an author. I am so thankful for the help and guidance that you've given me. Virginia, thank you for all your support and assistance with this project and for helping bring ideas out of me that I didn't know were there!

Last, but certainly not least, thank you to the two most precious gifts one could ask for; Jaidyn and Isaiah. Mommy loves you more than you could ever imagine and every move I make is with the two of you in mind. I love you more than anything in this world.

DEDICATION

This novel is dedicated to my daddy, Jerry L. Harris, the true definition of a KING…

Veronica-1

One year ago…

I was in my bedroom unpacking my suitcase. My weekend in Houston went really well. My sister Traci and I reconnected after almost twelve years from when we were in foster homes back in Missouri. She was just as pretty as I'd remembered; milk chocolate skin identical to mine; slanted eyes, and cheekbones like our mother's. Traci had made a life for herself in Texas and seemed to be doing well. We had had such a good time; I almost didn't want to return to Atlanta where I'd resided since I graduated high school.

My return was bittersweet. I was glad to be home in a way, but was still shaken by the news that the strip club I'd been working at was raided and my man was sitting in the county jail. Most of the dancers were arrested too, but ended up getting released after extensive interrogations. I considered myself lucky that I dodged a bullet, but I knew others wouldn't see it that way and I knew that wouldn't be the end.

On my way from the airport that day I received a call from Chico telling me that he made bail and would see me at home.

As I placed the last pair of underwear back in my dresser drawer, I heard a loud banging on the front door. When I rushed through the living room and looked through the peephole, Chico was staring at me from the other side.

"Baby, why didn't you just use your key?" I asked him as I turned the lock.

"I lost it," he lied, coming inside and slamming the door behind him, causing a picture of us that hung along the wall to fall to the floor and shatter immediately. I looked into his eyes and was sure of two things. One, he was beyond angry, and two, he stopped to get his cocaine fix before he came home to me.

Without warning, he wrapped his heavy hands around my neck and choked me, banging my head up against the door.

"Bitch, you set me up, huh?"

"I…I…" I attempted to speak but couldn't find my words.

"I know you did! You set me up and made sure you was outta town when the mu'fuckas came through my spot!" he roared, strangling my neck. I almost blacked out from the loss of breath. Once he realized I was close to unconsciousness, he released me enough to draw the first punch to my face. I fell to the hardwood floor, which gave him the opportunity to kick me in the stomach and ribs.

"After everything that I've done for you! Bitch, you ain't shit; I know you set me up and I know you was fuckin' around on me while you was gone too, wasn't you?" he shouted, allowing his insecurities to rear their ugly head. He paused his kicks to wipe his nose that had started to run, a result of the cocaine use. When I got up on my knees in an attempt to fight back for the first time, he became angrier and started hitting me with his large fists again like I was a nigga on the street, blacking both of my eyes and doing more damage to my ribs as the kicks got sharper.

My insides burned severely from the pain, I felt like that was it for me, and that was how I would die. That wasn't enough for Chico though; he had to leave a mark. He dragged me by my legs from the trashed living room back into our bedroom and then flung me on our bed. I was too weak to try and escape his grasp, let alone scream, and I knew if I did that would only make things worse so I just laid there while he ripped off my shorts and underwear, then forced himself inside of me. The discomfort was too much to bear, as his thrusts were sharp and fast like a razor blade. The silent tears that streamed down my face stung like fire

2

into my cuts and scrapes as he pounded into me repeatedly.

When he finished, he zipped up his pants and said, "Clean all this shit up, I'll be back," and then left the apartment.

Not even 48 hours later, Chico was arrested again for DWI and with all of his pending charges from the raid; he was facing eight years in prison. I wasn't sure what it was that made Chico think that I was his enemy after all we had been through; but even behind bars he was determined to get the message to me that things were far from over.

A few nights after he had been booked, I got a phone call from an unknown number. My first instinct was to ignore it but then convinced myself it could've been important so I answered.

"Hello?"

"Hello?" a female's voice answered. "Is this Veronica?" she asked.

"Yes, this is her, who's calling?" I asked, turning on my professional voice.

"So you can't answer the phone for me huh, Nica?" a familiar yet not-so pleasant voice shouted through the phone. I knew who it was right away by the nickname that he'd chosen to use.

"Ch…Chico… what…?" I said but he wouldn't let me get a word in.

"Yo, you dirty as hell for that shit you did, you know that, right?"

"I don't know what-" I began but he wouldn't let me get a word in edgewise.

"You know exactly what the fuck I'm talking about, bitch! The streets is talking and I know for a fact you set me up witcho police-ass. On my soul you betta pray I don't get outta this mu'fucka cuz when I do, I'm at yo head bit-," he yelled into the phone and before he could finish calling me a bitch I ended the call.

He was pissed and still convinced that I was the one behind the scenes, slowly trying to ruin him. Just the sound of his angry voice gave me goose bumps, and even though I knew he was locked up, the fear he had put in me years ago told me that I

3

needed to watch my back…and my front.

Though he was locked up and was looking at some serious time, Chico was well plugged in the streets of Atlanta and all he would have to do is make a phone call and I would be a distant memory with a snap of a finger. I had no family other than my sister who was all the way in Texas, hadn't seen my mother since I was a child, and my father had been killed in prison. I was alone, and being alone not to mention being scared for your life, was a dangerous combination.

Veronica-2

It was just my luck that the police had frozen any assets of Chico's, which left me penny-less other than my possessions and whatever cash I had. I stopped stripping per Chico's request or demand was more like it once we started living together. In turn he funded everything and I was given an allowance and access to his account, which was the one that was frozen.

My savings that I earned prior to our relationship was placed into a secure interest-baring account that I couldn't touch except if it was an absolute hardship. I'd assumed 'Abusive-Boyfriend-That-Had-Everything-In-His-Name' didn't count as a hardship to the bankers at Wells Fargo.

I sold almost everything of value in the apartment and moved into a tiny studio in Union City. The only thing that Chico had left me with was the seed that he planted in me the night he fucked me against my will. The cash that I stashed was spent on terminating that pregnancy.

After I began to mentally recover from the mess that was my life, I went to the bank with the excuse that I had lost my job and needed money to enroll back in school. I told myself that I needed to do something with my life and living in Atlanta as an ex-stripper wasn't the "something" that I was referring to.

My request was granted and after I proved to them that I

was accepted back into Morris Brown for the fall semester to finish my Bachelor's degree in Business; I felt like I was getting things back on track. It turned out that if I studied hard and took a full load of classes, I could finish by the end of spring and graduate. The only person that I remained in contact with from my former place of employment was a girl named Frankie who went by the stage name "Luscious". The girl Yvette that helped me get the job was a good friend at first, but she grew ill feelings as she watched me become one of the highest paid dancers at Libido.

Frankie called me one afternoon as I was leaving the Morris Brown campus headed back to Union City.

"Whasup Chick, long time no hear!" she screeched through the phone, her raspy voice extra chipper.

"I know right, what's been up with you?"

"Girl, not too much, just working. What's been up with you? Ever since Chico got locked up, it's like yo ass fell off the face of the earth," she joked.

"Girl, I been doing me for a change. I got back in school and just been focusing on that."

"Oh yea, that's good Roni. I know you never wanted to drop out of school."

"Yea, Morris Brown let me back in so I'm gonna take this and run with it, hopefully finish next spring."

"I'm proud of you, that's good."

"Thanks. What you got goin' on?"

"I actually called you with a proposition," she said, attempting to turn on the charm.

"Uh oh, I knew yo ass was up to something Frankie, what is it?" I asked, hitting the remote to my pearl white BMW that I was holding onto for dear life. That was the one possession that Chico paid for in full and was the only thing that was actually in my name.

"Well, you know I been working at Emerald City Gentleman's Club since all that shit blew up, right?"

"Yea, I remember you telling me that," I said, tossing my purse and backpack to the passenger seat, and then sticking the key in the ignition.

"Well, Saturday night there is a private VIP party and the owner asked me to find a girl that could dance and wanted to make some money."

"Frankie, you know I don't dance anymore," I reminded her and shaking my head as I put the car in reverse.

"I know Roni, but this is a one and done, I promise. One night, one party. You the best dancer I know other than me, and I know you could use the money."

"Actually, I'm doing alright," I lied, sort of. My rent was paid up through the end of my lease and so was my tuition, but that was it. I had gone through my entire savings and was holding on to my car before I ended up selling it.

"It pays $1000 plus whatever tips you make," she said. There was dead silence on the line. "Hello? Roni?" she said into the phone.

"Text me the address," I said and ended the call there.

All week I prepared myself to get back on stage and drop it like it was hot one last time. I stepped up my daily workout and broke in my six-inch heels around my apartment. By the time Friday night came I was ready, at least I thought I was.

I parked in the Emerald City Gentleman's Club rear parking lot and Frankie was outside smoking a blunt with one of the other dancers waiting for me.

"Roni!" she said, beckoning for me. I was wearing neon orange and white Adidas tennis shoes, grey leggings, my North Face jacket and my weave was up in a bun on top of my head. I clutched my Nike gym bag on my shoulder with sweaty palms as I walked to where she stood.

"Hey, girl," I said, stretching to give her a hug. Frankie was taller than the average woman, about five-foot-eight to be more precise. I was more on the average size, five-foot-five exactly. She introduced me to her friend Towanda a.k.a "Misty" and referred to me as one of my old aliases, "Raven".

"Come on, let me show you the dressing room. Here, Wanda," she said passing what was now a 'roach' of blunt to her friend before she linked arms with me and led me into the back door of the club. We went inside where the music was booming and she led me downstairs to the basement. Inside the space was huge. Half of the room was set-up like a gym and equipped with several treadmills, elliptical, weights and even a punching bag. The other half was a dressing area complete with ten vanities and huge lights that surrounded each one and clothing racks everywhere.

There were about six other dancers already down there getting ready, none that I recognized which was a probably a good thing.

"Everybody this is my home girl Roni, she gon' dance wit' us tonight so treat her right," Frankie's raspy voice said filling the room. Most of the faces were pleasant and smiling, a couple of them waved their hands towards us while they put on their faces. I smiled and waved to everybody and followed Frankie to where I could sit my down things.

"What outfits did you bring?" she asked, plopping down on a stool and motioning for me to sit next to her. I opened my gym bag and pulled out the outfits that I had, a few of them still brand new that I hadn't worn because of Chico's abrupt decision for me to stop dancing.

"I like this one," Frankie said, holding up a metallic halter bra that was only enough to cover my nipples, a matching thong, and six inch heels that tied up my legs to my upper calf.

"Yea me, too," I said.

"You should definitely wear that one tonight," one of the other dancers chimed in across from us. Frankie nodded and looked through the rest of what I brought. She chose a fuchsia see through bra and skirt for me to wear for the lap dance portion of the evening.

The housemother, Ms. B came down the steps with a tray of shot glasses, limes, salt, and a fifth of Patron to help the dancers mellow out. When I first started stripping, I also turned into a heavy drinker and had to be in a certain zone before I got naked for a room full of strangers. When I stopped dancing, I put down the bottle too, so my tolerance was significantly low and seeing that tequila reminded me of that. After my first shot, I had two more and I was beginning to loosen up and get a little more comfortable. I slipped into the fuchsia outfit that Frankie insisted I wear and used her curling wand on my weave. The heavy curls fell down to the middle of my back and once my stilettos were on I looked flawless.

"Is everybody ready?" a tall, slim, chocolate man asked when he reached the bottom of the stairs.

"Don't we look ready?" The dancer named Shay asked.

"Yea, Chuck, you say the same shit every night. We ain't new to this shit, we true to this," Towanda said.

"Well, make me know it then Goddamit. Let's go," Chuck shouted with a clap of his hands.

Everyone filed up the stairs, and Frankie and I were the last to approach Chuck.

"This is my friend I was telling you about," she said, looking up at him.

"Pleasure to meet you darlin'," he said looking me up and down, taking my hand and making me twirl around a little for him. When we were face to face again he kissed my hand and winked at me. "Don't break no hearts out there tonight."

"I'll try not to," I smiled shyly and he released my hand. Frankie walked ahead of me and Chuck watched my ass as I walked past him up the stairs.

"Goddamn!" he said shivering and then following behind us.

Before we walked past the curtain, Frankie stopped in her tracks.

"Here," she said, handing me a shimmering pink eye mask that was almost the same color as my costume.

"What's this for?"

"The theme is supposed to be 'your biggest fantasy' or some shit like that. It's better this way, especially for you. None of these bastards will see your face," she grinned. I took the mask from her hands and put it over my head and positioned it. "You ready?" she asked.

"I think so," I said nervously.

"Let's get this money," she said and then we walked past the curtains.

The room wasn't as dark as it usually was in most strip

9

clubs, the lights were yellow and brighter and we could see the face of every man in the room. The song that was playing was "Yonce" by Beyonce and the killer beat had all of the walls vibrating. I tried to escape all the thoughts that were in my head, and let the music take over my body. I started swaying my hips as I walked around the room. I didn't make it too far before a white guy grabbed my hand and wanted a dance. "This is easy," I thought. He had no rhythm whatsoever and I just shook my ass on his lap, then grinded against his small, yet growing erection. He peeled off a few twenties and tucked them on the sides of my skirt.

When I looked up, I saw my wing-woman Frankie with her leg lifted and shaking in front of his buddy over in a nearby corner. She gave me a knowing grin and then got back to what she was doing.

As the song transitioned, I gave my guy a little wave and met back up with Frankie and we scoped out the room. She found herself another contender quick, I on the other hand continued to look until a guy dressed in all black, seated in the very back on a red velvet love seat in the shape of lips, motioned for me to come over to where he was. I strutted his way, my hips calling him subtly with each step.

When I made it to where he was, I stood in front of him, his legs were slightly spread and he was wearing a seductive grin. Before I made my next move, he put his hand up to stop me and then stood, his tall frame towering over me even in my six-inch heels. Next he took my hand and led me past the rest of the guest and into "The Champagne Room", where anything goes. I swallowed hard as we walked inside and winced eternally at what I saw underneath the red lights. Bottle service was going, fifths of Goose, Patron, Dusse, and Rose was all over. Girls kissing girls, someone getting head in the corner, and one guy had a dancer completely naked while she twerked on the floor in front of him as he tipped her with one dollar bills.

That was something I wasn't prepared for. Not only was "The Champagne Room" $500 a pop to get in, but men expected certain things when they went in that room, things that I wasn't accustomed to doing. When I closed my eyes for a second, I felt my patron take me to the next level and I let the lyrics to the song seep into my head.

"Bandza'make her dance, bandza'make her dance. All them chicks popping pussy I'm just poppin bandz."

"What you want from me?" I asked over the music as I started to shake my ass a little.

"I'm thirsty," he said in my ear and then grinned down at me. I bit my lip but didn't respond as I looked at him.

"Sit down," he demanded.

"Why?"

"Just sit down," he told me and I rolled my eyes and plopped down on the black and white leather couch with no arms. I saw him reach for the unopened bottle of Dusse, then opened it with skilled swift fingers. "Now, lay back," he told me, more authority in his tone that time. I sighed and did as I was told. I felt him down at the other end of the couch where my legs were, then he took the bottle and carefully poured some of the slightly chilled alcohol into my navel. With the bottle still in his hand, he licked from where my skirt began up to my belly-ring and navel were, then slipped his warm tongue inside and slurped up all the cognac all while never taking his eyes off of mine.

"Damn, that was good," he said with a playful, sexy smile.

"I thought I was supposed to be dancing for you."

"Oh you will, I just had to get that out the way," he informed me as he sat up. "Now, how bad do you want these?" he teased, pulling out what looked two hundred ones from his deep pockets.

"As bad as you wanna give 'em to me," I said with confidence this time, once I was standing in front of him again. I knew this one wouldn't be a cakewalk like the white guy before him, but I liked a challenge.

I started off slow and squatted down in front of him, my hands on each of his knees and rubbing his thighs that felt toned and muscular under the thin material that were his pants. I grinded low on the ground, teasing him a little. He watched me carefully with serious eyes, but didn't react. His caramel skin glowed under the red lights above us and he licked his full pink lips at me. I knew I had to do something to blow his mind so he'd give all those ones to me. I rose slowly from the floor and then carefully placed a steady foot on the love seat one at a time so that I was standing over him, his face staring at my pussy that was covered in the tiny skirt that I had on. I shook in his face and dropped down a couple times, never eye contact with him.

Before he knew what hit him, I had turned around, had my knees on the love seat, my ass in his face, and my heels were locked at the back of his neck, pulling his head forward and shaking my ass at the same time. I did it fast but kept it in sync with the beat on 2 Chainz verse, so all he could do was embrace it. As I moved, I could feel his teeth playfully nip at my ass cheeks while I threw it in a circle and he loved every minute of it. I knew I had won.

When I finally stood, he took the entire stack of crispy ones and handed them to me.

"Thanks," I smiled moving a stray hair away from my face.

"Oh, I'm not done with you," he said, biting his bottom lip with hunger in his stare. My pulse quickened and I turned around and walked away.

I disappeared back downstairs after that dance to put up what I had earned so far and it was almost two hundred dollars for two songs. I guess stripping was like riding a bike because I definitely still had the chops to make some money.

As the night progressed, mystery man number two had monopolized my evening completely. He requested me personally and only wanted dances from me. Chuck was more than willing to accommodate him because he was probably a regular and obviously a big spender.

When it came time for the actual stage performances, I bid my admirer a farewell and went back downstairs to get ready. Towanda danced on stage first to some song that I didn't know but was apparently popular in the strip clubs lately.

Then Shay danced and then the one they called Baby Doll did her thing to "Get this Money" by Jamie Foxx, one of my signature songs.

When Frankie was up, she popped, shook, and twerked her

ass off to "Dance for you" by Beyonce.

On my turn, my nerves were returning and I had to take another shot of Patron before I could go out on stage.

Before the beat dropped for my song, the lights went out and the club went pitch black. When the song came on, the spot light shined on me and the rest of the lights in the club were red on everyone else. Bruno Mars song "Gorilla" blazed through the sound system and I did my own rendition of what the stripper in the video did when she danced to that song, wearing a silver mask that time. On the part when he sang "And what I got for you, I promise it's a killer. You'll be banging on my chest BANG! BANG! Gorilla!" I slid down the pole upside down just as the dancer did in video then pulled my legs down and twirled around the pole.

Dollar bills were thrown on the stage and I even saw some fives, and a couple twenties. Once I released the pole, I grinded on it from behind as I unfastened my metallic bra that only covered my nipples then tossed it behind me and shimmied my breasts for the crowd. I heard tons of whistles and cheers and more money was thrown on the stage, no one dollar bills; just tens and twenties.

I played with my breasts a little before I climbed the pole again and on the part right before the second chorus, I landed in a split, so naturally, the crowd really lost it.

For the bridge I had my back to the audience showing nothing but the metallic G-string I was wearing. When Bruno broke it down and the guitars blazed, I removed the G-string and bent over while shaking my ass. Between my legs, I saw my admirer at the edge of the stage and he was making it rain on me. Money was flying everywhere on the stage and I smiled at him before I climbed the pole again for my finale.

When my dance was over, the room went pitch black again and when the lights came back on all my money was bagged up and I was in a robe and back downstairs in the basement being congratulated by all of the dancers.

"Excellent show ladies, excellent show," Chuck said, clapping his hands as he walked downed the steps. "You all were phenomenal," he told us. He chatted briefly with each girl, eventually making his way down to me and Frankie.

"And you, young lady, did exceptionally well. I want you to come and work here for me. I'll match whatever they're paying you, wherever you're working."

"Oh, I don't dance anymore," I said, looking at his reflection in the mirror as I removed the makeup from my face.

"I think you should strongly reconsider baby, it's a lot of money to be made. I take very good care of my girls, ask Frankie," he assured me.

"I did the dancing thing before, Chuck and I have to admit the money was good. But I don't want this life anymore. I appreciate your offer, but tonight was a one and done for me. Thank you anyway," I said with a smile and continued to wipe off my make-up.

Frankie tried her hand at trying to convince me after Chuck disappeared and I reiterated the same thing to her. She wouldn't have been herself if she didn't try, and I loved her for that. I was done stripping. It had taken me to a place in my life that I never wanted and I had to leave it behind me before I got sucked back in. It was almost like a drug, you got addicted to the money and the glam that came along with it. Living in Atlanta and being a dancer allowed me to see all kinds of celebrities and Emerald City Gentleman's Club was far more prestigious in the strip world than Libido could ever have been.

"Thanks for coming tonight, it was good to see you, girl," she said, hugging me as we stood outside in front of my car.

"You're welcome," I replied.

"You sure you don't wanna hang with us tonight? We getting ready to go to Waffle House in a lil bit."

"Nah, I need to get home. I got homework and everything this weekend."

"Okay. You take care of yourself and don't be a stranger," she grinned down at me.

"I won't."

"And let me know if you change yo mind," she said and winked at me, then turned on her heels to go back inside of the building.

FIT *for a* KING– *P. Sharee*

I laughed and turned around once she was out of sight so I could put my bag in the trunk. Just as I reached up to close the trunk, I saw a black Mercedes Benz slither in my direction. The car stopped right behind me and the dark tinted window of the passenger's door rolled down slowly.

"You callin' it a night already?" a deep voice asked. I squinted slightly and saw that it was my little admirer from the private party in the driver's seat. I giggled to myself and said, "I am."

"Awww don't say that, especially since I finally get to see that pretty face that you been hiding behind that mask all night. Have a drink with me?"

"Um, I don't think so; I have a busy weekend ahead of me," I exaggerated. I really only had a couple homework assignments and a four page paper that all could be done in a half day.

"One drink won't interfere with your plans, I promise," he said, a promising grin on his face, displaying his pearly white smile. I had to admit it was hard to resist, it had been a while since I enjoyed the company of a man.

"Do you make a habit out of asking out women that you met in the strip club? Because I gotta say it's a little creepy," I joked and he threw his head back in a hearty laugh.

"Nah, I don't but you're not just any woman…and I told you I wasn't done wit you tonight."

"You did, and that's not creepy at all by the way," I smiled.

"Look, I'm not a creep, I swear. I came to Atlanta to handle some business and it was one of my buddies' birthday tonight so I told him I would come through," he said with honest eyes.

"Mmhm, and you came through and monopolized a dancer for yourself, huh?" I reminded him.

"I liked what I saw, and still do. You know we could discuss all of this over that drink," he told me.

"You just don't give up, do you?" I asked.

"Not when I see something I want," he said still wearing his sexy grin.

"Ugh. Fine," I said with reluctance in my tone. "Follow

me," I told him and walked around to the driver's side of my car and climbed in. I put the car in drive and sped out of the parking lot and the mystery man followed.

Veronica-3

The stranger and I settled at a low-key bar, off in the cut, up the road about five minutes away from my apartment. It was one of ATL's many after hour spots and the parking lot was half full

When I climbed out of the driver's seat, blues music escaped the little pub and leaked out into the parking lot. My mystery man got out of his wet-black Benz and stuffed his phone into his pants pocket. As I walked toward him, I inhaled his cologne that reeked sex. The smell was almost intoxicating and heightened all my senses. He was a deep caramel color with a sleek low haircut that had a natural curl to it. His lips were pink and slightly full and he was wearing all black, dress pants and button down shirt that was open at the collar revealing a thick gold chain that hung slightly from his neck…just so fuckable. When he put his hand in his pocket, his gold and diamond watch slid down his wrist and twinkled in the moonlight. I suddenly felt a tad bit under dressed, wearing my outfit that I initially wore to Emerald City Gentleman's Club before I changed into my costume. My face was plain with no make-up and my hair was back in a messy bun on top of my head.

Once I was standing in front of him, a grin spread across his face as he looked down at me.

"What?" I asked, a little confused.

"You're a lot shorter without those heels I see," he noticed, slightly amused.

"Yea, I am," I smiled and he opened the door of the bar for me, the music attacking my eardrums as we walked inside. He followed me over to the bar that had plenty of available seats and we sat toward the middle.

"What's your poison?" he asked me as the bartender waited to take our drink orders.

"Uh, I'll have a Red's Apple Ale, please," I told her and she nodded then looked over at him.

"Jack and coke," he said and she moved down the bar to prepare our drinks. "What's your name?" he yelled over the music.

"Raven," I said, giving him my alias once again.

"So that's the game we playin' tonight?" he asked, holding back a laugh.

"I don't know what game you're referring to. My name is Raven, I told you that when you asked me earlier tonight."

"Did you? Was that before or after you put that ass in my face?" he joked as he looked behind me at my booty on top of the barstool and I couldn't help but laugh.

"You didn't like that? Thank you," I said to him and then thanked the bartender for my beer.

"Like is an understatement, I fuckin loved it. You are…very talented. How long you been dancing?"

"I don't dance anymore, I did it for almost a year though," I answered then took a long pull from my drink.

"What do you mean you don't dance anymore?" he asked with furrowed brows.

"I was just helping a friend out tonight, I quit a while ago."

"Why?"

"It wasn't the life for me, in a nut shell. What do you do?" I asked, looking him up and down before I took another sip, letting the bottle suck in my top lip then snatching it away from my mouth. He watched my every move and took what seemed like an eternity to respond.

"Entrepreneur," he answered.

"Is that code for unemployed? Or drug dealer?" I asked and he almost choked on his drink.

"Not at all. I own a few night clubs, a chain of restaurants, and a few other businesses," he answered, reaching for a napkin to wipe his mouth.

"Hmm, that's interesting," I said and he took another sip from his glass, not taking his eyes off of me for a beat.

"Do you frequent any of the clubs here in Atlanta?"

"I used to. I don't do a whole lot of anything these days except for school."

"Oh really? Where do you go to school?" he asked a bit intrigued.

"Morris Brown."

"Really? That's good, one of my cousins went to Spellman. What are you studying?"

"Business," I said, feeling a little self-conscious about how he stared at me. I found myself fidgeting and removing invisible hairs from around my face and at the nape of my neck.

The small talk continued, but by the second round of drinks he started on how he had never been attracted to a dancer the way he was attracted to me, then went on to say how he loved my body and would be in town for a couple more days. He wanted to spend some more time with me and wouldn't give up on knowing what my real name was. I held fast and didn't reveal who I really was, and cut our evening short at close to two that morning.

"This was fun; I had a good time. Wait, what's your name. I can't believe I never asked, I apologize," I asked him as we walked towards my car. I had never been so caught up.

He laughed, as if he knew how mesmerizing he could be. The type that could literally talk the panties off of a woman. "It's Chase and I had a great time too, even if I still don't know your real name. I can understand your reasons; I know dancers or 'ex-dancers' should I say, get harassed by a lot of creeps that think that they're in love and shit."

"Yea we do." I laughed a little.

"That's cool sweetheart, I'm glad I got to spend some time with you outside of the club."

"Me too," I smiled up at him. He grabbed my hands and

entwined our fingers together and pressed his mouth against mine. My first instinct was to pull away, but couldn't. His lips were wet yet soft. Skilled. His tongue slid into my mouth, and mine followed. His large hands released mine and found my hips, then my ass giving it a squeeze.

The intensity of the kiss grew and I began to feel heat in my chest and between my thighs. When I tried pulling away, he wouldn't let me and deepened the kiss. He nibbled at my lips a little and my hands moved up to caress the back of his neck. Inside, I was feeling several different ways. It wasn't like me to kiss a stranger in public, especially someone whose name I barely even knew and who I'd met in the strip club a few hours before. That was definitely a no-no. I was also starting to feel…aroused, which I didn't know I was still capable of feeling after what had went down with me and Chico. In my mind, I had secretly sworn off men. But that night, my vagina was saying otherwise.

When he pulled away, only enough to speak, he looked me in the eye and said, "Spend the night with me," in a heavy husky voice.

"I…I can't," I said, looking up at him and into his intense dark and mysterious eyes.

"You can't or you won't?" he asked, cocking his head to one side with a grin playing at the corners of his mouth.

"Both. Don't give me that look," I warned him.

"What?" he asked, stepping closer to me and then stealing a kiss with moist lips. When he pulled away and looked at me again his eyes looked almost as if he was craving me and caused a throb between my thighs. With a sly grin he kissed me again and that time it took. All my inhibitions escaped my head in the form of invisible steam and before I knew it I was in the penthouse suite of the Ritz-Carlton Buckhead with this man tearing at my clothes.

"You smell so fuckin' good I can't wait to taste you," he said as he tugged my shirt over my head.

"Mmm," I moaned as he attacked my lips with hard passionate kisses leaving me panting and shamelessly wanting more. It had been months since I had been touched by a man so I was nervous; but when he pushed his tongue in my mouth and ran his hands down my spine I relaxed and fisted his short curly locks in my palms with that same hunger.

He snatched his lips away from mine, the moonlight from the massive window beamed on his face and he wore this look of confidence, like a predator that was finally close enough to feast on its prey. That look told me I was in trouble. Without warning, he dropped to his knees and started to remove my shoes. He yanked my leggings down with force as if they were an enemy of his, taking my underwear with them. He smiled as he was now at eye level with my pussy and his strong bare chest heaved up and down. His tongue darted out of his mouth as he used it to push my lips apart to reach my clit. I released a soft moan of approval and let him continue his work.

He gripped my hips as he continued to only lick with his tongue back and forth and his hands slowly moved to my ass. I pressed my head into the wall and let my arms dangle at my sides but they quickly found a place on his head when he placed each of my legs on his shoulders and lifted me up into the air continuing to devour me.

"Uhh!" I cried out into the dark empty hotel suite. This man was taking me on an unexpected ride. The last thing I thought would happen when I showed up to Emerald City was to leave with a stranger and end up in his hotel room while he fucked me with his tongue. But there I was and he had yet to disappoint.

His mouth worked on me and made me forget about where we were or the fact that we didn't know each other. All that mattered was here and now and after not having any sexual contact for as long as I had, I was almost embarrassed to come on his tongue the way I did.

"Fuck, this pussy tastes better than I thought," he said licking his lips. When he finished he released me so that I slid down the wall and landed on my feet.

The night was far from over. We fucked his suite up and did it in every place imaginable and it was almost as if neither one of us were capable of growing tired, like we were on ecstasy. Against the wall. On the love seat. Every which way in the bed. Once in the shower. When the sun came up we finally called it quits, or at least he did. As soon as I knew he was completely asleep I got dressed and took a cab to the bar where my car was still parked then headed home.

That was the last I saw of him. Frankie even texted me the next day saying that he showed up at Emerald City looking for me. I told her I didn't want to talk to him or see him, I was too embarrassed at what we had done to face him. That entire evening consisted of a one and done. My last time dancing and the first and only time that I had a one night stand with a stranger that I would probably never see again.

After my finale at Emerald City, I worked my ass off for the rest of the school year. I worked out hard and studied even harder. Not having a man in my life gave me the drive and motivation I needed to power through my last year at Morris Brown, and when spring came I graduated with a 3.2 GPA, but decided not to participate in commencement.

My sister Traci came to visit me and even kept an eye on any job openings at the Architecture firm that she worked for in Houston.

A few weeks before it was time for me to renew my lease, Traci called me.

"Hey Tray, what's up?" I asked with my legs folded Indian-style on my sofa bed. I was chomping on a salad and looking in the classified section of the Atlanta-Journal Constitution Sunday newspaper.

"Do not renew your lease!"

"You found me a job?!" I asked with excitement.

"Yes! I talked to the HR department and emailed them your resume that you sent me. She says that there is an opening as an Executive Administrative Assistant. I know that isn't what your degree is in, but it can get your foot in the door, Roni."

"OMG," I said lowly.

"What? What do you think?" she asked on the edge of her seat.

"When do I start?!"

"Yaaay!" she squealed through the phone. "Okay, I'm gonna text her and figure out the rest of the details," Traci said on the other end of the phone, she sounded more excited than I was. She talked to her associate in Human Resources and told me to expect a phone call from her that following morning so we could have an interview. She and I hit it off right away after Skyping for over an hour and I was expected to report to work the very next Monday.

It was like a miracle, a blessing from God. Everything had started to fall into place for me. I finally obtained my degree which was what I moved to Georgia for in the first place. Now at 27 years old, I was starting a new chapter in my life that was drama free. After the two of us getting lost in the DCFS system, my sister was back in my life and was my biggest cheerleader. She wanted nothing more than to see me do well and intended to help me in any way that she could. I was beyond thankful to have her back in my life.

Making the decision to leave would mean leaving all of my baggage behind and that was fine by me. Chico was still pissed that his club had gotten raided and that he was probably going to be doing a bid because of it. He had been trying to contact me ever since he was arrested and I was avoiding him like the plague. I had nothing to say to him and wanted nothing to do with his ass anymore. He pounded on me for the last time and raping me was the last straw. I wasn't interested in listening to his threats and even though the sound of his voice, and just the thought of him still scared the hell out of me, I figured I would be long gone by the time he ever got out.

FIT *for a* KING– *P. Sharee*

Nathaniel-4

Present Day…

Today was not my fucking day. The last thing that I wanted to do was sit through another long and tedious shareholder's meeting; but when you were the owner, president, and CEO of a company, that was one of the many things that you were forced to endure. I had also just lost another executive administrative assistant, the third one in the past six months. The first left on maternity leave and decided that she wanted to be a stay-at-home mother, the second one couldn't type worth a damn, and the third was a walking sexual harassment suit. She couldn't seem to stay away from the male employees and the last thing that I needed was another reason to see the inside of a courtroom.

Courtney in Human Resources promised me that this new person would stick and stay. She was the sister of one of my employees in our CAD department that had been with the company since she graduated college. She was dedicated and loyal to King Global Inc. Hopefully, that trait was genetic because I was up to my ears in pleasantries with every new assistant that I had to get to know and then fire or replace. I had a business to run.

As the CFO gave his closing remarks to the rest of the shareholders, I brought my attention back to the group and said my usual "Thank you for coming…blah blah…we appreciate your support here at King Global."

As everyone departed the conference room, I overheard Courtney talking to who I assumed was my new assistant.

"Here is your desk and this is Roxanne, she's Mr. King's other assistant and she'll be training you."

"Hi, you can call me Roxy. It's Veronica right?" Roxanne smiled her bubbly smile at the new girl. I could tell she couldn't wait to talk her ears off and give the office gossip once Courtney disappeared.

"Roni, please," she said having a seat at her desk.

"Roxy and Roni. This will be fun," Courtney smiled at the both of them and they all giggled amongst themselves. When she looked up, she saw me coming in their direction and beckoned for me. "Mr. King," she called, waving me over. I gave her a tight smile and walked in the direction of the three women.

"Good morning, Courtney," I said to her.

"Good morning. This is Veronica Banks, your new Executive Administrative Assistant. Veronica this is Nathaniel King, Owner, President and CEO of King Global," Courtney said introducing us. The one she called Veronica stood up straight from her new desk, her face eye level to my chin. I saw the complete and full view of her figure when she stood and smoothed out her clothes. Her hips were wide, but modest and covered in a pen-striped pencil skirt. From her front I could see the most perfect and round ass that you only saw in music videos, and one you could've set a dozen glasses on top of and they wouldn't have fallen. She wore a white blouse that was tucked in and her feet were covered in red lipstick colored pumps. As she stood before me, there was no question...she was beautiful. Fucking gorgeous, and not that generic super model gorgeous with tons of make-up, but a natural beauty. Full lips painted with a faint gloss, smooth milk chocolate skin with a hint of caramel, big bright brown eyes that turned lighter in the sun, and a short haircut that fit her face perfectly. My dick twitched in my pants just looking at her.

"It's nice to meet you, Mr. King," she said with the most angelic voice, her white teeth showing as she spoke my last name with a smile.

"Nice to meet you too, Veronica, welcome to King Global," I smiled, trying to keep my eyes from inching down past her face to where her full breasts teased me. I extended my hand to shake hers, and she accepted it with nervous fingers.

"Thank you," she smiled shyly glancing down at her shoes.

"Veronica relocated from Atlanta, so I'm sure she'll be here with us for a while," Courtney reassured me with raised eyebrows.

"Oh? Where in Atlanta?" I asked, inhaling the sweet smell of her perfume. It was a mixture of fruit and a light musk that made my dick a little hard and I lowered the file folder in my hands to cover my growing erection.

"Union City," she said looking up at me. I nodded at her politely but could not stop thinking about her fucking chest and that ass she had on her.

The introduction was brief; I had to excuse myself to a pressing and fictitious assignment back in my office which really was my enlarged dick that was straining against my pants from the sight of my new assistant.

I got myself off as quickly as I could in the bathroom of my office because I knew at 9:30 like clockwork, Roxanne and now Veronica, would be barging into my office for our daily briefing.

After I rushed to wash my hands and tried to get myself together, I took a deep breath and attempted to shrug off the obvious affect my new assistant had on me. No woman had turned me on like that in eons, who did this Veronica Banks think she was?

As I was coming out of the bathroom, Roxanne was ushering Veronica to have a seat in one of the leather chairs across from my desk before our morning pow-wow began.

I had removed my suit jacket, and was only wearing my charcoal gray vest and pants from my Armani suit collection.

"Sorry about that, ladies." I said, rolling up the sleeves to my white shirt and having a seat at my desk. "Roxanne, hit me."

"You have a video conference call at 10:30 with the group of investors from Dubai…and a lunch meeting with Intel at 12 noon sharp," she told me as she swiped her fingers across her iPad going through my calendar that she had organized. I couldn't help but notice that Veronica seemed to be on the wrong screen because her eyebrows were knitted together and she looked frustrated. I cleared my throat and said, "Ms. Banks, are you following along alright?" I asked and her head popped up wearing a look of panic on her alluring face.

"Um, yes I..."she attempted to say but in an instant I found myself walking from behind my desk and over to where she sat, her legs crossed and the iPad in her hands resting on her lap. When I was next to her, the fragrance that she was wearing hit me again and I felt my mouth water a little. I kneeled down beside her and inspected what was on her screen. Out of my peripherals, I could see her staring at my profile until she realized she was doing it and darted her eyes back to the screen in front of us both. I grinned a little at how nervous she seemed and navigated her to the correct screen.

"There you go. Don't be nervous, we're a team. It's okay to ask for help," I assured her with my signature warm smile.

"Oh, okay. Thank you, Mr. King," she smiled shyly. I guess that was her signature smile because it certainly almost had me forgetting where I was for a moment. I stood back up and found a comfortable seat on the corner of my desk, and gestured for Roxanne to continue. She crossed her legs so that her skirt inched up and revealed more of her bare thigh, another pathetic move I was all too familiar with when it came to Roxanne's attempts to seduce me.

"It looks like your schedule is clear after about 3p.m. depending on how long your lunch with Intel goes," she said, making eye contact with me, at that point, frustrated that her little gesture ceased to phase me.

"Good, I have a few properties I have to go and take a look at. I think that's it, unless you have anything else for me?" I asked, clasping my hands together.

"No that's it; I'll buzz you if anything else comes up," she flirted brazenly and rose to her feet.

"Okay. Thank you, ladies," I smiled at them both and they walked towards the door, Roxanne in front and Veronica behind her. I got the opportunity to see her ass in full view and it was as perfect as I'd thought. It wasn't enormous or one of those ghetto booties, but it was round, large, and looked firm like she worked out. She had a small waist, and her breasts were just right. A picture perfect body and a face to back it up. I wasn't sure how I was going to be able to focus with her around.

When the investors from Dubai's video call came through, I had both of the ladies join me back in my office so that they could take down any notes that I might miss.

All three of my 32 inch flat screen monitors that were on the far wall of my office were on and displayed two men and one woman from Dubai that were interested in investing in my next business venture, a technology firm.

Roxanne and Veronica sat on the sofa near the wall of monitors and took down notes as we discussed the details of the company. I couldn't help but steal glances of Veronica's smooth bare, crossed legs and thick thighs that hid under her skirt. This woman was what my moronic friends and brother would refer to as 'stacked'. Her body was impeccable and she seemed so sweet, polite, and poised. It had been a while, years since I had been attracted to a woman in that way, since Lauren actually.

As the gentleman in the center (monitor number two) looked over the figures I had sent him, I glanced at Veronica who was watching me with this look of admiration and we both smiled at each other and then looked away. She quickly got back to what she was writing, fluttering her long lashes.

My meeting ended so well that my potential investors were no longer potentials. We were all on the same page and ready to move forward. The rest of my day raced by, between my long lunch with Intel, and meeting with my realtor, my workday didn't end until about a quarter after six.

I had to go back to the office to grab my laptop and ran into Alaina as I was leaving.

"You still here?" she asked, catching up to me as I zipped my YSL briefcase.

"I had to come back and grab my computer. What the hell you still doing here?" I asked, raising an eyebrow at her.

"I had to go through a dozen spreadsheets and God knows

what else that was on my desk. I'm still not finished; I'm just going out to grab some food. What are you up to? Or who are you about to get into should I say?" she teased.

"Fuck you," I chuckled. "I'm about to hit the gym before I start to look soft, like your fiancée," I teased and she flicked me off.

"You ass."

"See you later."

"Bye," she laughed tossing her long locks over her shoulder and we both went our separate ways.

Alaina was the oldest of my two younger sisters, and one of the Senior Architect Managers at King Global. She was smart as a whip, and after she finished college I would have been a fool to let her go work for any company other than mine. I made her an offer she couldn't refuse and within a year of employment she had become assistant to the director, and eighteen months later she was the head of her own department. Not because she was my sister but because she knew what she was doing and was damn good at it.

When I stepped out onto the curb, my Mercedes CL65 was running and waiting for me with the top down. I put my computer and briefcase in the passenger seat, cranked my music and sped off.

Just as I was getting onto the expressway, a pearl white 5 series BMW zoomed past me, a few years old. The driver however was unmistakable and none other than my new assistant, Veronica. I finally had removed her from my thoughts the past couple of hours, and there she was again.

It got worse when I got to the gym that afternoon. In an attempt to workout harder than usual, every time I blinked, my assistant popped in my head. Blink. Her cleavage. Blink. Then her completely topless. Blink. Her ass in boy shorts. Blink. Her bare ass with nothing but G-String wedged between the cheeks.

I tried to shake it off by the end of my workout and wash all thoughts away of Veronica in the shower of the men's locker room, but failed miserably.

As the small-enclosed space filled with dense opaque steam, I closed my eyes tight and tried to think of something else, anything else but my new assistant. But it seemed like the more I tried not to think about her, the more my mind went against my wishes and I found myself slipping into a day dream that I couldn't seem to control, nor did I want to.

It all took place in the gym itself and I was in the exact same position, the men's locker room in the shower. I heard a light tap on the glass door and when I turned around I could see the curves of a woman's body through the steam. I wiped my hand over the glass enough to see that it was in fact Veronica wrapped in a cotton white towel and wearing a shy little grin on that gorgeous face of hers. I opened the door and stepped back so that there was room for her to join me and a slight draft followed her inside before she could shut the door.

"Mr. King," she said close to a whisper.

"You're a little over dressed don't you think Ms. Banks?" I asked her and then tugged at her towel so that it became undone and pooled at her feet.

"I guess so," she smiled, looking down at her adorable toes that were painted in pale pink polish.

"I wanna ask what you're doing here, but then again I don't care and all I want you to do is promise me...you won't run," I told her and then pressed my mouth to hers before she had the chance to respond. I urged her lips apart with my tongue and she offered me hers in return. I caressed her smooth skin and went straight for that ass when I cupped it and pressed her up against the glass shower wall. The pressure from the shower caused the hot water to cascade down my back and in one long thrust I was inside of Veronica and she was crying out in my ear while her bottom lip brushed my lobe. Her hand gripped my back and she clawed at my skin in a savage way that made me want even more of her. I could hear her pant "Mr. King," over and over again as I gave her my A-game. Just as I began to find my release, the water turned cold.

My eyes opened at the sudden change in temperature and when I looked down, my dick was in my hand and I realized that I was alone and there was no sign of Veronica.

FIT for a KING – P. Sharee

Nathaniel-5

After dinner that evening, I retired to my home office to look over some things before work the next day.

My phone rang and buzzed just as I was examining some blueprints that were sent over to me from an architect in Alaina's department.

"Hello…yea what's up…nah just looking over some work before bed, what's up with you...I guess so…see you in a minute," I said and ended the call.

Not even ten minutes later my doorbell rang and my cousin Kyle was wearing the goofiest grin when I opened the door.

"What up, Nate man?" he said coming inside.

"What's up? You alright, man?" I chuckled looking him up and down.

"Fan-fucking-tastic, cuz," he smiled as we headed upstairs to my bedroom.

"I can see that, you're grinning like a fuckin' idiot," I chuckled.

"You would too if you just got some head in the car on the way over here," he said with a toothy grin.

"You and Traci, huh? Y'all are just like some horny ass teenagers," I laughed and opened the French doors to my bedroom.

"Yea," he lied, averting his eyes and followed me inside the room.

"Where are you two going that you need to borrow a shirt anyway?" I asked him.

"Some lounge downtown," he answered as we entered the massive walk-in closet. "Damn this is a lot of shit," he said as he took in my wardrobe and shoes that was organized better than most department stores. He turned to his right where my shirts were organized by style and then by color. His eyes darted to a black Armani shirt with the price tag still dangling from it.

"Choose wisely young grasshopper," I advised and he laughed as he picked up the shirt. "That's a three hundred dollar shirt that hasn't been worn."

"I'll dry clean it before I bring it back, nigga, damn," Kyle assured me.

"Yeah, you better," I warned him before I walked out of the closet.

I let Kyle change and I went back downstairs to my office. Before he left my room he sprayed on some of my cologne that cost almost twice as much as my shirt that he was wearing and shuffled back downstairs then poked his head into the door of my office before he left.

"Alright, thanks man, good looking," he told me.

"Good looking my ass, nigga, you better dry clean my shit before you bring it back," I said and he threw his head back with laughter and said, "I got you," with that goofy ass grin. "Oh before I forget, what did you think of Traci's sister Veronica?" he asked. I removed my reading glasses from my face and sighed before I could respond. The mere mention of her name gave my dick a pulse and completely exasperated me at the same damn time, but I wasn't about to tell Kyle that.

"She's cool...seems shy," I lied but Kyle and I both knew what it was.

"Cool and shy, huh?" he asked. "So she isn't someone you would be interested in?"

"You know I don't get involved with my employees," I reminded him, which was also a reminder for me.

"That wasn't my question, but okay. I'll accept that answer

34

for now. Later, Nate."

I thought about my assistant again and couldn't shake that lil daydream that I had earlier about her and in the shower at the gym. It was almost as if I could feel everything that was taking place in my thoughts and it was odd and all too vivid. I hadn't had that strong of an attraction towards anyone like that in years. I told myself that I would do better the next day. I couldn't and wouldn't for that matter, sit and fantasize about what my assistant looked like naked or how good she would probably taste on my tongue. I had a business to run.

When I finally attempted to get back to work, my iPhone vibrated on the corner of my desk. I glanced at the caller I.D. it read "Unknown". I furrowed my brows and picked up the phone.

"Nate King," I said but got no response. "Nate King," I repeated, with more authority in my voice, but still heard nothing and then the call ended. I scrolled through my call log and noticed that was the third call I'd gotten like that in the past week and a half with someone calling from a blocked number and just listening to my voice, but not saying a word. I grabbed my Blackberry and made a call of my own.

"Yea, Mitch it's me Nate…I need you to look into something for me man…yea I've been getting calls from this unknown number on my personal line and whenever I answer, no one says anything…trace the calls for me and get back to me when you find something out." I told him and ended the call.

Every smart businessman had that one "go-to" guy a.k.a a "fixer", and Harvey Mitchell was mine. A former secret service worker and ex-sniper, he was the total package and well compensated for any work that he'd done for me. Mitch was loyal and sharp so whenever I gave him a job, I could expect nothing less than accurate and thorough results. I knew he would get down to the bottom of those mysterious phone calls sooner rather than later.

I temporarily shrugged off that thought and tried to busy myself with more positive ones

I glanced over at the family portrait of my mother, myself, and my three siblings on the left corner of my desk, and put Veronica in the back of my mind for a moment.

Sometimes when I looked at that picture of us, I thought about our absentee father and how we never really knew him. He was around long enough to get my mother pregnant three times but apparently not long enough to marry her; then disappeared when Alaina was a baby. My mother never offered an in-depth explanation as to what went wrong between the two of them and we didn't bother asking and pegged him as a deadbeat dad like all the other fatherless children in our neighborhood.

When she married my stepfather, I think that I was the only one that didn't necessarily approve. I felt like even though Robert Hathaway was wealthy and my mother actually loved him, I could see right through him and he still wasn't good enough for her no matter how much money he had. He and I never got along. I even did some teen modeling in high school (against my better judgment) to earn money to pay for my own college education because I didn't want any of his.

He had been known to have extra-marital affairs, even while my mother was pregnant with my baby sister, and always took her kindness for weakness in my eyes. That was the main reason why my visits were so seldom. I should've been the more mature man and put that to the side if my mother did; but a bigger part of me wanted to knock Robert out every time I laid eyes on his philandering ass.

Later that evening when I finally found sleep, I dreamed which wasn't out of the ordinary. My sleep was dark and all I could hear was a little girl crying and calling for her mommy.

"Mommy, I want my mommy," echoed in my head. When I finally see light and the darkness fades I see myself in the middle of the street barefoot with bluish-grey pajama pants on and a white t-shirt. A silver Mercedes SUV is coming towards me and no matter how much I try to move my legs are still. The Mercedes crashes up against my body almost as if I weigh as much as a semi-truck. My body shatters into a million tiny pieces and the spirit of me rushes over to the car. When I look inside I see Lauren in the front seat of the car with her body flung over the steering wheel and blood gushing from her head. In the backseat of the car in a Hello Kitty car seat is my baby Kristina who looks like she is sleeping. She has a few cuts from the glass shattering but otherwise looks okay and like she's taking a nap.

I woke up in a cold sweat with heart palpations. The t-shirt that I was wearing was drenched with sweat and my chest heaved up and down. That recurring dream had me shaken up and when I looked to my left I remembered that I was alone. I reached for the bottle of pills that was on the nightstand next to my bed and took two.

I sighed as I stared up at the ceiling above me, unable to get back to sleep that night. There wasn't a day that didn't go by that I didn't miss my wife and daughter. Though it had been seven years since their car accident, I still struggled with the grief daily. I missed the sound of Lauren's voice, her touch, even her smart mouth. I missed the way my baby girl giggled whenever I would tickle her and how she dragged out her words when she said "Daddy". We had only been married for a few years before the accident and the time with them that I was robbed of, left me with a hole in heart not to mention a mountain of regret.

FIT *for a* KING – *P. Sharee*

Veronica-6

I stood in front of the full-length mirror of Traci's guestroom, my new bedroom for the time being; and contemplated on what I would wear to work the next day.

"That's cute. Hey, did you check the mail today?" Traci asked me as she leaned in the doorway.

"Yea I did, something came for a 'Yasmin Bishop' or something," I told her as I held up a navy blue pencil skirt and an ivory colored cardigan in the full-length mirror. "Whose-." I began.

"Wrong address…I'll put return to sender on it and take it to the post office tomorrow," she interrupted, avoiding eye contact.

"Maybe a nude pump with that," Traci said, coming inside the room completely and changing the subject all together.

"Yea, I think that would be cute," I agreed and then reached for the hanger on the bed.

"Did you see Mr. King when we were on our way home earlier?" she asked me, plopping down on the bed.

"In the Benz? I thought that was him getting on the expressway."

"Girl, yes, and he was looking in the car, too."

"He was?" I asked with excitement. "I mean, he was?" I rephrased with less enthusiasm.

"Don't try to switch it up. Let me find out you checking for your boss, Roni!" she teased and playfully kicked me in the butt.

"I'm not…checking for him," I lied and sat down across from her, folding my legs on the bed.

"Yes, you are. You can't even say it without a smile," she continued and I shook my head in denial. "Don't be shy about it. Every straight woman has a thing for Nathaniel King. And the gay guys and I've even seen lesbians check him out. So trust, it's not a big deal. I mean look at him."

"He is fine as hell, I'll give you that."

"Fine ain't the word."

"He is a bit of a pretty boy though Tray, I don't know. You sure he ain't playin' for the other team? On the down low or something?" I joked.

"No, he's very much so heterosexual," she giggled.

"He must be a whore then," I assumed.

"Maybe. He was married but his wife and daughter died like six-no seven years ago," she told me and I placed my hand over my heart.

"Aww, how did they die?"

"Car crash. According to office gossip, he just stopped wearing his wedding ring like a year ago."

"Wow. I know that had to be hard."

"Yea. He doesn't talk about it so don't mention it," she warned me.

"Mmm," she said clutching the bottom of her stomach.

"You okay?" I asked her.

"Not really, I haven't been feeling good, the past couple days. I don't know if I'm getting the flu or what," she told me.

"Have you been to the doctor?"

"I went to urgent care yesterday and they ran some tests, I told them to email me my results so I don't have to wait for something in the mail-"

"What kinda tests Tray?" I interrupted, a little worried.

"Nothing too bad Roni, relax. Just some blood work and an STD screen."

"You think you may have something?" I asked carefully and avoiding eye contact. Those kinda questions were already extremely personal whether we were sisters or not.

"I hope not, but you never know with Kyle's whore-ass," she joked and we both laughed but I knew she was serious.

"Shit, I'll be right back," she told me and rushed into the kitchen to the whistling teapot over on the stove.

My heart ached silently for Nathaniel King's loss. I could only imagine how hard it must've been to pick up the pieces and move on with his life after losing his wife and child.

Traci wasn't wrong, I was definitely attracted to him. He was the definition of a pretty boy. His skin was deep flawless caramel and his black hair laid on his head in a perfect Caesar haircut. Through his suits I could tell he worked out and was fit. He was two or three inches past six feet and wore the most intoxicating cologne that I had ever smelled on a man. Earlier that day when he kneeled down beside me, I could barely hold it together and just being in his presence sent some sort of electrical current through my body.

Later that night after we finished our tea, I lied awake in bed and stared up at the popcorn ceilings. I thought about my sister's warning concerning my new boss. The last thing that I needed to do was fantasize about the man's signature that would be on my paycheck, but I couldn't help it. Physically, he was perfect and very difficult not to look at or daydream about. I almost wished that I didn't have to work so closely to him, that way I would have room to breathe normal air instead of "Nathaniel" air that made my knees slightly weak.

I wasn't even remotely interested in a man since my fallout with Chico; that was until now. My one nightstand did however linger in my head from time to time though. His swag mixed with that hint of arrogance was what made me cave, which in turn made my panties practically melt off in his hotel suite the night that we met. Sometimes I wondered if I should have given it a chance and at least saw what he was about before I threw him away and treated him…how most men do women. He was fine, obviously had some coins, and the sex had been good, so what was wrong with me?

That next morning Traci was up and dressed before I was

and had to go in early, which meant I would have to rely on my memory and GPS to guide me to King Global.

Once I was dressed in what I had picked out the night before, I grabbed my purse and keys and headed downstairs to my car. Luckily, the trip from Traci's apartment complex was almost a straight shot to work and I got there right on time.

"Hold the elevator, please!" I shouted as I rushed towards the gold bank of elevators. Someone's hand caught it and when I got close enough, I saw that the hand belonged to Nathaniel King.

"Good morning, Ms. Banks," he smiled down at me.

"Good morning, Mr. King," I said lowly. My eyes did a quick scan and saw about seven other occupants in the elevator. My nerves settled at the fact that we weren't alone. The pep talk that I had with myself the night before and in the car that morning were replaying in my head as I eased to the back of the confined space. Things like "He's your boss, be professional!" and "As fine as he is, he probably has women lined up around the block," not to mention "A guy like him would never go for someone like you, he looks like he prefers models or someone that doesn't eat."

By the time the elevators reached the 16th floor, Mr. King and I were the only two people left and we were both going to the 20th floor, his floor. My heart was beating so fast and hard, I glanced down at my chest to make sure you couldn't see it through my shirt.

"How was your first day?" he asked me casually.

"It went okay. I survived," I joked a little.

"I see that, you came back," he smiled.

"Yes, I did."

"Is Roxanne talking your ear off yet?" he grinned and I giggled a little before I said,

"No, not yet," with nervous laughter.

"Just wait, she will," he said looking over his shoulder at me. He was a few steps in front and my back was to the wall of the elevator counting the seconds in my head before I could get away from him. That morning he smelled of the same cologne from the previous day mixed with soap and a hint of mouthwash. I could have relished in that scent all day, every day. I bet his morning breath wasn't even bad he was so damn perfect.

At the 20th floor, the elevator's doors opened and he motioned for me to exit first, and then he followed. Feeling slightly confident in my strut, I envisioned Mr. King watching me walk and enjoying the view. In my mind he was in to models, but in reality he was still a man, and every man enjoyed looking at a nice ass.

As she typed as fast as the speed of light on her keyboard, Roxy asked me, "So you and Mr. King rode up together on the elevator?" once he was in his office.

"Uh...yea we did," I said powering my computer on, a little perplexed by her question.

"Couldn't you just...eat him up girl?!" she said, still staring at her screen and pecking away at her keyboard.

"Uhh..." I said trying to hide a smile.

"I've been throwing it at him since I started and he won't budge. He said that he doesn't get involved with his employees. It's unprofessional, but I'm not convinced. Then again, I've never seen him show interest in anyone else, and you know I would know," she told me. I didn't respond, just listened.

Roxy was attractive and had a nice body, too. She was about my height and her complexion was a shade or two lighter than mine. Her breasts were bigger and looked like she had gotten them done. She was curvaceous and wore her hair in a bob style with blonde highlights. I on the other hand was still getting use to my short hair. I had been wearing weaves since I moved to Atlanta, but finally took my extensions out about a week before I moved to Houston. I had my hairdresser chop my hair off and give me a style similar to Halle Berry's. My natural hair was almost at my shoulders before I cut it, but needed a change.

As I drafted an email that Mr. King wanted sent to the Human Resources department, I couldn't help but watch the time in the corner of my computer screen. It was 9:28am and I knew at 9:30 he would be expecting Roxy and me to barge in his office for our morning meeting. After enduring the elevator ride, I wasn't sure 30 minutes was enough elapsed time before I had to look at him again.

Just before I gathered up one of the iPads, Roxy murmured

something to me about forgetting her thumb drive in her car and
that she would be right back; which in turn meant that I had to face
Mr. King alone until she returned.

"Damn," I said to myself. I adjusted my skirt and cardigan
after I stood, grabbed the iPad and turned on my heels to go to Mr.
King's office. Before I entered the second set of double doors, I
tapped on the glass lightly.

"Come in," he called and I opened the door slowly and
peeked my head inside.

"Mr. King, are you ready for our briefing?" I asked quietly.

"Of course, Ms. Banks, come in please," he told me,
looking up from the dual monitors on the right corner of his desk.

"Roxanne had to grab something from her car, she should
be back any minute," I told him.

"That's fine, we can start without her. Please have a seat,"
he smiled up at me and I sat down in the same leather chair that I
had the day before. I took a deep breath before I began and he just
grinned at me.

"Still nervous?" he asked.

"No," I lied.

"Good," he grinned almost as if he could tell I was lying.
When I unlocked the screen I found myself having the same
trouble as the day before and when he looked up from his monitors
again he could tell I was stuck.

In an instant he was rounding his desk and sitting next to
me, his scent wafting to my nose causing my lashes to flutter at its
sweetness.

"May I?" he asked and I nodded but couldn't seem to
formulate a verbal response. He leaned in closer and helped me
navigate to the correct screen using his hand to guide mine. There
was that "Nathaniel" air again and I found myself feeling warm all
over and difficulty catching my breath. I barely heard what he said
as we went over his calendar for the day and it all seemed to
happen in a blur. My mind was so hypnotized by this man's
presence I couldn't see straight.

"Now, that wasn't so bad, was it?" he asked as I stood from
the chair.

"No, it wasn't." I said lying through my teeth for the second time that morning. "I'll be at my desk if you need anything Mr. King," then rushed toward the double doors. He paused for a moment and then said, "Have you been on a tour of the building yet?"

"No, not yet," I said turning around.

"Well, I think today would be a good day to take that trip," he said and I saw him start to unbutton his black suit jacket and then remove it. He hung it on the arm of his chair and then walked towards me. "After you," and opened the doors for me to exit his office. "Roxanne, I'll be out of my office, I'm going to do a walk around of the departments, Ms. Banks is accompanying me," he told Roxy. Her jaw dropped a little at the nature of his statement and then she nodded.

"Okay, Mr. King," she said and then shot me a fake smile as I walked past her desk. I shrugged my shoulders and followed our boss.

Instead of taking the gold elevators that everyone used, we took a different set that was around a corner from them that were invisible to the untrained eye. He held the door open for me and waited for me to step inside completely before he joined me and allowed the doors to close.

The space was a lot smaller than the standard elevators and was a dull grey color inside.

"I figured we'd take the service elevator, we'll be waiting forever if we took the gold ones," he said just as it started to descend. The take-off caught me off guard and I felt my stomach jump. I grabbed the railing beside me. "Yea, this one is…old." he said at my reaction.

"I see," I said looking over at him.

He looked even sexier without his suit jacket. I couldn't help but wonder what was underneath the rest of his clothes. Did he have rock hard abs? Tattoos? Any scars or war wounds from his younger years? I licked my lips at the thought and saw him watching me from the corner of my eye. This space was too confined and I found it difficult to breathe as my thoughts consumed me. From my peripherals I could see that he was still watching me in amusement. I think he liked the fact that he made me nervous. He had to know that he had that effect on women, Roxanne practically threw herself at his feet to get his attention and it didn't seem to faze him one bit. But with me, he seemed to enjoy my reaction to him almost as if it was the highlight of his day.

I inhaled deeply, searching for all the air I could find. It was too quiet and I felt like I was suffocating. I was trapped in this small elevator with this man that was too beautiful to be real. Everything about him panted sex. His face, his voice, his scent, even his walk.

"I thought I'd start at the bottom and work my way up," he said and his words dripped with seduction. "Start on the ground level and work our way back up to the 20th floor I mean," he corrected himself after he'd heard how his previous statement sounded.

"Okay," I said looking above to see that we were almost on the ground level. In my mind I willed the elevator to hurry up and get us there so that I wasn't forced to be so close to this man...alone.

The first floor consisted of the lobby area where all employees entered the building through the double set of revolving doors. The floor was completely marble with gold fixtures around the entire space. The second floor was where the first and second year interns were stationed but they floated all over the building wherever they were needed. The third floor housed the third year interns, and the floors four through ten were where the architect designers and project managers worked. Floors 11 through 15 were comprised of the senior managers and on the 16th floor is where I met Alaina King, the head of the department.

"Veronica Banks this is Alaina King, the Senior Manager and head of this department. Alaina, this is my..."

"Your new assistant, I assume? Nice to meet you, Veronica," she smiled graciously and extended her hand to shake mine. I accepted it and returned the smile.

"Nice to meet you, too, Alaina," I told her.

"Oh and I guess this one forgot to mention that I was his

sister. He's such a dick sometimes," she said referring to her obviously older brother. Alaina looked close to my age, and Mr. King seemed like he was probably in his mid-thirties. I was a little surprised at how candidly Alaina spoke, but also found it refreshing in that moment.

"She is not my sister; she's my mother's daughter," Mr. King said and I giggled a little.

"You ass," she said and swatted her brother's arm with her hand. Alaina was gorgeous. She had this beautiful dark hair identical to her sibling and wore it up in a twist held together by what looked like two wooden pencils. Her skin was a peanut butter color and she had slanted hazel eyes. She was wearing a red Dolce and Gabanna pants suit, which she too had her jacket tossed on her desk and wore a black sleeveless blouse and black Jimmy Choo heels.

"I was just doing a walk through and giving Ms. Banks a tour," Mr. King informed her.

"Ms. Banks? Why so formal, Nathaniel?" she asked walking back over to her drafting desk to continue what she was working on. "She's not some old lady, damn. 'Ms. Banks'," she said mocking him.

"Does it bother you that I call you Ms. Banks?" he turned to me and asked. I suddenly felt like I was being put on the spot and couldn't quite find my voice.

"I..."

"See, I told you," Alaina chimed in.

"What would you prefer? Veronica? Is Veronica okay?" he asked attentively and I nodded.

"Yes, that's fine."

"Okay then, Veronica," he smiled and I almost melted under his gaze. We did that thing again, where we stared at each other for a long pause and when Alaina noticed she cleared her throat.

"Nate, come take a look at this," she told her brother. He snapped his head up and took a few long strides over to where she worked. When he reached her, he looked down at an almost blank blueprint.

"What am I looking at Alaina?" he asked, looking over at her.

"Since when do you give tours of the building to your assistants?" she asked under her breath.

"What are you talking about?" he asked.

"Doesn't someone from HR give the tour in the second week for all new hires?"

"I decided to do a walk around and brought her along, what's the big deal?" he asked confused.

"You're into her," she concluded with a sly grin.

"What?! Don't be ridiculous," he hissed and then stood up straight. "That looks good; let me know when it's finished," he said coming back towards me. "We can go now."

"Don't run this one off!" she called to him and he turned around to flick her off as she laughed.

The elevator ride back up the 20th floor was more difficult than the one before. I'm not sure if it was my imagination or not, but it seemed like Mr. King and I had established a new level of comfort. He stood closer to me, so close that our arms brushed up against each other's and I felt like I was getting high off of his scent alone.

When the elevator jolted to a stop, I lost my balance. I reached out for the rail and missed, instantaneously Mr. King's arms were around me in a close cradle.

"Are you alright?" he asked looking down into my eyes with his intense brown ones. My chest swelled as I tried to catch my breath. This man had me speechless once again and all I could do was nod my head in an answer to his question. The doors were open and after staring at each other for a long pause, he helped me stand up straight and took my hand leading me off the elevator.

When we rounded the corner towards the reception area, he stopped and asked me if I was okay for a second time and I nodded again with a smile. He returned my smile and carefully released my hand then walked ahead of me. When I looked up, I saw Roxy watching me with squinted eyes. Her expression faded and she offered her signature fake smile before she continued her conversation with one of the receptionists.

I rushed to the bathroom before I returned to my desk. I needed to escape that *Nathaniel-air* and smother the flames that he'd ignited between my thighs. The fever he gave me in the elevator only heightened the attraction I had for him and I needed to do something to calm myself down before I got back to work. My pulse settled as I caught my breath and stared at myself in the mirror. When I licked my lips, I clenched at the thought of Mr. King doing more than just catching me before I fell. I glanced around the bathroom and under the stall doors and saw that I was alone.

I turned on my heels and went inside the very last stall on the left, then locked it from the inside. When I slid my skirt up over my ass and hips, I pulled down the lace nude colored panties that I was wearing and saw that they were moist. I bit my bottom lip and couldn't help but smile at what my boss was doing to me. It was something about seeing how wet I was solely from my thoughts of Mr. King that made me want to take it to the next level.

Slowly I ran my index finger over my slick clit and shivered slightly under my own touch. I closed my eyes and rubbed back and forth and let one finger slip inside my warm and wet center which made me bite my lip for a second time. While my eyes remained shut, I envisioned my boss's head between my legs and his tongue licking swiftly and his mouth gently sucking my clit while using his fingers all at once. I uttered a soft moan as I slipped a second finger inside myself, pretending they were his fingers.

"Uhh," I panted, echoing throughout the empty bathroom. I was so far in my zone that I didn't even hear the bathroom door open, or someone's heels clicking on the tile floors. My fingers worked faster and I felt myself close to edge until I heard, "Roni?"

My eyes and mouth shot open. I cleared my throat and knew that that voice belonged to Roxy.

"I-I'll be out in a second," I told her trying to sound as calm as I could considering the compromising position I was in.

FIT for a KING—P. Sharee

Veronica-7

"I'll have water with lemon, please, and a turkey club sandwich," I told the waitress as my sister and I sat at the outdoor café, having lunch a block away from King Global.

"That sounds good, I'll have the same," Traci told her and the waitress took our menus and walked away to put our order in.

"So, how is it going?" she asked, crossing her long thin legs that glistened in the sun. She was wearing a pale blue dress that stopped at her knees with a thin white belt around her waist.

"It's going okay. I met Mr. King's sister today."

"Alaina? Yeah, I love Alaina," she told me.

"I like her, too; she seems really down to earth and real."

"She is."

"It's so cute how they tease each other," I giggled.

"Did she come up there today to give him shit about something?" Traci assumed.

"No, he took me around the building on a walk-through and we stopped on her floor," I told her as the waitress brought over our drinks.

"He took you on a tour himself?" she asked with surprise.

"Yeah. Is that bad?" I panicked a little.

"No, but it is unlike him. Usually, somebody from Human Resources does that your second week. Hmm," she said and I could tell she was thinking further on the matter. I took a sip of my water and studied her face.

"What? What is it?"

"I think he might be in to you, Roni." she blurted out and I spit my water out on the sidewalk in shock. Traci shook with laughter at my reaction.

"What would make you think some crazy shit like that?" I asked wiping my mouth and nose with a napkin."

"I've been here for a long time and I've never seen him give an employee, least of all, one of his assistants a tour of the building. Oh shit," she said all at once.

"What now?" I asked confused and slightly agitated.

"Don't look, but he's coming this way," she said and I turned around and saw him coming towards us, talking on his phone.

"I just told you not to look," she hissed.

"Shit," I said, my nervousness filling the bottom of my belly as I was now aware of his presence.

"Okay…yes, I will make sure I get it to you by the close of business today…right…okay…bye," I heard his deep voice from behind me. "Afternoon ladies," he said, standing in front of our table.

"Good afternoon, Mr. King," Traci said, smiling up at him with her hands underneath her chin.

"Good afternoon," I said to him.

"Ms. Banks…I mean, Veronica," he said, correcting himself and grinning at me. "Is this your sister?" he asked knowingly.

"Yes, this is Traci."

"I use to work in CAD," she informed him.

"Of course, you were just promoted, right?"

"Yes sir, last quarter," she said with pride.

"Keep up the good work," he told her.

"How is Veronica doing?" Traci asked and I shot her an evil look.

"She's doing great actually, better than she thinks she is. She's a fast learner; I need more people like that on my team," he

52

said, not taking his eyes off of me.

"That's good to hear, right Roni?" Traci said, raising her eyebrows.

"Yes." I said, giving her a look and then smiling up at the perfect man that stood before me.

"Excuse me," the waitress said with two plates in her hands. "Two turkey clubs," she said and sat the plates down in front of us.

"Oh, excuse me. I apologize, you ladies enjoy your lunch," he told us. "Veronica, I'll see you back upstairs," he said, touching my shoulder before he went inside the café to order his lunch.

"Thank you," Traci and I said in unison to the waitress. She smiled and then disappeared but not before she sized Mr. King up with a smile of approval.

"I knew it," she said leaning in to the table.

"You knew what?" I asked placing a napkin on my lap.

"I was right, he is into you," she said so only the two of us could hear.

"You are crazy." I told her before I took a bite of my sandwich.

"Are you telling me you didn't notice how he was looking at you? How he couldn't take his eyes off of you?" she said in almost a whisper.

"I think you're exaggerating," I told her and when I took my eyes off her for half a second; I saw my boss staring at me from inside of the eatery and smiled when our eyes met. I gave him a shy smile and turned my attention back to Traci.

"He was just staring at you, wasn't he?" she asked watching me.

"He's just being nice, Traci relax. I mean weren't you the one that said 'be careful' and that he was a bit of a whore?"

"The whore-thing was an assumption, a theory really based solely on his good looks. I don't know it to be true. And I said be careful because I figured your little crush was one sided, but now I'm rethinking things. He is a nice guy but he doesn't pay this much attention to anyone at King Global. He has a one track mind, business."

"He's just being nice," I told her and picked at my food. I couldn't eat, I had lost my appetite. "What could he possibly see in me anyway?"

"Have you seen you? You have the body of a fuckin' video vixen. Gold. An ass that won't quit, flat stomach, do you hear me?" she declared. "Not to mention you have a pretty face and you're educated. You have a lot going for yourself Roni, can't you see it?" I didn't respond, just listened.

For the rest of the day, I tried to block out all the nonsense that my sister had tried to fill my head with. She was being silly, or was she? It was foolish of me to think that a man like him would be interested in someone like me when he could have any woman that he wanted. He was rich, handsome, and brilliant. His persona howled sex and power. Traci had it all wrong. Nathaniel King was not into an ex-stripper.

Later that evening, Traci's boyfriend Kyle came over and ended up staying the night with her. Since I had been in Houston, every black man that had crossed my path had been fine as hell and Kyle was no exception. He was coated in this deep caramel skin and had a set of lips that made every woman that saw them think of one thing. I guess his handsome face and playboy swag was to be expected, after all, he was related to Mr. King.

As I was coming out of the bathroom, I could hear Traci giggling from behind her closed bedroom door. When I went back into my room, the paper-thin walls allowed me to hear the tail end of a conversation she was having with Kyle.

"I think your cousin likes my sister," she blurted out.

"Who Nate? What makes you say that?" I heard him ask.

"Well, when we saw him at lunch he was just…giving her a look like he was…smitten."

"You sure? You know Nate is an all-around friendly dude, he was probably just being nice." Kyle said.

"Yeah, I don't know about that, Bae. Roni said he took her on a tour of King Global," Traci explained. "He never gives his employees a tour. HR does that," she said and then paused when Kyle's phone started ringing.

"Aren't you gonna answer it?" I heard Traci ask.

"Nah, I don't recognize the number," he lied.

"All the more reason to answer the phone, Kyle," she snipped.

"If it's important they'll leave a message, I'm spending time with my woman right now."

"Mmhm," she said rolling her eyes.

"Fuck that phone," he said and I could hear Traci giggling again.

I silently agreed with Kyle's revelation. Mr. King liking me was just Traci's imagination going into overdrive. Her boyfriend's opinion was all the confirmation that I needed, so I busied myself the rest of the evening with trying to find something to wear to work the next day.

As I thumbed through my last unpacked suitcase, my mind wandered to the life that I'd left behind in Atlanta and the relationship that had ended itself. As my thoughts strayed I found myself thinking about how things used to be before I feared Chico, before he turned into the monster that didn't hesitate to raise a hand to me.

One memory in particular that stuck in my head was the first time that we became intimate.

Since we'd been dating he had told me that he wanted things to be different with me, he didn't want us to rush things like he had done in his past relationships and I agreed. Several months of dating had passed and the most that we had done was kiss. He called me one night on edge after a heated argument with someone.

"Baby what you doing'?" his voice dragged and he sounded like he was catching his breath.

"I was trying to get some studying done but I can't focus. What you doin'? Why do you sound out of breath-?" I asked but he interrupted.

"I need to see you, I'm on my way over," he told me.

"Okay," I responded and he ended the call.

I couldn't help but wonder what was bothering Chico. Since I'd met him he had always seemed calm and kept a cool head for the most part, but that night his tone was different and even on the phone I could tell that he wasn't quite himself.

Not even ten minutes had passed since our call before he was banging on the front door of my apartment. I hopped off the couch and ran over to the door, hoping he wouldn't wake my roommate with his loud knocking. When I opened the door, he stared down at me with a pained expression on his face and his eyes were heavy and red. The grey V-neck shirt that he was wearing looked a little torn at the collar and his broad shoulders were slumped. His body language was unreadable and I wasn't sure how to greet him.

"What happened to your shirt?" was the first sentence that I could form.

He didn't respond, he just came inside and shut the door behind him. When he turned around so that he was facing me again, I tried to say something else but before I could he was holding me by my waist and his lips were pressed against mine. I didn't protest or try to force him to talk, I realized that he was talking to me using his body instead of words.

His kisses had me in a haze and when he cupped my ass and carried me towards my bedroom, I wrapped my arms around his neck and surrendered to his lips and touch. The waiting was over, I could tell, and Chico was ready for us to take a step further in our relationship, which was highly anticipated. We knocked over the lamp that was on my dresser next to the door in my bedroom and it made a loud thump when it hit the floor but surprisingly didn't break. He laid me on the bed and kissed me from head to toe. He stood at the foot of the bed and stared at me as he tugged his shirt over his head revealing his well-built physique from the defined pecs to the washboard abs. Chico had the body of a weight lifter and whenever I got to see was a treat within itself.

Our first time wasn't gentle or super slow like I had envisioned it to be but it certainly wasn't disappointing. Chico's thrusts were strong and made my body yearn for more. When he tugged my hair I could feel the passion in his touch. When he bit my shoulder as he went deeper I could feel the closeness between the two of us. His stare told me that there wasn't anywhere else that he'd rather be in that moment than right there with me and that he loved me inside out.

Our climaxes were like tidal waves crashing against each other and when he laid on top of me with nothing but sweat between the two of us, the redness in his eyes had faded and he looked like he was back to himself.

"When you got here you looked like something was wrong, now you look okay. What happened babe?" I asked him as he rested his chin between my breasts.

"It's not important. What's important is what I'm about to say now," he began.

"What?"

"I want us to move in together," he exclaimed with a straight face. I paused for a moment, I wasn't sure what to say. "Nica, say something, don't get quiet on me," he said with his thick brows furrowed in a frown, using the nickname that he chose for me.

"I-I don't know what to say-."

"Say yes."

"Don't you think it's a little soon for us to live together?"

"All I know is I love you and I wanna wake up to this pretty face every day. I hate being away from you Ma, you know that. Don't you love me?" he asked, flipping it on me.

"Of course, you know I do."

"Then that's it, that's all that matter," he said with a grin and rolled me over so that I was on top.

That was the Chico that I knew and loved, the man that I had fallen in love with and that treated me like a princess in the beginning of our relationship. I wasn't sure why he changed but I know it had everything to do with his cocaine habit, which I later learned that that night was the first time that he had gotten high before he came to see me.

Now Chico was sitting in the Fulton County Jail awaiting his sentence and I was four states away with a new job and hopefully a better future ahead of me. A part of me missed him or maybe it was the security that he represented. When I was with him, I wanted for nothing, but it all came with a price. I didn't miss the yelling or him going upside my head every time I looked at him wrong or sneezed too loud. His excessive drug use had turned him from the man that I had fallen for to the monster that I dreaded and that thought I had set him up and made him think I was his enemy.

I looked for my sheer fuchsia blouse to wear to work. "I know it's here somewhere," I said to myself and then my voice trailed off when I found something in my suitcase that was fuchsia but was definitely not a blouse. I pulled the string until the entire garment was out of the suitcase. I held it by its straps and examined the shear see-through bra, which was the same thing that I performed in when I danced at Emerald City with Frankie over six months ago.

My mood went from anxious about seeing Mr. King the next day at work to being nervous for my next week or so at my new job. I wasn't exactly sure how long I would be able to hide the fact that my last place of employment was a strip club and that my past was anything but wholesome. My ultimate fear was that if Nathaniel King was into me like my sister was convinced he was, how long would it be before the truth came out?

I was awakened out of my sleep at about three that morning by Traci yelling and doors slamming. I snatched the covers off of me and got up, but just as I reached for the door I listened to what was being said from the other side.

"Traci, will you please calm down and let me explain?" I heard Kyle say.

"Explain what?! That you're still fucking around on me like I knew you were? Explain to me that you're a liar that can't keep his dick in his pants?!" she shouted from the hallway.

"I swear I didn't know baby, you gotta believe me," he pleaded but she interrupted.

"You are a fucking liar and I hate you! Save it Kyle, you were just with the bitch Uptown at some lounge! I saw the text messages and shit in your phone! I can't believe you did this to me and I can't do this anymore. Get out!" Traci told him, it sounded like she was shoving him and his back was hitting the wall where my room was.

"I swear nothing happened between me and that girl. I told

you that the last time I fucked up was the last time-," he pleaded but she interrupted.

"Save it Kyle, text messages don't lie and the same number that you said you didn't recognize is the same one that you have at least a week's worth of messages between you and whoever this bitch is. You were just with her Uptown at some lounge! I can't do this anymore. Get out!" Traci told him, she sounded like she was near tears.

"Traci-."

"Just go, get the hell out!" she insisted and after the ruffling of what sounded like some clothes, I heard footsteps until the front door shut. Traci shuffled back into her bedroom and closed her door quietly, and I could hear her sobbing until she eventually fell asleep.

FIT for a KING—*P. Sharee*

Nathaniel-8

With each passing day, I found Veronica more and more difficult to resist. She was everywhere, all the time, and I couldn't seem to shake away my thoughts and desires to spread her hips. It had been about a month since she started working for me and the cold showers and intense workouts weren't working anymore.

The fact that she did her job exceptionally well, and seemed to be a perfectionist like me didn't help the situation. It was like an aphrodisiac. There was nothing more attractive than a hard working woman. Everything about her turned me on from the way she walked and talked, how she dressed, her shyness, even the way her name rolled off my tongue.

I couldn't even hide my growing interest anymore. Whenever I needed something I would call her instead of Roxanne's chatty ass. I kept her busy with simple errands while Veronica and I worked on whatever little task I came up with just to be close to her. Whenever Roxanne needed to leave early to pick up her son, I would make Veronica stay late just to be near her.

On that particular Friday afternoon, I had grown extremely frustrated. That day she had worn a subtle yellow skirt, a sleeveless blouse with a low neckline and multicolored flowers all over it and a white blazer that stopped where the skirt began and buttoned right underneath her inviting breasts. I think the humidity outside mixed with the heat & desperation I felt to be closer to this woman threw me off my square.

My office door was cracked so I could hear her and Roxanne gathering their things at the end of the workday so they could go and start their weekend. I panicked and practically sprinted out of the door to see them headed towards the elevators.

"Veronica!" I called to her. She and Roxanne were laughing about something and turned around in unison when they heard my voice.

"Yes, Mr. King?" she asked, still wearing a smile from whatever was so funny.

"I need you to look over this spreadsheet you emailed me; I think I saw a few errors," I said referring to the errors that I created on my own to buy some alone time with her.

"Did you? I tripled checked it—of course I'll look at it again," she said all at once.

"You want me to wait for you?" Roxanne asked her.

"No, I'll call you," she told her.

"Okay. Have a good weekend, Mr. King," Roxanne said and then disappeared onto the elevator, mumbling something under her breath.

"You too," I told her and allowed Veronica to walk ahead of me. "I have it pulled up on my computer in my office," I told her as we walked past her desk and she set her things back down.

"May I?" Veronica asked if she should could sit down at my desk.

"Yes, of course," I told her and she sat down and she looked at the spreadsheet that I had pulled up on my dual monitors.

She squinted a little bit as she examined what was in front of her and then I saw her reach for the mouse and highlight a few fields, and made the necessary changes. I hovered over her while she worked, taking a deep breath and taking in her sweet perfume. I saw her visibly tense up as she continued to work.

"It looks like I transposed some of the dates in a few columns…but now everything should be perfect," Veronica said as she finished up what she was doing. "See," she said sitting back a little admiring her handy work. Veronica brushed up against my shoulder when she did that and she immediately sat up straight. "Sorry," she said a little embarrassed. "Don't apologize," I told her. I leaned in a little closer and placed my hand over her hand on the mouse to scroll down and pretended I was checking for any other mistakes. As I searched, I sniffed her hair and it smelled as good as the rest of her did, her hand trembled slightly and felt miniature underneath mine. The loud and unexpected sound of thunder roared through the room and she jumped a little. "Everything looks good from where I'm standing," I said, looking at the side of her face. "Thank you."

"You're welcome," she said and turned to face me and our lips slightly brushed up against each other's. She gasped lightly and placed her hand over her mouth and said, "I'm so sorry."

I shook my head with a grin and said, "Stop apologizing and move your hand." She shook her head, "No," almost as if she was afraid of what would happen. "Veronica, move your hand," I said with a chuckle and she still refused. "Fine," I said and pushed her hand down with mine so that her full pretty lips were mine for the taking.

"Mr. King–," she attempted to say but before she could finish my lips were pressed against hers.

At first it seemed like I was the only one doing the kissing, and then I felt her kiss me back. The rain began to fall and landed on the windows of my office in large heavy drops. I inched closer to Veronica, wanting more of her mouth. I cupped her face in my hands and deepened the kiss.

I could tell she was into it when I heard and felt her moan in my mouth a bit. My hands moved from her face and down to her hands, ushering her to stand. Our tongues slid into each other's mouth and I pressed her up against my desk, pushed the keyboard to the side, and sat her on top. I slid her skirt up and wedged myself between her thick thighs, running my hands up and down her smooth skin.

"We. We. Shouldn't. Be doing. This," she said between kisses.

"I. Know." I replied.

"So. Why. Don't. We. Stop?" she asked.

"I. Can't. Stop," I admitted. I pulled my lips away from hers and started to kiss her neck and unbutton her blazer. Once the single button was free I pushed it off her shoulders and sucked on her neck a little harder. What we were doing wasn't enough and I needed to feel closer to this woman; I needed to feel her.

I sat down in my chair, pulled her on top of me so that she was straddling my lap and swallowed her in a deep kiss as my hands fondled her breasts and moved down until they were between her thighs where she was warm and her panties were wet. I groaned into her mouth with approval and pushed her panties to the side and began to stroke her clit with my finger. It became slicker under my touch so I used another and stuck it inside of her. She felt so tight around my finger that I knew whenever I got the chance to feel it for myself I would lose it.

"I love how wet you are for me already," I said against her lips.

"Mmm, Mr. King," she moaned just as she had in my daydream with half closed eyes. The line of employer-employee no longer existed between she and I. The both of us were finally letting our guards down and acting strictly on passion.

I inserted a second finger into her and she grew even wetter as her clit throbbed from the strokes of my thumb. I wanted her to come one good time before I propped her on top of my desk and had that pussy for an early dinner. When I looked up at her, her facial expression was unmistakable and I knew my wish was about to come true. I felt her insides grip my fingers tighter as she cried out "Mr. King!" her body creaming and her juices dripping down my fingers and into my palm.

"I can't wait to taste this pussy," I said through clenched teeth then I heard my iPhone ring and buzz from my desk. I looked at it and then looked at Veronica.

"Aren't you gonna get that?" she asked licking her full lips.

"I'm kinda in the middle of something," I grinned and she giggled and shook her head at me. I was relieved when the phone silenced so I could keep my head in the game; that was until it started ringing and vibrating again. That time I looked at the caller I.D. and the name on the screen and that told me the call was business related. I groaned with frustration and reached for the phone.

"Jim? What's the word?" I asked, answering a call from my accountant. "Uh huh...okay...good, good, so everything went through...excellent..." I said into the phone but watched Veronica's every move. She had eased herself off of my wet fingers and began to button her blazer. I offered her a puppy-dog look and she smiled but continued to readjust her clothes. "So everything is in place? Great...yes of course, we'll get together Tuesday and revisit everything...alright...bye." I said and ended the call. Veronica had a blank expression on her face.

"I should go," she told me.

"Where do you think you're going?" I joked as I stood up from my chair and shifted my now semi-hard dick in my pants.

"I need to get home. I'm going out tonight and I have no idea what I'm wearing," she said, looking up at me. I loosened my grip on her and said, "A night on the town, huh? Where? To a club or just a bar?" I asked, trying not to sound too eager.

"Some place called...Matrix or something," she told me and a grin spread across my face. "What? Do you know that place?"

"Yeah, I've heard of it," I lied, sort of. "So, you two are having a girl's night?"

"I don't really do the club thing but Roxy really wanted me to come and my sister thinks I need to get out. The only thing that I've done since I moved here is go to dinner and come to work," she admitted.

"Yeah, you definitely should get out, there's a lot more to Houston than just King Global."

"Said the King of Houston," she teased and we both laughed.

"You're cute when you're trying to be funny," I took in her stance and wanted more than anything than to finish what we had just started. "Enjoy yourself tonight, Veronica," I told her.

"I'll try. You don't go out?" she wanted to know.

"Not really, the club scene was never really my thing."

"I know what you mean," she told me and then licked her

lips, making me want her even more. "I guess I'll see you Monday, Mr. King," she smiled at me and heading to the door. I followed her out to her desk as she grabbed her things.

"Enjoy your weekend," I said, returning her smile. "Oh and Veronica?" I called to her and she turned around to face me.

"Yes?" she asked. I brought my two moist fingers that I had just used on her up to my mouth and slowly sucked away the traces of her arousal that tasted just how I imagined.

"You taste sweeter than I thought you would," I said with a wink after my fingers slid out of my mouth. She gave me a seductive grin and bit her lip then walked away.

I was even more sexually frustrated than I had been before. I had finally gotten a taste of her, and I felt like a fiend. I needed more, much more than just a kiss and a finger fuck. Veronica had conquered my mind without even knowing it and I knew her body would be my kryptonite.

When I left my office, I skipped the gym and decided to work out at home. There was nothing on my schedule for the weekend and I couldn't stop thinking about my assistant.

I committed myself to an hour on the treadmill and my usual amount of crunches and push-ups, deciding before I started that the free weights were out of the question.

At around nine that evening, I found myself completely exasperated and without anything to do. My usual group of friends were all having "date-night" with their significant others and I was a prisoner of my own filthy thoughts of her.

My mind had been telling me to suppress whatever attraction I had for this woman, and remain professional. My body said I had to have her; I needed to at least see if there was anything to it. My mouth desired hers, my hands itched to touch and caress her skin, and my dick twitched and yearned to feel her insides.

"Fuck!" I yelled, my voice echoing throughout the room. "Fuck it," I said and hopped off of the plush sectional I had been laying on watching a rerun of "First Take" on ESPN.

I went upstairs to my bedroom and explored the contents of my massive walk in closet. After careful consideration and trying on four different versions of the same thing, I ended up choosing a pair of black acid washed jeans, black Ralph Lauren Polo shoes, a black and white t-shirt by YSL and a light leather jacket.

When I was ready to head out, I pulled out my wet black Aston Martin and headed towards the expressway. I made one phone call on my way to my destination via Bluetooth as I drove.

"Yea Lance, its Nate…I'm coming through tonight so prepare the usual." I said and then ended the call.

FIT for a KING– P. Sharee

Nathaniel-9

By the time I arrived at Matrix, it was minutes away from midnight and the line was wrapped around the building.

The valet was waiting out front and approached my door when I put the car in park.

"Good evening, Mr. King." The tall biracial young man said as I stepped out of my car.

"What's up, man?" I asked, shaking his hand and sliding him a $50 dollar bill in the process.

"Thank you, sir," he said, nodding his head as I rounded the car so he could take my place in the driver's seat.

I stepped up onto the curb and took a few long strides up to the entrance of the club.

"Mr. King, welcome," Lance, the manager of Matrix said and greeted me with a handshake.

"Thanks Lance," I said, looking past him at the growing line to get inside.

"Enjoy your night Sir and let me know if you need anything."

"Will do." I told him and the bouncer unhooked the velvet rope to allow me entry.

The club was beyond packed and Latin music blared through the speakers, making the wall's vibrations coincide with the beats of the bass. I immediately started to rethink my decision to come out but then reminded myself why I was here. I couldn't wait until Monday to see her again. I knew I would spend my weekend being a dud and thinking about her the entire time anyway so why not torture myself a little bit more?

The second level housed a private VIP area where the music wasn't as damaging to my eardrums, but still fairly loud. Two waitresses serviced that particular area along with one bartender.

"Here you are, Mr. King," one of the waitresses dressed in white said and set down a chilled fifth of Jack Daniels.

"Thank you," I said with a smile and handed her a twenty, the valet had gotten my last fifty and she certainly hadn't earned a hundred dollar bill, not yet at least.

I poured myself up a shot and took in the scene. I scoped the crowd for Veronica or Roxanne, and even Veronica's sister Traci. I wasn't sure who else would be with them but I figured if I spotted one of them, I would be led to the one I was seeking. The crowd was filled with every ethnicity imaginable, black, white, Hispanic, Asian, even Arabic. But then again that was the kind of club that Matrix Houston was. It appealed to mixed crowds and was named one of the hottest and most happening nightclubs in Texas for the past three years.

About a half hour in, I grew a tad bit impatient. I still hadn't found who I was looking for and my last two shots of Jack had about the same effect on me as glass of water. I poured up my third and stood with it as I looked over the balcony into the crowd. Looking for Veronica was like playing 'Where is Waldo' in this crowded club. Once I took my shot to the head, I held onto my empty glass as I searched and then froze when I found my target.

There she stood, in the center of the dance floor, my sole reason for making an appearance at Matrix that evening. She had the most carefree look on her face and was wearing that smile that made me melt. Dressed in a red mini dress that fit her voluptuous body like a glove and black patent leather peep-toe stilettos, Veronica danced to some song that talked about sex and grinding on each other in the worst way. The way she moved her hips and sang along to the lyrics made me question the shy persona that she had been displaying since we'd met.

Roxanne, Traci, and Veronica danced with each other until the song became blended with some up-tempo techno song and then I saw Veronica and Roxanne head in the direction of the restroom. That was my chance and the only problem would be avoiding Roxanne's nosey ass so that I could get Veronica alone.

I rushed down the steps and by the time I reached the bottom they were inside the ladies room. My phone buzzed in my hand and the caller I.D. read "Unknown" again. I shook my head, silenced the call and waited around the corner from the restrooms until Veronica emerged a couple minutes later.

I played with my phone around the corner from the restrooms until she emerged a couple minutes later. She waited outside for Roxanne while she fumbled with her clutch I knew it was now or never if I wanted her to myself.

"Veronica," I called from where I stood leaned up against the brick wall. Her head popped up from what she was doing and when she saw me a smile spread across her face.

"Mr. King?" she asked, looking up at me. With nervous fingers she smoothed down the back of her short hair, which was intact just as it had been at work that day, and she was wearing very little make-up which was a turn-on.

"Come here," I ordered as I beckoned for her with my index finger, wearing a mischievous smirk.

She glanced over her shoulder to see if Roxanne was behind her and when she saw that she wasn't, she rushed over to me. I took her hand in mine and then ducked around another corner into a dark empty hallway and planted a fiery passionate kiss on her soft lips. I wasn't sure what had come over me but when I saw her up close, I couldn't help myself. She was the only thing that I wanted in that moment and I was confident that she wanted me too.

When I finally pulled away we were both short of breath and damn near salivating for each other.

"Come with me," I insisted.

"But, my sister and…Roxy will wonder where I went," she

told me.

"Send your sister a text, tell her you're with me and tell her not to tell Roxanne. She's nosey as hell," I said and she giggled and then removed her black iPhone from her clutch and typed out a text then stuffed it back in the small purse. "Come on." I said and took her hand again and led her down the hall and into the door of the stairwell that led to the roof top VIP.

The roof was for exclusive guests like me and those that could afford the VIP treatment. When we got to the door the bouncer saw who I was and let us in.

"How you doing tonight, Mr. King?" The huge Rick Ross look alike asked me.

"I can't complain, man," I told him, and then saw his attention turn to Veronica. His eyes noticeably slid down her body and I shot him a knowing look.

There were only about a dozen other people on the roof seated at the glass counter-high tables for two. Veronica and I went to the very back of the space to what I called my oasis when I visited Matrix. It was a little nook complete with sheer white drapes, a glass cocktail table, and speakers so that you could still hear the music playing from downstairs. There had been a bottle of Cristal chilling and the oasis had its own bouncer.

This one was white and a lot taller than the one that guarded the door.

"Sir," he said and stepped aside to allow us entry.

"Thank you." I said as we stepped inside then took a seat on the crisp white love seat.

"I thought you didn't do the club scene, Mr. King," she flirted as she crossed her long milk chocolate legs while sitting across from me. I laughed to myself before I responded with,

"I usually don't but tonight I...had a change of heart," then reached for the Cristal that had been chilling and poured up two glasses.

"Oh really?" she asked with a raised brow accepting her glass.

"Mmhm," I said, licking my lips. "I saw you on the dance floor."

"You did? Oh no, you have to excuse me when I've been drinking," she said, covering her face and returning to the shy version of herself that I knew from the office.

"No no, I liked what I saw, no complaints over here."

"Oh." She said with her perfect lips stuck in "O" position, I wanted to kiss them again she looked so fuckin' sexy.

"I feel like you're too far away, come here," I ordered as I wrapped my arm around her waist and scooted her body closer to mine discarding the champagne. Without thinking, just like downstairs a few minutes before, I attacked her lips with a tongue kiss. I had never been so into someone the way I was into Veronica, it was almost like she brought the animal out of me. When I kissed her I didn't care that she was my assistant and that I had a strict policy about not dating my employees, all I wanted was her.

I pulled her onto my lap and the kisses and touching grew more intense. We were picking up where we had left off earlier in my office and I was down for whatever she was.

"What are we doing, Mr. King?" she asked once she snatched her lips away from mine.

"Huh?" I said, suckling her bottom lip back into my mouth.

"What are we doing? What is this?" she asked as she straddled my lap, her warm center right above my growing throbbing erection.

"Kissing, touching…" I said, kissing her neck after each word.

"Mr. King…I'm serious." she said, holding back a smile.

"First of all, cut that Mr. King shit; we're not on the clock," I told her. "And what do you mean what are we doing? I like you."

"You like me?" she repeated.

"Yes, you don't like me?"

"I…you're my boss."

"And?" I said raising a brow.

"And I thought you didn't get involved with your employees," she said slapping me with my own words.

"I don't…I didn't until you."

"Why me? You don't know me outside of work." she said,

73

easing her way off my lap and I felt my jaw drop just a little with silent defeat.

"Why not? Look at you, pretty face, and a beautiful body. You're intelligent and sweet, how shy you are is adorable."

"You seem like you would go for more the model type or something."

"I'm attracted to all women, but you..." was all I could say as I looked her up and down. She smiled and looked down. "So you don't like me?"

"I didn't say that," she said, her eyes shooting back up to meet my gaze.

"So, what's the problem?" I asked, placing my hand on her thigh, her skin as soft as rose petals.

"So, we like each other? What does that mean? I work for you...are you looking for something that's just physical? Because if so, I'm not sure we..."

"I never said that. I don't know what any of this means, but I know I had to just get it out. What are you looking for?" I wanted to know. She paused for a while before she spoke again.

"I don't know either, but I know I'm not up for a fuck buddy. My last relationship was...toxic, so before now I had kinda sworn off men. I haven't been with anybody in a while so the next person that I do decide to become intimate with will have earned it," she said plainly, taking a sip from her glass. She set the champagne flute down and licked her lips, our eyes locked with each other's.

"I understand," I said, unable to take my eyes off of her.

I inched a little closer to her and then kissed her lips. We pulled away at the same time and looked at each other, then kissed again. Her lips were soft and moist from when she had licked them and it was almost as if she was dissolving in my mouth. She moaned as she had done earlier in my office and I wrapped an arm around her waist.

Her hand came up to my face and rested on my cheek as our tongues danced in each other's mouths. In an instant she was above me and straddling my lap again. My hands found her ass and squeezed and caressed it, closing my eyes tight at the feeling. It was firm like she did squats regularly, but still had just enough softness and jiggle that I loved. Her arms were around my shoulders and I groaned in her mouth and ran my hands up and down her legs with a mix of frustration and lust.

Just as she began to suck and bite my bottom lip, the bouncer guarding my oasis opened the sheer curtain enough for me to see his face.

"Excuse me, Sir," his husky voice spoke. I reluctantly pulled away from Veronica's lips and looked past her at the bouncer with an irritated expression. "Sir we have a…situation downstairs," I knew exactly what that meant.

"Okay," I said and then returned my attention to Veronica, "I have something that I need to take care of, I'm gonna have you escorted outside along with Traci and Roxanne, you all need to leave the club."

"What? Why? What's going on?"

"I'll explain later but I wanna make sure that you're safe, just trust me," I said calmly.

"Okay," she said with confusion. I stole one last kiss and then helped her up so that she was on steady legs.

"Gimme your phone," she removed it from her clutch and handed it over without hesitation. I quickly dialed my number and let it ring long enough until I felt it vibrate in my pocket and then ended the call and handed it back to Veronica. I looked at her and kissed her long and hard one more time and then said "Alright, I gotta go," then gestured for the bouncer to escort her out of Matrix.

Before I left the rooftop I stopped at a steel locked case that required a code for entry near the exit. I entered a four digit number and grabbed my bulletproof vest that I kept there incase shit ever got out of hand while I was making an appearance. I pulled the white YSL t-shirt over my head and strapped the vest on and then headed down the back stairwell.

Chaos crowded the main floor and it looked as if a riot was taking place. All the bouncers that were dressed in black suits were breaking up the rift raft but shit was still crazy. I did the only thing that I knew would get everyone's attention and ran behind the nearest bar, opened the safe next to the fridge at the end and took out my chrome 40-caliber handgun to fire off five rounds in the air. When everyone heard the shots go off they started scattering like roaches and the club emptied out in what looked a stampede.

I ended up hitting one of the light fixtures with my cowboy move but I knew I had to act fast if I wanted whatever that was going on to cease.

"What the fuck was all this shit about, O?" I asked Omar, my head of security.

"Nate, man, I don't know, it sounded like some baby mama-baby daddy shit but I'm not sure. That's what Lance thinks."

"It looks like we're gonna have to have a stricter policy at the door. I shouldn't have to pull out my piece to clear shit up around here. You need to call a mandatory meeting with your men so that this shit doesn't happen again, is that clear?" I yelled.

"Yes Sir."

I walked past Omar and made my way to the entrance of the club. Crowds of people were being ushered away from the sidewalk and away from Matrix and the Houston police were now on the scene. I scanned the clusters of people to see if I saw Veronica and I sighed with relief when I saw her assigned escort helping her, Traci, and Roxanne into a taxi.

I pulled my phone out and scrolled to the last missed call that I had.

Veronica-10

"Okay, I'll see y'all later. Text me when you make it home," Roxy said waving bye to Traci and I.

"I will," I told her and she climbed out of the taxicab that we'd shared after leaving Matrix. We watched her walk into her apartment building and then allowed the driver to pull off.

"That was crazy what happened at the club; I can't believe there was actually a riot," Traci said as the driver turned the car around and headed towards our destination.

"I know, I did not expect that at all," I agreed.

"Where did you and Nate sneak off to? I had to make up some shit and tell Roxy you met up with some guy and he took you to his VIP."

"That wasn't far from the truth."

"What happened? Don't leave anything out. Did y'all finish what y'all started earlier in his office you lil freak nasty," Traci teased.

"No, we just kissed and talked. He told me that he…likes me."

"Hell I told you that. I told Kyle the same thing and he tried to play it off with his lying ass," she said pursing her lips up with a hint of anger.

"What's up with you two anyway? You haven't talked to

him?" I asked, remembering the whole "herpes" blow-up a few weeks back. I hadn't really asked Traci about it, but the day after it happened she had a breakdown and confided in me and told me how she felt about the whole thing. My heart went out to her and I was just as angry with Kyle as she was for what he'd done.

A few weeks back, she called me and told me she had painful, open sores on her vagina and how Kyle was the the only one who could have done that to her. Sure enough, after she Googled the symptons, and a quick visit to a local clinic, Herpes was the diagnosis. I kept telling her, "No mistakes. Just lessons learned." But I knew it wasn't helping.

"Hell no. Once I went through his phone and saw all kinds of text messages and pictures from different bitches. I told him they could have his nasty ass and that I was done. Thanks to him I'll be taking fucking Valtrex for the rest of life," she spat.

"Damn Tray that's messed up, I'm sorry he-."

"He's the only one that should be sorry, I'm good," she said, trying to convince us both. Her phone began to ring from her lap and she rolled her eyes when she saw that it was Kyle calling. "That's his sorry ass right now," she said and as soon as she answered the phone the only words that came out of her mouth were curse words as she gave Kyle the tongue lashing of his life for the tenth time about his cheating ways.

I shook my head at her and then felt my phone buzz on the seat where it sat next to me. The screen displayed an unknown Houston number that I didn't recognize.

"Hello?"

"Did you make it home safe?" Nate's voice said from the other end.

"Hey? Almost. How did you get my number?" I smiled.

"A magician never reveals his tricks," he joked. She'd forgotten that she gave him her number at the club.

Just the sound of his voice combined with the alcohol that I had consumed that evening was all I needed. His concern for my safety made me warm all over and our conversation had my complete undivided attention I hadn't even realized we made it home as quickly as we did.

"So, Nate," I said stepping out of my heels one at a time.

"So, Roni," he said and I could hear his turn signal in the background.

"What is this thing…that we're doing? What do you want from me?"

He laughed loudly into the phone and said, "I want to get to know you."

"Really? That's it?"

"Don't get me wrong, I am a man. And I would be lying if I said I didn't want to put a plate underneath you, and have my way," he told me and my eyes widened with surprise as he spoke honestly. I felt myself tighten between my legs at his confession.

"But as I said, I do like you and I'm willing to go at whatever pace you're comfortable with," he told me.

"I appreciate that," I told him, turning on the faucet so that I could wash my face and get ready for bed. The time on my phone said 2:20 a.m. but I was wired.

Nate and I continued to talk while I got ready for bed and wrapped my hair up. By the time he got home closer to three, we were still on the phone and having the best convo. Our conversation started off about work related stuff, to where we both went to college and how he started King Global. We went from that to briefly discussing his wife and daughter and I told him a little about my relationship with Chico but I managed to dodge how we truly met.

He went on to tell me how he hadn't dated much since Lauren passed (his late wife) and how his family was worried about him for a while. He spoke highly of his mother and siblings and how he never really knew his father and wasn't too fond of his stepfather. I told him about how Traci and I had reconnected nearly two years ago and how it was the one of the best things that happened to me in a really long time. I told him how I hadn't seen my mother in over ten years, but I didn't tell him about my days as a stripper. I didn't think it was the right time to visit that skeleton.

Before I knew it, the sun was coming up and we were still laughing and talking like a couple of kids.

"Do you realize that we've been on the phone for over four

hours? The sun is coming up," I informed him.

"Damn, you're right. I hadn't even noticed. I haven't talked on the phone this long probably since high school," he grinned.

"I know, me either." I agreed.

"It's easy to lose track of time when you're anywhere around," he told me.

"Yeah, you have that same effect on me," I admitted.

"I'll let you get your beauty rest. Can I see you later?" he asked, catching me off guard.

"Um, let me see if my sister has anything planned for us today and then I'll let you know." I lied.

"Okay, I'll text you later to see if you're free," he told me.

"Okay," I said and hung up.

I set my phone on the table next to the bed and sighed. I couldn't believe the night I'd had, hell the last 24 hours to be precise. My boss and I had crossed the line of professionalism and apparently neither of us cared. We had gone from what I thought was him being nice and innocent flirting, to tonguing each other down in his office (not to mention the finger fucking) and on the rooftop of a club. We spent the remainder of the evening and early morning hours talking on the phone like two teenagers and enjoyed every minute of it. Was I dreaming? Had he actually told me that he liked me and wanted to get to know me on a more personal level? I was starting to think that Traci was right all along when she said that he was into me on my second day at King Global.

I decided to keep whatever Nate and I had going on between the two of us and my sister, of course. Roxy was cool, but I didn't know her well enough to trust her yet. Besides she was a gossip, and even though she claimed she had a new man, she still had a fire burning between her legs for our boss.

Once I finally fell asleep, I didn't wake up again until almost one that afternoon.

I stumbled out of my bedroom and across the hall to the bathroom to brush my teeth and wash my face. As I stared at myself, I couldn't help but still feel the memory of his arms around my waist, his lips on mine and on my neck. I was trying my best to hold on and keep it in my pants, but I wasn't sure how many more of Nate's kisses and touches I could endure before I would let him put that metaphoric plate underneath me and feast.

After I showered, I noticed that I missed a text from Nate and grinned ear to ear as I read it. He asked me if I wanted to see a movie that afternoon and after I agreed he informed me that he would pick me up in about an hour.

I tossed my phone on the bed and rambled through the closet and dresser drawers. I needed to find something cute yet accidentally sexy that would coincide with the Texas heat. I tried on I don't know how many capris, shorts, skirts and dresses. I finally settled on a loose linen jumper that was colorful with spaghetti straps. I wore a denim half jacket with it and black gladiator sandals that had rhinestones on the straps.

While I was in the bathroom fixing my hair, I heard Traci's bedroom door open, and then her face appeared in the doorway.

"Where are you going, Miss Thang? I was gonna ask you if you wanted to go to lunch or something," she said scratching her head.

"To the movies," I told her sitting the flat iron down and then combing the back of my hair down.

"Oh," she said lowly. "With Mr. King?" she asked, raising her eyebrows and making them dance, veiling her disappointment.

"You are silly," I laughed, reaching for my cherry lip-gloss. "And yes, I'm going to the movies with Nate."

"Oh, he's 'Nate' now?" she teased.

"Hush," I said as I painted my lips with the gloss in the mirror.

"Girl, I'm just playing," she giggled as she ran her fingers through her hair. "Sooo, you never told me about last night, what happened? You were too busy cackling on the phone."

"I know. We talked until like six this morning."

"That's cute," she grinned.

"I know, right? He told me a little bit about his wife and daughter. But we spent most of the time just laughing and joking. He's funny."

"Sounds like y'all are really hitting it off," she gave me a warm smile.

"It's crazy, right? Me and a man like him?" I said twisting the lip-gloss cap closed.

"Don't sell yourself short, honey. I mean he's fine and all but you're no slouch," her eyebrows knitted together as she spoke.

"How do I look?" I asked turning to face her completely.

"Really cute. Turn around," she said twirling her finger and I did. "I wonder why I couldn't get as much ass as you did, that thing has a mind of its own, I swear."

"You didn't get the ass because you got the boobs," I said touching one of her breasts and making it bounce underneath her shirt. We laughed at each other and I walked out of the bathroom.

My phone was vibrating on my bed when I walked in and I anxiously picked it up when I saw who was calling.

"Hello?" I said.

"Hey, you ready?" Nate's voice said into the phone.

"Yeah."

"I'm downstairs, which apartment are you in?" he asked me.

"That's okay, I'll be right down." I told him

"Okay," he replied and then hung up.

Outside the Texas sun's radiance kissed my skin and I saw a black Aston Martin parked in front of the curb. It looked like one of the cars that James Bond drove, too pretty to actually be driven. Nate stepped out of the driver's side and came around to where I stood. He was wearing a black V-neck t-shirt that hugged his muscles just right, dark gray Levi's and black and white Polo loafers. The light wind wafted the scent of his cologne and body wash to my nose and I had to close my eyes as I inhaled. Black Ray Bans covered his eyes and he was wearing a thin silver chain with a cross that hung from it on his neck.

"Hey," I said as he embraced me in a warm hug then a kiss on my cheek.

"Hey, you," he said looking at me, his face inches from mine. "You look beautiful as usual," he told me as he ran his hand down my arm.

"Thank you." I said, smiling shyly at his compliment, thankful he couldn't see my eyes behind my shades.

"Shall we?" he asked, opening the passenger door for me. "We shall," I said with a giggle. He smiled at me and shut the door once I was inside. I studied the interior of his car and everything was sleek and still had that new car smell. It was all black and had ample legroom since it was a two-seater. Nate got us deluxe tickets to an action comedy that starred Kevin Hart and Jamie Foxx. Our seats were up on the balcony of the theater and we shared a tub of popcorn along with my cherry slushy and Nate's bottle of water.

Halfway into the movie my phone vibrated with a text and it read:

I've been wanting to kiss you since I stopped kissing you last night

I smiled down at my phone and typed back:

I never wanted to stop kissing you

I could see him grinning from the corner of my eye when he looked down at his phone and typed something back right away. When my phone buzzed he had sent me a winking smiley face emoji. He inched as close to me as he could in his seat and took my phone and shoved it back in my bag and then grabbed me by the chin and pressed his lips to mine. There was that electricity again, flickering through my lips and into my bloodstream. It was like his lips were meant for mine. I covered his bottom lip with both of mine and sucked and nibbled on it. He slid his tongue inside of my mouth, forcing mine into his and he inhaled as I exhaled. I was the first one to pull away once I felt myself start to really get into it. We both snickered afterward and wiped the moisture away from our respective mouths.

"You gotta stop kissing me like that," he whispered next to my ear and I smiled and said,

"Why?"

"Because," he said getting closer so that his breath was on my skin as he spoke, "You make me want to kiss…other places," and then nibbled on my ear tugging at my lobe with his teeth. I took a deep breath and felt that familiar warmth between my legs return.

After the movie and our little…make-out session in the

Cinemark Theater downtown, we got a slice of pizza at this little pizzeria nearby, then drove to the beach and walked around while we ate frozen yogurt. Being with Nate felt like no one else was around, like no one else existed and we were in our own world. It was like a breath of fresh air and I was afraid to exhale because if I did, it all could end.

My evening ended with a heated kiss from Mr. King on Traci's doorstep that left me breathless, I reluctantly went inside of the apartment and locked the door behind me. As I made my way to my bedroom, I felt my phone vibrate from my purse. I was hoping it was Nate, but a little surprised at the name that the caller I.D. displayed and answered.

"Hey Frankie, what's up girl-," I began.

"Roni, have you heard from Chico?" she interrupted in a low voice, almost as if she was sneaking on the phone. The mere mention of Chico's name still made me shiver.

"No, you're the only person from Atlanta that has my new number," I reminded her. "What's going on?"

"I heard he hired Ericka Lucas to represent him," Frankie told me and I froze momentarily. Ericka Lucas was one of the most successful and prominent black litigators in Atlanta and she specialized in Criminal Law. She had been known to get off some of Georgia's biggest kingpins with charges ranging from drug raids to multiple homicides. Ericka was damn good at what she did and if I didn't know anything else, I knew that Chico was in good hands and probably wouldn't step foot in a prison once she was done.

"You know what that means," Frankie continued.

"There's a good chance he's getting out," I muttered in a shaky voice.

"I would bet my last on dollar on it," she told me.

Veronica–11

I arrived to work the next morning still uneasy from Frankie's phone call about and the news on Chico's defense attorney. How was it even possible that he could be getting out after all the evidence they supposedly had on him? But then again, in Atlanta it wasn't what you knew, it was who you knew and Chico knew a lot of people, all the right ones if he was able to get Ericka Lucas to represent him.

Roxy was sitting at her desk moving her mouse around and extremely focused on whatever she was doing when I walked in. We exchanged pleasantries, her not taking her eyes off the screen and I sat down quietly at my desk as I tried to calm my nerves. She pecked a bit at her keyboard and then finished what she was doing. "So," she began as she switched over to my desk as I sat down. "Are you ready to tell me what really happened when you disappeared on us at Matrix?" she said so only the two of us could hear.

"What? I told you I met up with this guy from my and Traci's apartment building who has a lil crush on me," I lied, turning on my monitor.

"Mmhm," she said giving me the side eye.

"Please, I'm not the only one that was busy Roxy. What about that guy that was all over you when we got there? What was his name?" I said, getting off the subject real quick.

"Who Julian?" she beamed from ear to ear at the mention of his name.

"Yea, what happened with y'all? I remember you couldn't keep your hands out of those dreads of his."

"I gave his sexy ass my number and we hung out Saturday. I call him my chocolate drop," she said fluttering her false lashes and placing a hand over her cleavage that was peaking from her teal blouse. "I still don't believe you though Roni," she reminded me with squinted eyes.

"No need to lie..." I said cutting myself off when Nate entered the room. He looked as good as he always had in one of his expensive suits. This one was light grey and made him look more fuckable than usual. It was almost as if his entrance was in slow motion and I had to fight my flesh from going over to him and sticking my tongue down his throat.

"Good morning, Mr. King," Roxy said standing up from where she had been leaning on my desk. The desperation for our bosses attention seeped through her pores it was so pathetic.

"Good morning Roxanne, morning Veronica," he smiled.

"Good morning, Mr. King." I said lowly, giving him a half smile before he disappeared into his office. My mind shifted from my worries about Chico and Roxy's talk about her new boo, to the weekend that I had spent with Mr. King. He turned out to be everything that I imagined and more; I knew I could never get enough of Nathaniel King and the more time I spent with him the more I wanted him to spread my hips.

Not long after our day started, Roxy and I got to work prepping for a board meeting scheduled for 10 am. The top executives gradually poured into the conference room that was adjoined with Nate's office as I made sure there was plenty of coffee, water and refreshments at their disposal after being informed that I would be taking the minutes for that meeting.

Nate took his seat at the head of the table and sat before the room of 12 board members which consisted of mostly white faces with a few black sprinkled in. He had a solid team that worked under him and in the short time that I had been there, I'd learned that he was a hardworking man and one you did not want to disappoint.

I sat to his right and started pecking away on the MacBook laptop that accompanied me in the meeting to keep the minutes. I had the seating chart completed already and the time filled in, ready to go.

Nate started the meeting with his usual speech about the company and then he went on to mention what areas he felt needed improvement as well the strong points. He turned the meeting over to the vice president and senior vice president.

As I typed, I wondered why this was something that Roxy enjoyed? I found it extremely boring and the things that they discussed sounded like it was in Spanish. I didn't mind sitting next to the man in charge which may have been the incentive that Roxy felt.

Everything about Nate breathed dominance and control when he was in the boardroom. He knew his company inside and out and didn't mind rolling up his sleeves and getting his hands dirty whenever he had to.

Forty-five minutes in I saw an alert at the bottom of my screen that told me I had an email. I furrowed my eyebrows and quickly clicked on it.

When I opened the message it said that the sender was from NKingTut@msn.com. I kept my expression neutral and read the message:

You are extremely sexy when you're focused. Don't be mad, but I made you do the minutes so I wouldn't have to endure Roxanne's pitiful advances…and so that I could have you next to me…otherwise I would be asleep by now.

P.s. I'm jealous of that dress, I wish I could hug your body the way it does.

NK

I casually glanced in his direction and saw that he was staring down at his blackberry which must've been how he emailed me. I typed up a quick response and sent it right away then notated something from the meeting that I was still surprisingly keeping up with. He replied with an 'LOL", showing he couldn't' multi-task.

So you drafted me, huh? So selfish, Mr. King. Just kidding,

I bet there isn't a selfish bone in your body. And speaking of bodies, mine would much rather have you wrapped around it than this ole' thing;-)

I typed and then clicked send. He sipped his water and read my message and a slight grin spread across his delicious lips. After he swallowed and returned the cap to the bottle, he picked up his phone.

Yes, you were indeed drafted. And yes I can be selfish when it comes to getting what I want…and I want you.

When I read his message my heartbeat quickened and I started to feel warm again. What was this man trying to do? Ruin me completely? My new "virginity" was holding on by a single thread, and after reading his words I was ready to surrender.

With a slightly shaky hand, I reached for my own bottle of water that was half-full and almost downed the rest of it. I didn't know what to type back so I took more notes from the meeting and then heard the senior vice president say,

"Nate, what are your thoughts on a possible expansion?" he asked and Nate looked up from his phone and switched gears with a snap of a finger.

"I've always been open to the possibility of an expansion, if the numbers are in place," he answered. "And we all know that numbers don't lie, don't we?" he said to the room with a grin and there were a few quiet laughs.

"If you refer to page four of the prospectus, there are some rough numbers based off of last quarter," the head of the accounting department told him.

"I did and I need something a little more current and a little less…rough," he replied. "Was there anything else that we needed to cover?" he asked and glanced at his Movado on his wrist to reference the time, then around the table.

"I think that was everything," the vice president said.

"Very well. I'll be talking with you all individually very soon, probably sometime this week. Thank you for coming. Veronica will forward you the minutes no later than…?" he asked, waiting for me to respond.

"Oh, it should be the first thing tomorrow morning," I said

with a smile.

"Great, we usually have to wait until the end of the week," The senior vice president said to me with a smile.

"Mr. King, did you need anything else from me?" I asked as Nate and I stood at the same time.

"Yes…if you could wait for me in my office, I'll be right in," he told me. I nodded and then charged out of the conference room and went through the doors that adjoined Nate's office. I sat down and started editing the minutes that I took during the meeting and waited for him to come in. Right before I began to edit my spelling and grammar, he charged through the same doors I had and locked them behind him.

"Come here," he demanded. Initially I hesitated, and then uncrossed my legs and walked towards him. Once we were facing each other, like a magnetic force, our lips locked and his hands rested on my hips.

"Are sure we should be doing this? Here at work?" I asked, with nervous laughter in between his fiery kisses.

"I'm the boss, remember?" he smiled down at me.

"What if Roxy walks in or..." I told him and he cut me off with another moist kiss, sucking my bottom lip into his mouth.

"I love these lips," he told me and I moaned into his mouth as I closed my eyes.

"Mmm," I said, reluctantly pulling away.

"What? The door is locked, Veronica," he assured me with a hint of annoyance in his tone.

"Okay, but you said you needed me for something," I reminded him.

"You keep interrupting me," he said holding me by the waist and we both laughed.

"Oh," I said, realizing what he had meant.

"Actually, I want to invite you and your sister to a gathering I'm having at my house this weekend. Nothing major, just a few people. No one from here will be there so we can…be us, or at least be more like this…I hope," he told me.

"What time?"

"Three o'clock. I'm cooking out and we'll be out by the

pool so feel free to wear a bathing suit," he smirked.

"Okay, I'll be there," I said with a smile. "Now let me get back to work." I told him.

"Fine," he said, stealing another long kiss then letting me go. I turned on my heels and put a little extra pep in my step because I knew he was enjoying the view.

Before I returned to my desk, I took a detour to the ladies room and paused in front of the large mirror that covered the entire wall above the sinks. What was this man doing to me? Purposely requesting that I take the minutes in not one but two major meetings in the same day just so he could be near me? Stealing kisses from me in his office?

As I gazed at my reflection, an uncontrollable smile spread across my face. I was feeling Mr. King and I couldn't help but squeal inside at the fact that he was definitely feeling me, too. Once I adjusted my blouse and skirt and gave myself a once-over in the mirror, I left the bathroom and headed back to my desk.

Roxy and I worked through lunch and I prepared the conference room, replenished the refreshments and set up everything that was needed for the second meeting. I made sure the flat screen monitor was working properly and that my template was pulled up on the laptop so that I could record the minutes for the afternoon meeting.

I tried keeping myself busy as my mind tiptoed around the thought of Chico getting out of jail. Frankie's voice echoed in my head throughout the day and I replayed our conversation over and over in my head. "You know what that means don't you?" and "I would bet my last dollar on it," stuck with me the most. I appreciated her warning, but her news was the last thing I wanted to hear.

As I adjusted the volume on the monitor in the conference room, I heard the door open, which made me jump a little since I was already on edge. I assumed it was Mr. King but didn't turn around. When I adjusted the vertical blinds, I caught a glimpse of the visitor out of the corner of my eye and it wasn't Nate like I assumed.

"I'm sorry, I didn't mean to startle you. You must be Nate's new assistant; I'm his brother Chase King," he said, walking towards me with his hand extended. I turned in the direction of the man's voice and could've been knocked over with a feather. He looked more stunned than I and when he said "Raven?" I blinked rapidly but was frozen for a moment. "You work for my brother now?" he asked with confusion. I was still in shock.

Suddenly, flashbacks started to replay in my head like an R rated movie and all I could see was me and this man's lips on my body, me pressed up against the wall and my thighs resting on his shoulders as he ate me inside out. The sweat. The nakedness. The passion; it all flashed before my eyes in a matter of seconds. This was my one nightstand in the flesh, staring me in my face and you would have thought I'd seen a damn ghost. When I finally snapped out if it and joined reality again he had already asked me a couple questions that were still unanswered because I had been in such a trance.

"Huh?"

"I said you live in Houston now…and work for my brother?" he repeated.

"Uh...yea. When I finished at Morris Brown my sister got me a job here as one of the executive administrative assistants," I muttered.

"That's great, I'm glad you're doing well. You are a hard woman to track down, you know that? I gotta give it to your friend, she played dumb really well when I came back to Emerald City looking for you," he smirked, showing his pearly whites.

"So, Mr. King is your brother?" I managed to say as I quickly passed out the handouts for the meeting that was about to start; ignoring his comment about Frankie.

"My younger brother, yes."

"Listen…Chase," I began almost forgetting his name already. "I'm trying to make a new life for myself and I don't want anyone here to know about...," I started to say as I made my way around the table.

"So, you're asking me not to say anything to Nate about how we met and how we…."

"Please?" I said, looking up into his dark eyes that were canopied with thick curly lashes similar to his brother's.

"One condition. Have a drink with me."

"Okay," I agreed without a second thought.

"A-hem," Nate said, clearing his throat as he entered the room. "Are you harassing my assistant? They are hard to come by and the good ones are few and far in between," Chase turned to face his brother.

"Tell me about it. What's going on, bro?" Chase said, shaking hands with Mr. King whom he favored.

"Work. You must be here for the meeting with Microsoft?"

"I told you I wouldn't miss it."

"Good. My brother isn't in here bothering you, is he?"

"Not at all, Mr. King," I said with a little twinkle in my eye as he focused his attention solely on me. "If you two will excuse me I have a few things I need to grab from my desk before the meeting," I told them both and exited the room like my underwear was on fire to get away from the Kings.

The entire meeting I felt like I was on pins and needles. The last thing that I expected to happen at work, was for my one nightstand to show up at my place of employment…not to mention be the older brother of my boss who I was falling for more and more with each passing day. I held on to my silent prayer that Chase King would keep his word and not tell his brother about what happened between us back in Atlanta and then returned back to my desk immediately after to bury myself in work.

As he was getting ready to leave the 20th floor, he looked like he wanted to say something to me but instead he stuffed his hands in the pants pocket of his suit and waited for the elevator.

Before I left work for the day, Chase made sure to call me at King Global and tell me where to meet him for our drink. I didn't expect for him to cash in on our little agreement so soon, but then again he wasn't the type to squander an opportunity when it was something that had wanted or was interested in. His interest couldn't be hidden that afternoon when he saw me again, and a part of me was glad that we were having a drink so that I could let him know exactly where I stood.

Our meeting place was a ritzy hotel downtown and as I accepted the ticket from the valet, I could have sworn I saw my sister

Traci climbing into the back of a taxi. I made a mental note to ask her about it and then went inside to meet the other Mr. King.

I found Chase at the bar looking refreshed and wearing a lazy yet sly grin on his full lips. He was sipping his and apparently his brother's signature drink. That damn Jack Daniels and Coke was like water to the Kings. I would have been lying if I said he didn't look appetizing in the dark navy Tom Ford suit he was wearing, but I was there for one reason and one reason only.

"Why did you want to meet at a hotel?" I asked as he helped me onto the barstool beside him.

"I was...in the area." he said getting the bartender's attention. "What's your poison and keep in mind they don't have that cider shit you drank the last time we did this," he joked and I couldn't help but giggle.

"I'll just have club soda," I said crossing my legs and his eyes slid down my body and lingered on my partially exposed thigh. I cleared my throat and gave him a look.

"You can't just have club soda," he objected. "White wine for the lady," Chase told the bartender and he nodded and started on my drink.

"Thank you," I said with a gentle bat of my lashes.

"You're welcome, Raven," he said with a knowing smile and I covered my face with my hand in embarrassment. "Or Veronica? Which is it?"

"It's Veronica," I said to him.

"So, why was that so hard for you all those months ago Veronica? Did you think I was a crazy stalker or something?" he asked as he turned his body to face me.

"I mean we did meet at a strip club," I joked and he threw his head back in a hearty laugh. "But seriously, I didn't think that I would ever see you again so it didn't matter what my real name was at the time," I explained.

"We weren't going to see each other because of you, I was interested. Very interested, still am," he informed me as he brought his glass up to his succulent mouth and took a long slow sip.

"Chase," I began but he raised his hand before I could finish my thought.

"Don't bother, I already know what it is sweetheart," he replied as he set the glass down on the bar. "You and Nate have something going on right?" he guessed and I was quiet but didn't confirm nor deny his conclusion. "I know and its cool, a little shocking but I get it," he continued and I raised one of my brows at his response.

"Don't curse me out or anything, I just meant that my brother has always had this crazy notion about not dating people that work for him. But it's more than obvious that that shit is out the window, and I can definitely see why," he said licking his lips and giving me that same look he had given me months ago, the look that against my better judgment allowed him to fuck me up against the wall of his hotel suite that faithful night.

"As long as we're on the same page-," I began but he held his hand and stopped me once again.

"While I was sitting here waiting for you, I was thinking that I'm kinda getting the short end of the stick here,"

"How's that exactly?" I asked with squinted eyes.

"This drink, it isn't enough. I feel like you ran away from me that night because you were scared and you felt the chemistry that we had between each other-."

"Chase look-."

"You can't deny it and I know that I'm not that crazy, I felt it too," he tried to convince me.

"So what is that you want?" I asked in an icy tone and a glacial expression on my face to match. A devious smirk stretched along his mouth and he laughed to himself before he responded. He took a quick sip of his drink and said,

"I haven't decided that yet, I'll let you know," and licked his lips with a smile.

I couldn't believe Chase's nerve. He and I had met months ago and slept together once. What were the chances that he was still into me after all this time or that we would even see each other again? The fact that I was now indebted to him somehow left a nasty taste in my mouth. It also made me question how someone with the kind of motives that Chase had, could share the same DNA as someone like Nathaniel King?

Nathaniel-12

"Hey," Veronica said once she and Traci were inside the house.

"Hey you, glad you made it.

What's up Traci?" I said with a wave, then kissing Roni's cheek and hugging her with one arm.

She smelled incredible as usual and was wearing an orange fishnet swimsuit cover up. Underneath, I could see a matching bikini with boy-short bottoms and a top that tied behind her neck and back. Her feet were in gold flip-flops and her toenails matched what she was wearing. Right away I wanted to conquer every inch of her body with my mouth and say the hell with the rest of the people by the pool.

"Hey, Nate," Traci responded. "Which way is the powder room?"

"Straight through the foyer, first door on the right." I told her and she was walking away before I could finish my sentence.

"You picked a good day to have a pool party. It's really warm out," Veronica said looking up at me.

"Yes, it is," I said, biting my bottom lip at the sight of her as I led her past the grand entryway and into the chef-style kitchen.

"What?" she asked as I stared.

"You look good enough to eat."

"Good enough for your metaphorical plate to go underneath

me, huh?" she teased and we both laughed.

"Precisely. It's ready whenever you are, I promise," I told her as she leaned up against the granite countertop near the sink.

"I'm sure it is," she laughed. "Your home is huge…it's really nice," she said looking around, her attention fixated on the contraption above the gas range that held pots and pans.

I stepped closer to her so that our bodies were pressed against each other and her warm breasts were on my bare chest then brushed my lips against hers. She smiled between the subtle pecks and just as I was about to grab her ass and deepen the kiss,

"Okay, I'm ready," Traci called as she emerged from the powder room around the corner. I bit my own lip with angst and looked at Traci with a tight smile.

"Alright ladies, come meet everyone," I told them.

When we stepped outside, Veronica and Traci followed me down the cobblestone steps to the infinity pool. I caught Roni admiring the lush landscaping of the backyard and the wait staff as they prepared the food and drinks for everyone. There was a game of basketball going on in the pool between the guys, and the ladies that were in attendance were laid out on the chaise lounges sipping margaritas of all flavors.

"Hey, everybody, this is Veronica and Traci. Ladies that is my sister Alaina who you already know. My cousins, Mia and Nikki, and my younger sister Savannah. Over in the pool is Ricky and Vince and you already know Chase and Kyle," I told them and I saw Traci purse her lips up at the mention of Kyle's name. "There is plenty of food and drinks so have whatever you like and there are also some extra towels if you need them to dry off."

"Traci, Veronica!" Alaina beckoned them to where she sat and I sighed internally. I wanted to have Roni to myself, but I let her breathe and mingle with the rest of my friends and family. They walked over to the table where Alaina sat drinking a mango margarita.

"Nate, come on and get in on this game, man." Ricky called to me. "Oh, and I see your girl showed up," he said while Chase and Kyle played hot potato with the basketball made for the pool.

"Yeah," I replied.

"Wait, wait, which one is you dawg? They both looking good from where I'm standing." Vince said, chiming in on the conversation.

"Orange bikini," Chase answered for me with a devious grin, tossing the ball to Vince now.

"Goddamn," Vince said with approval. "She made up like a stallion, I swear," he said with a little too much enthusiasm for me.

"Ain't she?" Chase agreed licking his lips and I gave them both the side eye.

"What that pussy do is the real question?" Vince asked and I hesitated before I answered.

"What? What y'all talking about?" Kyle wanted to know.

"Just how Nate ain't smashed his fine ass assistant yet," Chase gloated.

"Aww, hell naw." Ricky said.

"Damn, Nate, you still ain't hit?" Kyle teased.

"Kyle, nigga I know you ain't talking. Tryna be a player and now you lost not one, but both of your girls when they found out about each other," I teased and the guys all gave a collective "Damn" at my testimony.

"Wait, you fuck with her sister?" Chase asked with raised eyebrows.

"I was…but nowadays she ain't tryna hear shit I have to say," he told us.

"I ain't know that, you and Nate tag teaming like the good ole' days, huh?" Chase joked with uncomfortable laughter.

"She's just pissed right now," I told him.

"Right. Now back to Nate not handling that there. What the fuck, man? Are you crazy?" Vince asked.

"No, I actually like her so I'm trying not to make sex a big deal. Plus she works for me..." I informed them.

"It is a big deal, though," Vince said.

"That ass alone is a big deal," Chase added, looking in the direction where Roni sat with our sisters and biting his bottom lip.

Not long after their arrival; Traci, Roni, and Alaina got up from their seats, looking slightly buzzed.

"We're playing," Alaina demanded, coming into the water,

one careful step at a time.

"Traci..." Kyle said, swimming over to the edge of the pool.

Traci pulled her swimsuit cover over her head and revealed a black, monokini that could have been classified as a two-piece because of all the cutouts it had on the sides and the entire back was missing. She ignored Kyle and jumped into the pool, splashing water all over him.

"Dayum," Ricky and Vince teased as they shook with laughter.

"Cold blooded," Chase sang and I tried to stifle a grin but failed.

"You coming in, Ms. Banks?" I asked Roni as she was the only one left besides Savy who was still on her phone and Mia and Nikki who hadn't put anything more than their feet in at the other end of the pool since they'd arrived.

"Yeah," she answered and slipped her toes out of her sandals and pulled her swimsuit cover over her head revealing her creamy milk chocolaty-caramel skin. The jewel from her belly ring shined in the sun and I wanted to dip my tongue in her navel at the sight.

She took cautious steps as Alaina had and descended into the cool blue water in what seemed like slow motion. All the other guys noticeably watched her with an exception of Ricky who was already tossing my sister, his fiancée, around in the water.

"What about me, Roni, Alaina, and you, Traci?" Chase said, assigning teams apparently. "And the rest of you suckers on a team," he continued.

"I guess you the boss, huh?" Traci said to him with a grin.

"Always," he said returning her flirty smile making Kyle tighten his jaw at the mere sight of Traci paying Chase any attention. I saw Roni roll her eyes unconsciously at being on the same team as Chase and wondered what he had done already to rub her the wrong way.

The game started and I was the least focused, my focal point was dressed in orange. The ball was passed to me and due to my lack of concentration, Roni caught it instead and scored on me.

"Ohhh! That's what I'm talking bout!" Chase said raising his hand for a high-five and she reluctantly obliged him. I saw him whisper something near her ear which seemed to have no effect on her, but looked like it made Traci visibly uneasy.

"Nate, what the fuck man?" Vince said to me.

I could've cared less about a game of 'beach basketball' at that moment. Veronica was my focus and now that I had her on my turf without distractions from King Global, I wasn't about to squander the opportunity or let Chase get too close for that matter.

The tattoo that she had on her back in between her shoulder blades written in Chinese caught my attention and when I was close enough, I placed a moist warm kiss there.

"Are you trying to distract me, Nathaniel?" she asked from over her shoulder and I realized that that was the first time I'd heard her say my whole name and it turned me on.

"Something like that. Is it working?" I asked and continued to kiss her; my lips moving across to the middle of her back then to her other shoulder.

"Something like that," she grinned. I slowly pulled her by her waist so that we were far enough from the others then turned her around in the water so she faced me. I pressed my lips up against hers then she pulled away after only a peck.

"What?" I asked, furrowing my eyebrows at her hesitation.

"Here?" she asked a little perplexed.

"No one is watching us, they're playing the game. And so what? Are you embarrassed to kiss me in public?" I asked, reversing it on her quick.

"No, but I just thought you..."

"Good," I smiled and she wet her lips with her tongue and swallowed me in a deep passionate kiss that ignited fire through me. I cupped her ass in both hands under the water and squeezed it hard. When I pressed her up against the cement that surrounded the water and wedged myself between her thighs, she wrapped her arms around my neck and greedily pushed her tongue in my mouth. Our public displays of affection proved that neither of us cared about who was around, it wouldn't and couldn't stop us from whatever we wanted to do.

The water was cold, but all I felt was heat between us and I wanted nothing more than to pick Veronica up and carry her up to my bedroom and do only what could be described as sinful things to her body.

When the staff informed me the food was ready to be served, we all gathered around the table that was set up outside after we dried off and sat down to eat. There were grilled steaks, burgers, and brats, chicken breasts, and shrimp kabobs; not to mention deviled eggs, potato salad, garden salad, baked beans, and corn-on-the-cob.

I couldn't help but notice how Chase kept looking at Roni and how Traci watched Chase, both trying to be somewhat discrete about it but did a horrible job. He had kept it no secret that he was interested in her from the day that he met her and learned that she and I hadn't…become physical yet. It was also no secret that my brother always wanted what was mine. My mother said as toddlers we fought over everything and that lasted well into our teen years and was apparent as adults as well. Veronica was off limits and he knew it, now whether he would honor that was a different story.

She had a hell of a hold on me. Her smile and laugh alone made me putty in her hands and she had no idea. She had the most loving personality once you got past her shyness and I adored her sense of humor. I was beginning to adore her.

After another game of beach basketball and a few more drinks, my guests started to depart. Mia and Savannah were the first to leave, and then Alaina and Ricky followed close to seven.

"Babe, let me talk to Nate really quick?" Alaina told Ricky in his ear.

"Okay, I'll be out in the car, baby," he told her, kissing her on the mouth. I migrated to the kitchen sink to wash my hands when my sister came over and stood next to me.

"I thought you were leaving," I said, looking over my shoulder at her.

"I am, shut up," she told me. "So what's going on with you and Roni? Are y'all like together?" she asked.

"No, not exactly," I said a little confused.

"Are you sure? I mean you were worried that she might not show up,"

"I wasn't worried," I corrected her.

"Don't lie, I saw you check your phone a half a dozen times before they got here. And then the kissing her every chance you got. I've seen the way you watch her," she said as if she had me figured out.

"I mean I do like her, if that's what you're getting at."

"Duh."

"So, what's your point?"

"It just seems like a little more than like to me, but what do I know?" she said giving me a teasing grin and nudging me with her elbow.

"Meaning?"

"Meaning I saw how Chase was looking at her too and if you drag your feet…" she told me and I knew the rest.

"Oh, I'm not worried about that," I said, offering her a reassuring smile.

"Okay, but you know how you and your brother can be when it comes to …well anything,"

"Thank you for your concern, Alaina."

"I like her, by the way," she added.

"I can tell," I told her.

"Just thought you should know," she said, walking backwards out of the kitchen and running into Roni as she was coming around the corner.

"Bye," I laughed, shaking my head.

Roni came into the kitchen after confirming her and Alaina's lunch date for the following Tuesday. I caught her by the waist and bent my neck to meet her lips. The kiss was nothing but tongue and lip biting. When she sucked my bottom lip between her teeth, I lost it. I picked her up and she wrapped her legs around me. We continued to kiss as my dick hardened in my shorts. I needed to taste her so I carried her to the first room I could find that had a lock on the door.

We went inside and I turned the lock then laid her on the edge of the bed and slowly slid her dress up, revealing a pair of black panties that had strings with tiny bows at the hips and lace all over. My appetite for her took over and all the composure I had left, vanished when I ripped her underwear off in one tear. She looked down at me with the same hunger in her eyes and I kissed her lips again. When my hands found her warm and full breasts I gave them a gentle squeeze. I pushed her dress up farther and then pulled it over her head. The bra she was wearing was barely a bra and I could see her nipples through the shear material. I planted wet kisses between them as I pulled them out one at a time. When I covered her nipple with my mouth, I heard a tiny moan escape her and she arched up so that I could achieve a mouth full.

"Please don't tell me this is the kind of shit you wear under your work clothes?" I said before I switched to her other nipple and sucked and teased it with my teeth. She laughed inwardly and bit her lip and raised one of her perfectly arched brows.

"Stop. I already have enough trouble trying to stay focused with all your…assets parading around," I told her and she smiled down at me. I made circles around her areolas with my tongue and then slowly kissed down her torso past her slightly defined abs. I stopped at her belly button and suckled the ring that decorated it, and then dipped my tongue inside her navel as I had envisioned myself doing earlier that day.

When I reached her pussy it was as pretty as I knew it would be. Perfectly waxed and mine for the taking. I lifted her up and grabbed both of her knees then spread her legs apart so that her feet were on the edge of the bed. I blew gently on her clit and she squirmed a little. That excited me and I dove in with my mouth extra moist and French kissed her clit. I felt her quiver above me and I closed my eyes and inhaled her sweet scent. I intended to pace myself but in that moment I wanted to devour her.

I grabbed her by the waist and got down on my knees and kissed her inner thigh. She started to breathe heavily with every touch of my lips. When I made my way back to her pussy, I kissed every crease and fold followed by sliding my tongue up and down. I lightly sucked on her clit letting it slip from my mouth then taking it back in.

She squirmed even more and moaned uncontrollably. That motivated me, and I began to flick my tongue fast as if I was singing to it which sent her over the edge. She clutched the bedspread between her fingers and arched her back off the bed. I continued what I was doing until I felt her juices begin to flow. Her moans got a little louder as she came and I licked and savored every last drop of her arousal. Her body seemed to relax and she tried to close her legs but I stopped her.

"Un-un, I'm not done with you yet," I said lifting my head up so that she could see my face and its seriousness. She sat up on her elbows and gazed at me with heavy lazy eyes. "Lay back," I demanded and lightly shoved her down. I got back into position and went back to work on her.

She smelled so good and tasted even better. I wanted her to cum again and again, and hard. If what she had said was true about not having been with someone in a while, she was in for a hell of a time with me. I intended to give Veronica nothing but my A-game. I wanted to conquer her body like no one else had and give her the most intense and sensual sexual experience that I could.

I sucked and licked slow that time and teased her with my tongue. I saw her bite her lip when I pushed my tongue inside her and let out a soft moan. Her hands found my head and she massaged it while she greedily pushed herself into my face wanting more of my mouth. I smiled at her effort and started to suck a little harder while I fucked her with my tongue. When she came that time, it was a twice as much than before. Her legs shook and her moans became hoarse. I felt her hands leave my head and she started to scoot away from me as I sat up and wiped my mouth.

She grabbed one of the pillows above her and curled up into ball with her eyes closed.

"You okay?" I asked her with a grin playing at the corners of my mouth.

"Mmhm," she told me and slowly opened her eyes. I lay next to her so that we were face to face and ran my fingers up and down her side. "You are something else."

"I am? How so?" I smiled. She reached her index finger over to my mouth and ran it across my lips, then left it there.

"I think you know," she told me and then I let her finger slip into my mouth and sucked it. When I finally let it slide out of my mouth she took it into hers and sucked it a little. I closed in the space that was between us and kissed her lips. "You taste like me," she smiled as our foreheads were pressed against each other. I licked my lips and said, "I love the way you taste and I could eat you all day, mmm," I said and kissed her again. Just as I climbed on top of her, we heard voices from the hallway and then a loud banging on the bedroom door.

Nathaniel-13

My phone rang at around two am and I reached for it on my nightstand. I assumed it was mysterious "Unknown" caller; either that or Mitch calling me with more information on the trace he ordered. So far, all he knew was that the calls were coming from a burner phone somewhere in France, he just wasn't sure where but was still digging deeper into the matter. When my eyes focused, I read the caller I.D. and then answered.

"Hey you...yeah I was, I'm up though…no you're fine what's wrong...okay…of course…yes I'm sure…alright, bye." I said and ended the call then returned my phone back to the nightstand.

Before I went downstairs, I brushed my teeth. I grabbed a bottle of water and camped out in the media room to watch an episode of First 48. Halfway through the episode my eyes began to feel heavy then I heard the doorbell ring. I glanced at the iPad with all eight security camera views on it to confirm who it was, then got up from the couch and slow dragged to the door to answer it.

"Hey," I said once I opened the door.

"Hey you," Roni said to me with her shy smile, staring down at her feet. "I'm sorry I called so late…but I wanted to see you and I couldn't sleep…and I couldn't stop thinking about earlier and how we left things...," she said, stringing all her words together as she often did when she was nervous. I shut her up the only way that I knew how which was to kiss her.

She moaned and wrapped her arms around my neck. Any sleep or exhaustion that I had felt before she arrived had disappeared.

"You won't get any sleep around here either," I warned her before I picked her up and carried her inside. I shut the heavy door behind us with my bare foot causing it to slam, then carried her all the way upstairs to my bedroom, not taking my lips off of hers.

She had called me and asked me if I was awake nearly 45 minutes before and asked if she could come over. Our alone time had been interrupted earlier due to Traci's desire to escape Kyle's shameless attempts to get her to listen to him. Because they were in one car and her sister needed her, Roni left me with a hard-on and secretly pissed at Kyle for fucking things up with Traci.

She couldn't get to me fast enough and when I saw her, there would be no turning back this time. Her skin was so soft and smelled of one of those intoxicating body washes that made my mouth water. She was wearing next to nothing in a pair of grey leggings and a shirt that showed her midriff with no bra and her black flip flops from earlier.

When we reached my room, it was pitch black except for the beam of the moon through the drapes. I laid her in the middle of my unmade bed and trailed my kisses to her neck. She ran her hands under my shirt and lightly scratched my back with her nails.

"You don't know how fuckin' bad I want you," I told her, pulling her shirt over her head revealing her naked breasts.

"Just as bad as I want you," she panted, her breath fresh with a hint of citrus.

She reached for my shirt and tugged it over my head then tossed it to the floor. I bent to kiss her long and hard then kissed my way down her body and tugged her leggings down along with her panties. Once they were off, I immediately went for her pussy and picked up where I'd left off earlier that evening. I had no mercy on her and licked, sucked, and kissed like the delicacy it was, making her come on my lips. She moaned and caressed my head, appreciating every moment of pleasure that I was giving her. When I finished, I kissed between her thighs and slowly climbed up her body until my face found hers.

She looked as if she was high, eyes low and heavy once again. Her hand clutched my bicep then moved over to caress my chest before it slid down to my pajama bottoms and tugged at the waistband. She started to pull them down as much as she could and then with her foot she pushed them down to my ankles. I lifted a little to kick them off, and then reached over to the night stand where my phone had been to pull open the drawer. I snatched off two Magnums with my teeth then ripped those two apart and closed the drawer. Roni watched me anxiously but stayed quiet as I handed her the condom.

"Put it on," I told her as she accepted it and she hit me with that shy and timid look of hers.

I could have done it myself, but I wanted her to touch me. I wanted her to see what I was working with and what was about to work on her. She looked down at my dick and then her face shot back up at me with a hint of fear. I gave her a half grin and then saw her visibly swallow hard before she removed the condom from the wrapper. As she rolled it down my length, I sucked air in between my teeth from her touch alone. She lay back afterward and I lowered myself onto her.

"What's wrong?" I asked her.

"It's just been a while for me and you're so…"she said and then widened her eyes. I smiled at what she was referring to.

"I am, but I won't hurt you. I promise, baby," I assured her with sincerity

"Okay," she said with a sweet smile.

"Do you trust me?"

"Of course," she said and I covered her lips with mine and kissed her soft and slowly.

I teased her clit with my dick as I kissed her, making her even wetter and then placed it right at her opening. I moved slowly to guide myself in but it was so tight. I dipped my tongue into her mouth to try and distract her as I slowly pushed in and it halfway worked. She rubbed my lower back and as I went in more she began to scratch it with her nails again. Her mouth opened and she looked up into my eyes, but no sound escaped. I continued to ease my way in and brushed her cheek with the back of my hand to try and comfort her at the same time. Once I was in all the way, or as much as I could, I began to stroke her slow and steady. She felt incredible, so warm and so tight and soaking wet from my mouth and her own arousal. I wasn't sure if I would be able to last but I was damn sure going to try.

As I moved inside her, I kissed behind her ear then trailed my lips to her inviting breasts. I teased her nipples with my teeth until they were hard, reminding me of two Hershey's kisses. She rubbed and caressed my arms and ran her hands over the tattoo on my chest, then reached for my face and brought it to hers kissing me again. I laid on her a little and then grabbed her by her ass and lifted her off of the bed so she could feel every inch of me.

"Uh!" she moaned, snatching her lips from mine. "Oh my God!" she cried out, then biting her bottom lip to try and hold in her sounds. When I realized what she was doing I used my teeth to make her release her lip.

"No. I wanna hear you, every moan, and every sound. It's just me and you," I told her then long stroking her so I was deeper and she gasped and screamed,

"Nate!" she panted, biting my bottom lip. She was wetter now which told me that she had came.

"Did you-?" I had to ask for my own confirmation.

"Mmhm," she moaned weakly, rubbing my chest again then running her nails over it and scratching, which I loved.

"You feel so fucking good; I could never get enough of you," I confessed as I spread her legs wider and gripped her thighs.

"Me too, it's so…so…" she said, trying to finish her thought but didn't; the pleasure so blinding she couldn't see straight.

"Sooo good, so perfect," I added.

"Yes," she moaned. "Yes," she repeated with a lazy smile and I couldn't help but smile back. I pressed my chest against her and continued to thrust at a steady pace, until I sped it up a little and caressed her body.

I took my thumb and moved it in a circular motion over the sensitive flesh of her clit as I continued to fill her with as much of me as I could. Her arms were above her head in surrender as sweat dripped from my forehead down on to her neck and trickled down between her breasts. I felt my spine tingle and my orgasm build in the pit of my stomach. When I looked at her, her face was scrunched up as if she was holding it in and then her muscles tightened around me and her eyes rolled back. I felt her release squirt out that time and that tipped me over the edge.

"Oh my fucking, God," I groaned, my voice bouncing off the walls of the bedroom.

My thumb was soaked from her wetness and I almost blacked out when I came just as hard as she had. I closed my eyes and was frozen in one position that I was in for a minute as I filled the condom with every drop of my release. She breathed heavily and reached up to wipe the sweat from my forehead. Her other hand cupped my cheek and I turned my head slightly to kiss the inside of her palm.

Once I was able to move again, I pulled out and collapsed on the bed next to her.

"You okay?" I asked her as I ran my hand up and down her thigh.

"Yeah. I think so," she sighed in a hoarse voice with a half grin.

"I didn't hurt you, did I?"

"A little," she began and I furrowed my eyebrows and turned toward her. "You made it hurt so good. That was definitely worth the wait," she told me, turning on her side and laying her head on her outstretched arm. I ran my fingertip down her curves and rested my palm on her hip.

"Definitely. I feel like I can move a mountain," I confessed and she giggled a little. "I'll be right back," I said and tore myself from the mess of the sheets and her, and went into my bathroom to dispose of the condom.

Traces of her release were on the base of the condom, my pubic hair and the bottom of my stomach. I chuckled to myself and then flushed the condom that was so full I was surprised it didn't break.

I washed my face and then joined Roni back in the bed

where I found her wrapped in my cream satin sheets waiting for me. I climbed in the bed and pulled a blanket over us, then pulled her over to me and she laid her head on my chest. I kissed her forehead when she looked up at me and her smile could've melted me.

"Your heart is beating fast," she observed.

"It's not every day that I have sex like that." I said, telling her the partial truth.

In actuality, it was her that had my heart beating out of my chest. Being that close to her and experiencing what we had just done had my world upside down. It felt like she was a part of me now and I wasn't sure how to handle that.

After Lauren died, I eventually started dating again. Nothing ever became serious and I always kept whatever woman that I was involved with at bay.

Veronica was in a completely different league. The day that I laid eyes on her she was a mystery to me and someone that I didn't want to want because of our work relationship. I couldn't help it though, and I didn't want to.

Now she was in my bed, laying next me in post-coital bliss and I didn't want her to leave, ever.

I heard her hum as she snuggled into my side more, eventually drifting off to sleep. I lied awake staring at the vaulted ceilings above me and tried not to think too much which was nearly impossible.

At about four that morning after I had finally fallen asleep, I turned on my side so that I was spooning Veronica and started to feel my dick harden as it was pressed up against her ass. The one kiss that I planted on her neck turned into two kisses, then three, and before I knew it she was awake and the other condom that I had torn off was on.

The next morning I was awakened by a collection of kisses all over my face. When I opened my eyes, Roni's angelic face was smiling above me and my morning wood was starving for her.

I groaned as soon as I slid inside her and matched her movements above me. She grabbed the back of my neck and I pressed my lips to her exposed throat.

Once we both achieved a steady rhythm, without warning she pulled back a little and in one gesture she hit the splits on my dick and my jaw dropped at her effortless move.

"Goddamn, you're flexible, did you use to strip?" I joked, sort of.

"Maybe," she said, continuing what she was doing and giving me a wink. I didn't dwell on that little remark in that moment but she definitely wasn't going to get off that easy.

We tore ourselves away from the bed long enough to shower, and have some leftovers from the barbeque. I couldn't let Roni's little trick that she pulled in bed go any longer without addressing it.

"Sooo, are we gonna talk about that little move you sprung on me this morning?" I asked, coming over to the sink where she was.

"What about it?" she asked knowingly.

"Did you? Used to strip I mean?" I asked and she swallowed hard before she answered with,

"Yes, I did," looking down at her feet like an embarrassed little girl.

"Hey," I said, lifting her chin with my finger.

"It's not something that I'm proud of..."

"I already knew, Veronica."

"You did? How?"

"When I saw the way you were dancing at Matrix it sparked my interest so I looked into you a little."

"How come you didn't say anything?"

"Because I wanted you to tell me when you were ready and because your past is your past. We all have one. I don't care about what happened before I met you, my only concern is the version of you that I'm looking at right now," I said and she practically leaped into my arms and swallowed me in deep kiss. We had round three or four in the kitchen and she didn't end up going home until later that evening.

FIT for a KING-P. Sharee

Veronica-14

When I got home that night after leaving Nate's house, I felt like I had been living on a cloud the entire time that I was with him. The night and day that we spent together was perfect and without a question the best sex ever. That wasn't saying too much, considering I hadn't been with very many men, but it was plenty in my opinion. I was no virgin, but after abstaining for close to a year, being with someone like Nathaniel King had ruined me for any other man after that.

I opened the front door to Traci and Kyle asleep on the couch after watching a movie, I assumed. I carefully shut the door and attempted to tip toe to my room but Traci stirred on Kyle's lap and looked up at me.

"Roni?" she whispered.

"Shh, go back to sleep," I told her then walked down the short hallway to my bedroom.

After I slipped off my flip flops I searched for my bathrobe behind the door. Unknowingly, Traci followed me and was slipping through the cracked door. I jumped when I saw her.

"I thought I told you to go back to sleep," I said to her a little startled.

"You looked freshly fucked," she smiled her voice a little raspy.

"I am," I grinned as I searched the top dresser drawer for

some underwear.

"Get over here and tell me what happened," she demanded. When I turned around to face her I could not mask what I was feeling even if I wanted to. Traci was the only person that I trusted and that I felt like I could be completely candid with.

"We made love all night long and then all day. And I'm sore as hell and can barely close my legs but I don't care. Tray, it was incredible. He is incredible. It was slow and he kissed me the entire time and caressed my body. Multiple orgasms, phenomenal head. He called me baby and just…uhh," I sighed, sounding like that teenage girl again.

"Awww," she said, covering her mouth with both of her hands. She fanned her face as if she was fanning away tears. "Y'all made love? Not just fucking, made love?"

"Yes."

"So, are y'all like…together?"

"I don't know we didn't really label it but..."

"It sounds like it to me, honey. You made love and I'm sure he made it clear that he didn't want you giving that pussy away to anybody else," she concluded on her own. I knew this would happen, I told you."

"Relax, we not getting married or anything," I laughed to myself. "But I do love being with him, and not just sexually."

"That's good, like you aren't just his lover, you two are actually friends."

"Exactly. We laugh and joke and everything," I said all bubbly.

"I have something to tell you," she began.

"What is it?" I asked.

"I'm pregnant," she blurted out

"You're what?! Pregnant?" I repeated in disbelief. "Oh my God, Tray!" I squealed reaching over to hug her.

"I take that as you're happy about this?" she laughed a little.

"Of course, aren't you?"

"I mean this isn't exactly my ideal situation or how I envisioned myself starting a family but I guess I am happy, yeah," she smiled.

"I think it's a blessing and I am sooo excited I'm gonna be an auntie," I told her all at once. "What did Kyle say?"

"I haven't told him yet. I wanna wait until after I go to the doctor and make sure, you know?"

"Right."

As I soaked in a much needed steaming hot bubble bath that night, I thought about the news that Traci had shared with me. She and Kyle were about to become parents and I couldn't have been happier for them. In the same breath, I couldn't help but think about things that would eventually change and how exactly I would fit into the picture.

When I stepped on to the 20th floor that next morning, I was exhausted and my body felt like I had done a day and a half of that "Insanity" workout that I once was obsessed with. I was still a little swollen and sore; even my hips were tender from all of his kisses and thrusts. I attempted to dress comfortable but settled on a burgundy pencil bandage dress that reached my knee and peep-toe heels.

As I strutted over to my desk, I noticed that Roxy wasn't there which was surprising since she was always the first one in the office, especially on Monday mornings.

I sat down and powered my computer on and felt my phone buzz from my purse. When I took it out, my screen said that I had a text from "King Tut". I smiled and swiped the screen so that I could read what he said.

Good morning baby, how did you sleep?

I typed back immediately

Good morning to you…and I slept okay, it would've been better had it been with you.

As he texted back, I heard the elevator open and then he came waltzing through the elevator doors with Roxy a few steps behind him.

"Good morning, Veronica," he smiled his same smile but somehow it wasn't the same. It felt a little bit warmer, more personal.

"Good morning, Mr. King. How was your weekend?" I

115

asked him with a smile as he approached my desk.

"Fantastic; I didn't even wanna get out of bed," he told me with a wink and then walked into his office. I did a cartwheel inside. I didn't wanna get out of your bed either, I thought.

"Morning, Roxy," I said with a smile. She looked almost as exhausted as I felt.

"Good morning," she said flatly.

"What's wrong?"

"Kenyon kept me up practically all night running a fever, I think he has a little bug. I barely got any sleep and can't get rid of this headache," she told me, referring to her three year old son.

"Oh no. Were you able to break his fever?"

"Yeah, it finally went down this morning so I took him to his other grandma's house, my head is killing me though."

"Why didn't you just call in?"

"That's what Julian said too. I'll be fine. I just took some Bayer Migraine so that should kick in soon," she tried to convince me. Even though Roxy felt like shit, she wasn't dressed like it. She was in a magenta skirt with a pale pink cardigan and a white top underneath with nude heels. Her hair was laid like always and she had on her usual amount of make-up, too much. Her eyes looked tired behind the mascara and lashes, even her posture was a little off.

My phone buzzed on my desk and I anxiously picked it up and read Nate's next text.

My bed felt empty without you last night while I lay in our sex sheets. They smell just like you, I think I'll keep 'em on a little longer. And what is up with that fucking dress you're wearing, Ms. Banks? Do you want me to call you in my office and spread those hips of yours again?

I tried to stifle my grin and typed back quickly.

Is that a serious question because I think you already know the answer…and what's wrong with my dress?? It happens to be comfortable, Mr. King. I couldn't wear something too tight thanks to the throb between my thighs.

Greedy is an understatement, I wanted to sleep in it…hell I did sleep in it. I can still taste you on my lips and tongue, and now my dick is on hard. Smh at what you do to me Veronica…

I tightened between my legs and shoved my phone in my desk drawer. After I checked mine and Nate's emails, I started going over the calendar on the iPad and saw that Roxy had made travel arrangements for him later that week to go to Los Angeles to check on three possible contracts that he was considering. She arranged for his jet to be ready and that his house in Malibu was to be prepared upon his arrival.

When we walked into his office for our 9:30am briefing, he was on the phone.

"I don't care…I have final say so on all new contracts…exactly and I expect you to have any prospective bids on my desk by noon!" he shouted then ended the phone call. Roxy and I carefully sat down across from a clearly agitated Nathaniel King.

"I apologize about that ladies, some people tend to forget whose name is on this building or who signs their paychecks, for that matter," he said to us with a chuckle and we both laughed a little. "Please," he said, signaling for us to begin.

"Today we have the employee appreciation luncheon up on the rooftop." I told him. "The caterers are already setting up and everything will be ready no later than 11am." And he nodded with approval. "There are blueprints for you to look over and I already forwarded your emails of priority this morning," I finished.

"Okay. Roxanne, what do you have?" he asked and she began filling him in on what he had to look forward to for the remainder of the week.

Roxy spelled out his information about his trip to L.A for that Thursday and he informed me that he would need me to accompany him due to the amount of business he had to get done over the weekend. Roxy couldn't go because of her child and babysitting arrangements and it was apparent that she was less than thrilled that I would be attending instead.

"Thank you very much, ladies," he said and dismissed us from his office. "Oh, Veronica, can I take a look at something on your iPad for a moment? I need to double check a few things concerning the luncheon," he called to me and I stopped in my tracks as Roxy walked out of the door in front of me.

"Sure," I smiled then turned on my heels and switched over to his desk.

He pressed some button that was in front of him and I heard a click that signified that the door to his office was locked. He stood up, towering over me and covered my lips in a warm and passionate kiss. His hands immediately cupped my ass and he gave it a two-hand squeeze, pressing his body into mine.

"I needed that the moment I woke up this morning," he told me, his breath smelling like coffee and mints.

"You too, huh?" I said, smiling up at him.

"You like getting me hard? Wearing this fucking dress with this ass looking edible," he grinned, smacking it playfully.

"Ba-abe, stop," I squealed, realizing it was the first time I used a term of endearment in reference to him.

"That's cute," he said, holding me by the waist and grinning down at me.

"It just…came out I guess," I shrugged.

"It was natural like when I say it to you. I like it," he assured me and kissed my forehead.

"Okay."

"I'll let you get back to work," he told me and gave me a quick peck on the lips then I walked out of his office and out to my desk not realizing that Nate wasn't far behind me.

As I was about to sit down, I saw a slim white guy dressed in a grey polo shirt and khaki pants coming toward mine and Roxy's work station carrying a huge bouquet of my favorite flowers, peach roses. I gasped at the sight and he stood in front of both of our desks and said,

"I have flowers for a Miss…Veronica Banks," he read from a piece of carbon paper.

"T-That's me," I said, holding my hand up slightly confused.

"These are for you," he smiled and just as he handed them over, Nate came out of his office with his light blue shirt rolled up to his elbows. He raised his eyebrows when he saw the flowers.

"Thank you," I told the delivery guy when I accepted the vase of flowers. Roxy's jaw dropped when she saw that they were for me, then a smile spread across her face. "Hold on one second," I told the delivery guy while I sat the flowers down and reached for my purse.

"Let me," Nate insisted and pulled out a wad of money held together by a white gold money clip with the initials "NSK" in script across it. He peeled off two twenties then handed it to the guy.

"Thank you very much, Sir," he said and got my signature then left.

"Roni, who sent you flowers, girl?" Roxy asked me from her desk wearing a huge grin. I glanced at her then Nate and reached for the card. "Read it, Roni," she encouraged me.

I read it to myself then aloud as they both watched me. "Just because it's a Monday and just because you're you," I read and Roxy placed her hand to her heart.

"Aww," she said returning to her upbeat and dramatic self just like that. "Who are they from?" she wanted to know.

"Just...this guy I've been seeing," I answered, thinking on my feet.

"Really? Who?" she probed with a knowing look on her face. I gave her a look and Nate smiled and shook his head at the two of us.

"That was really nice, whoever the guy is. He's a lucky man," Nate turned to me.

"I'm just as lucky," I said and he winked at me.

"If anyone needs me, I'll be on the rooftop. I would like to make sure that everything is coming along for the luncheon," he added then disappeared onto the elevator.

"Okay, now Mr. King is gone, you can tell me who sent you these roses. I didn't know that you were even seeing someone," she said, eying me suspiciously.

"Damn, you are nosey," I giggled at her effort.

"Who is he?"

"The guy from Matrix."

"Mmhm," she said, not sounding convinced.

"Anyway, girl we have work to do," I reminded her, trying

to change the subject, a little more uncomfortable with her line of questioning.

"Mmhm, "she repeated. "I'll let it go for now," she told me.

"Don't you have a headache you should be trying to get rid of?" I asked her focusing on my computer screen.

"Oh, it's gone now."

"I bet."

"You and your guy should get up with me and Julian soon; I would love to meet him," she offered. I shuffled some papers on my desk and averted my eyes when I said,

"He's really busy, but I'll ask him," I lied.

"Good," she said giving me that suspicious look of hers.

The employee appreciation luncheon turned out exquisite. The rooftop was covered with dozens of round tables with white linen cloths and silverware. There was a buffet line with about eight servers and warming pans filled with food. The tables had white tea lilies floating in water as centerpieces and all of the employees were instructed to wear name tags upon entering the roof.

About 90% of the people employed by King Global had actually shown up and the 10% that wasn't there were either manning the phones or hadn't shown up for work that day.

Before everyone started to eat, Nate made a little speech about how much he appreciated the incredible team he had at King Global so we all would be receiving a bonus due to the how well the numbers were from the last two quarters.

"I'll be right back," I told Roxy when I spotted Traci across the room. She had even started to look pregnant in the face now that I knew she was. Her weave was pulled back in a neat ponytail and she was wearing a black pants suit with a tan blouse and nude pumps.

"I completely forgot this damn thing was today," she said once I reached her.

"Yeah, I guess everyone is getting a bonus."

"Girl, you are gonna give every poor bastard around here a hard-on with that thing," Alaina teased, coming up to Traci and I as we stood near the exit.

"I know, right?" Traci agreed.

"Stop exaggerating," I told them both.

"No exaggeration honey, that ass is colossal," she teased.

"Let's get something to eat and people watch," we laughed and followed her to the buffet line.

The meal was catered by Nate and Chase's restaurant "Angela's", named after their mother. Nate told Roxy and I to put together a meal and we chose garden salads, grilled chicken breast, vegetable medley, and baked potatoes for everyone at the luncheon. We also had cheesecake and white cake with white frosting for desserts.

We found a table towards the center of the rooftop that was empty and had girl talk.

"So, you got roses, huh?" Alaina asked me before she took in a forkful of salad.

"Damn, how did you know?" Traci asked before I could answer.

"You know mouth of the south can't hold water," she said, nodding her head in Roxy's direction who was off to the side flirting with some tall dark skin guy that seemed into her.

"Of course." Traci said rolling her eyes.

"I heard her saying something to Courtney from HR when I got up here, you better watch that one, Roni. I know you two work together but she is always in someone else's business and I know she is itching to know if you and Nate have something going on." Alaina advised me.

"Yeah, I told you she was messy," Traci added.

"She was asking a lot of questions when the flowers were delivered," I told them taking a sip of my water.

"That's what I mean," Alaina told me and I thought about what her and Traci were saying. Roxy was a little too interested in who sent me flowers and seemed more than suspicious with my answers.

My thoughts were shaken away when Alaina mentioned something to me and Traci got up to visit the dessert table for the second time. With a quick scan of the roof I saw Chase come waltzing through the entrance/exit with his phone up to his ear. He appeared to be in deep thought as he listened to whoever was on the other end of the phone, but his look of focus faded when he and I made eye contact. A flirtatious, yet inappropriate smile spread across his face when he saw me and he licked his lips before I could turn away.

Seeing Chase reminded me of how uncomfortable I was at Nate's pool party whenever I caught him staring at me, or even when we were in the pool and he whispered "I still remember how sweet you taste". I pretended to be unbothered by his little advances because the last thing that I wanted was to draw attention to the two of us.

When I casually looked up again in his direction, I could see him heading towards where Traci was near the cheesecakes and I was dying to know what he had to say to her, especially since I was almost certain I saw her leave the same hotel that he and I had drinks at couple weeks back.

"I'll be right back," I told Alaina as I excused myself from the table with my half eaten salad and headed toward the trash. When I was close enough to zero in on Traci and Chase's conversation but not too close so that it was obvious that I was eaves dropping, I inadvertently got an earful.

"I thought I was gonna have to track you down," his deep voice said in almost a whisper.

"What are you doing here?" she tried to ask nonchalantly with a fake smile plastered on her face as she talked through clenched teeth.

"I have some business with my brother," he lied. "Are you avoiding me?"

"I've been busy; I have a lot going on."

"A lot like how you didn't tell me Roni was your sister or that you were fuckin' with my lil cousin?" he asked, still smiling.

"I didn't know who you were Chase and besides…we didn't do a lot of talking when we first met," she reminded him.

"True," he laughed to himself remembering their tryst. "Have a drink with me so we can really talk."

"I can't. Besides, wouldn't you rather talk to Roni? I saw how you were watching her at the cookout," she said angrily.

"Jealous?" he teased. "I mean I am attracted to her, but she's with my brother and that has nothing to do with me and you…"

"It has everything to do with it, I guess you feel good that you got to have both sisters huh?"

"Traci-," he began.

"There's nothing else to talk about and I'm not mad. We fucked once, before I knew who you were and before I knew that you had already fucked my sister. I-I was upset about Kyle…and you, you were there. It was a moment of weakness. I'm back with Kyle now so let's just…pretend that day never happened," she told him still wearing her fake smile as she walked away from the dessert table with her cheesecake.

My suspicions were confirmed. That was Traci that I saw leaving the hotel, the same hotel that Chase had asked me to meet at for our drink. When I met him at the bar he had been wearing that freshly fucked look and it was because he had just fucked my sister less than an hour before. I couldn't necessarily blame Traci because she had no idea that he was my one night stand and I too had fallen prey to Chase's charm and good looks so I could relate. But now it was more than obvious that she knew the truth about everything and had chosen not to tell me.

FIT for a KING– *P. Sharee*

Veronica-15

Alaina and I met for lunch the following afternoon, just to talk and get to know each other a little better. She informed me that her and Nate's college friend Ricky were engaged and would be tying the knot in less than a month and wanted me and Traci to come. I graciously accepted the invite and gave her our address so she could send a formal invitation.

When we got back to King Global Alaina had taken the elevator with me up to the 20th floor so she could look around and give Nate shit before she returned to her office.

"Come on, Roni," Alaina said, not even giving Roxy a glance and barged through both sets of doors to Nate's office with me a couple steps behind her. We both stopped in our tracks when we saw a woman with long dark hair sitting in one of the chairs across from Nate's desk and he was leaned against the corner with his arms folded across his chiseled chest.

"I didn't realize you were with someone..." Alaina said, looking at her brother.

"Its fine," he said in a monotone voice as he massaged the top of his nose with his thumb and index finger. "Alaina, you remember Ashley, Lauren's baby sister?" he said and my jaw dropped. Lauren's baby sister? Then the woman that was facing Nate turned around in her chair with wet eyes and waved her hand to Alaina in a childlike manner.

"O-Of course," Alaina said, wearing a perplexed look as she marched over to where this 'Ashley' sat. "How are you?"

"I'm…okay," Ashley said in a low voice, almost like a whisper it was so faint.

She stood to hug Alaina and had a tiny frame to match her even tinier voice. In the Louboutins she was wearing she still wasn't as tall as Alaina who was my height, five foot five. Dressed in a black and white pencil skirt, black heels, and a blouse that was half- black and half- white, her long, jet black extensions stopping in the middle of her back; she was stunning. She was pretty and had fair skin, a complexion lighter than both Nate and Alaina who I considered light-skinned in comparison to the milk chocolate shade that I was.

I felt like my feet were stuck in tar and I couldn't move even if I wanted to. When I finally found my voice again I said, "Mr. King, I'll be at my desk if you need me," and his attention quickly shifted from his sister and sister-in-law to me.

"So, Ashley, what brings you to Houston?" Alaina asked.

"Well…it's a long story," she began. I didn't feel all that comfortable around the sister of Nate's dead wife and she definitely gave off a vibe that she didn't want me there.

"I'll be at my desk," I mouthed to Nate as he walked in my direction. Just as I turned on my heels, he caught my arm. We stood near the three monitors on the wall of his office.

"What's wrong?" he asked so only the two of us could hear.

"I was just trying to get back to work and besides, this all seems…family related," I pointed out. From the corner of my eye I could see Ashley watching me through squinted eyes as she half listened to Alaina.

"Not really. How was your lunch?" he asked, quickly changing the subject on me.

"It was nice; I like Alaina," I told him. "She invited me to the wedding."

"Beat me to the punch I see," he grinned.

"Oh, you were gonna invite me?" I asked, raising a brow.

"Of course."

"That's cute."

"Would you have said yes?"

"Of course," I smiled. "Now, I'll be at my desk if you need anything, Mr. King," I flirted and left the room before he could catch me again.

Alaina emerged from Nate's office a couple minutes later and ten minutes after that, so did Ashley and Nate. Her tears were dried and she looked like she had gotten exactly what she wanted which she probably always did.

"So, be here Monday morning at 8:30am, business casual right?" she said, turning to face Nate who had walked her out of his office.

"Yes," he said, his fingertips at the top of his nose again with a hint of exhaustion.

"Great, I'll see you then. Thanks again Nate, I really appreciate it and I promise I won't let you down," she assured him and then leaped into his arms to hug him. He hugged her tiny frame briefly then released her.

"You're welcome," he said and then she strutted past mine and Roxy's desks.

"See you Monday, Roxanne," Ashley smiled.

"Okay girl, congratulations!" Roxy smiled at her from where she sat as if they were old friends or something.

"Thanks," she said and headed towards the elevators.

Later that evening, during dinner at Nate's house, he informed me that Ashley had shown up to his office in tears about a huge break-up between her and her boyfriend, who was supporting her financially. She was pretty much left with nothing and was looking for his help. Instead of shoving some money her way, he offered her a position working on the 19th floor as a receptionist and she graciously accepted.

I totally understood what Ashley was feeling and could relate to her situation. I didn't however get how she and Roxy seemed to be besties already. That was until Nate informed me that the two of them had met at Texas State University during Ashley's freshman year. Apparently Roxy dropped out when she was a sophomore and never went back so they lost touch.

During dinner, however, I couldn't help but wonder how

Nate was feeling about his late wife's younger sister showing up, out of the blue. If Lauren was anything like Ashley, she had been gorgeous; which in return made that recurring question I had about what it was that Nate saw in me? I mean he was now aware of my past which was a relief within itself and it didn't seem to have an effect on him, so what was it about me that kept him interested?

When I made it home that evening I saw Traci racing to the bathroom as I came through the front door. I sat my purse on the kitchen table and went to where she was.

"Tray-oh," I said all at once when I found her hurled over the toilet. I got down on my knees beside her and gathered her hair in both hands while she threw her guts up. I rubbed her back in efforts of trying to soothe her and when she was done, she sat with her back against the wall and I handed her a piece of tissue to wipe her mouth.

"You okay?" I asked.

"As okay as I can be, but I still feel like shit," she smiled weakly.

"What did they say at the doctor's this morning?"

"It's too soon to tell how far along I am since I just missed my period but I made an appointment for a vaginal ultrasound."

"That's good," I said and paused for a moment before I spoke again. "I wanna ask you something."

"What is it?"

"I saw you and Chase talking at the luncheon…and I saw you leaving the hotel that I told you I met him at for a drink-."

"Roni," she attempted to interrupt me but I stopped her.

"Is it something going on that I should know about?"

"Me and Chase…we did mess around, but that was right before you told me who he was. I would never intentionally get involved with anyone that you had dealings with,"

"I know, but why didn't you just tell me when you realized who he was?"

"I don't know, I was going to though I swear," she said truthfully.

"It's okay, it's not like I want him. It was one time, I just wish you would have said something."

"I'm sorry. But there's actually something else I want to tell you," she began as she sat up straight.

"What?"

"Don't judge me,"

"Promise. What is it?"

"I'm not sure if the father of my baby is Kyle…or Chase," she blurted out and I just stared at her, unable to find words. "Roni say something."

"Whoa," was the first thing that came to mind. "W-What are you gonna do?" I asked.

"I mean, I'm pretty sure its Kyle's but I'm gonna look into my options as far as DNA tests. I've been doing my research," she informed me and I took a deep breath and said,

"Well, you know I'm here for you, no matter what," then reached over to embrace her in a warm hug.

"Don't say anything to Nate, I wanna tell Kyle myself."

"Okay, I won't."

"We should have a spa weekend this weekend. Have some sister time, on me," she offered.

"I would love to, how bout next weekend instead?"

"What's wrong with this weekend," she wanted to know as we both stood up from the floor.

"Nate and I are going to be in L.A., we leave Thursday and come back Sunday," I explained.

"Oh," she said trying to hide her obvious disappointment. "What's in L.A.?"

"He has some business there and wanted me to come and help keep him organized I guess, I don't know," I shrugged.

"Oh okay, that's fine," she said and left out of the bathroom.

Though I temporarily put to the side my frustration with Chase and Traci's little fling and the fact that my one night stand could be my sister's 'baby daddy'; I felt bad that Traci wanted to have sister time and that I had plans with Nate. I know she felt that that was the norm these days and that the two of us barely saw each other since me and Mr. King became…whatever we were. I told myself that once I got back from L.A., I would make our spa weekend happen and it would be my treat instead.

Thursday came before I knew it and I was beyond excited to go to L.A with Nate. The more time that I spent with him, the more I began to believe that he was in fact a King and that his last name carried weight. We took his private jet that was remarkable and even had its own personal flight attendant. The part that surprised me the most was the bedroom that was quite spacious considering it was on a plane and was complete with a king sized bed, of course. By the time we landed, Nate and I were both still on cloud nine. We had wrecked the room on the plane and given the flight attendant something to do once we were done.

There was a white Range Rover waiting for us when we stepped off the plane with the engine already running. Nate shook hands with the pilot as the L.A staff retrieved our luggage and loaded the SUV with our things. The sun was beaming bright as I squinted through my sunglasses. I was instantly hot and couldn't wait to get out of my jeans…again.

Once Nate finished his conversation with Hank his pilot, he took my hand and walked me over to the passenger's side of the car and opened my door for me then sprinted around to the driver's side and hopped in. I ran my hand over the sleek interior of the Range and inhaled the new car smell.

"You like?" he smiled as he buckled his seatbelt.

"I love Range Rovers, the way they look, how they drive."

"Oh yea, I might have to let you test drive this one then, huh?"

"Do not joke with me," I told him.

"I'm not," he said with a smile and then peeled out, taking us straight into the Los Angeles traffic once we were out of the airport.

The time difference from Houston was about two hours so it was only a little after 11am in California as opposed to the 1pm it was back home. I wondered what we would do during the down time that Nate didn't have anything planned.

A normal driver would have taken a good 45 minutes to get from LAX to Malibu, but not Nate. The way he weaved in and out of traffic like a bat out of hell we made it there in 30 minutes flat.

We drove up a fairly steep hill and from the crack in my window I could smell the ocean. California was gorgeous, even the air was beautiful. Nate pulled up into a tile covered driveway of a large Mediterranean style home that over looked the beach. Once he put the car in park, he turned off the engine and looked over at me.

"I thought that I would be staying in the hotel that I reserved," I said, looking over at him.

"I know what you thought," he grinned over at me.

"Is that not happening anymore?" I wanted to know.

"You were never staying in a hotel, Veronica. I did that so Roxanne wouldn't get suspicious, or even more suspicious than she already is," he informed me.

"Oh," I said calmly but jumped up and down inside with excitement.

"Did you honestly think that I would let you be away from me?"

"I...," I attempted to say and he interrupted me with a heated kiss. "I guess not," I said when we pulled away.

Once we were inside, Nate swept me upstairs and bypassed a tour of the crisp white living space with an immaculate view of the ocean from every window in the house, and took me straight upstairs to the master suite, leaving our luggage in the Range outside.

I closed my eyes for a second as I inhaled his cologne. He began kissing my neck with feather light kisses and moved his hands to my zipper. He slowly unbuttoned them and slid the zipper down with his thumb and index finger. With ease he hooked a finger on both sides and pushed my jeans down to my ankles and then got on his knees in front of me and unlaced my shoes, taking each one off and tossing them.

"I love these fucking jeans," he said, as they were the next thing to join the pile of clothes.

I figured he would completely remove my panties next but he didn't. Instead he pushed them to the side where my clit was and started to lick slowly. His licks turned into subtle sucks and with his other free hand he pushed one index finger inside of me.

When I clinched, he inserted another all while he kept his mouth on me. The silent house was filled with my soft moans and the noise his mouth made from the suction that he was giving to my pussy.

His mouth and fingers practically had me dripping and I rubbed his head as I came. This turned him on even more and before I could blink, I was on his shoulders and pressed up on the nearest wall as Nate started fucking me with his tongue.

Déjà vu.

"Uhh!" I cried out uncontrollably. This man was my kryptonite. He sucked and kissed my clit like it was his favorite dessert and he was trying to savor it with every lick. I held on to his head and tugged at his ears I was in such a frenzy I almost wanted to escape Nate's mouth the pleasure was so intense.

My second orgasm sent me crashing down and moaning his name. He sopped up my juices and I slowly slid down his body until my feet reached the hardwood floors.

"Huh!" I panted with my head up against the wall. He looked at me with desire in his eyes and a smile playing at the corners of his glistening lips. I felt like I couldn't move, my legs were as limp as spaghetti noodles. He bent slightly and swooped me up and laid me on the massive king sized bed.

He slid on the condom that he had gotten from the pockets of his jeans and pushed himself inside of me with no warning and I practically screamed when I gasped at the intensity of the pressure. His thrust was strong and powerful and my body succumbed to his right away. He put my legs over my head and my toes brushed the padded headboard above me.

He pulled almost all the way out and then pushed back in, our sex noises filling the room. When he slid out he flipped me over onto my stomach and I put my ass in the air for him to get back where he needed to be, where we both needed him to be. He gave my ass a smack that was not only loud but stung a little. It felt good though and when he thrust inside me deep, he did it again and I looked back at him and bit my lip to let him know that I liked it.

The bed squeaked a little as Nate drilled into me and I felt myself near the cusp of my orgasm once again.

"I…I'm…," I began and Nate cut me off and said, "I know baby, I feel it, too. Come for me," he told me still going strong. I wanted him to go with me so I tightened my muscles around him and he gripped my ass hard then gave it another smack. "Fuck! What are you doing to me?" he groaned. I bit my lip again and threw it back on him one time, then squeezed him again. I could tell he was there too and on his last powerful thrust he lost it and I cried out then bit the pillow that I was holding onto as he panted hard.

Afterward, we laid there next to each other trying to catch our breaths. That was where the contemplating ended with me and in that profound moment I knew that I needed to come clean about the remaining skeletons that were in my closet if I wanted to even consider a future with this man.

FIT for a KING– P. Sharee

Nathaniel-16

Our lunch with the owner and head chef of Ink almost turned into dinner it lasted so long. He wanted Veronica and me to try just about everything on the menu and we did.

We left at about 6pm and afterwards decided to go back to the house and regroup, though I had something else in mind.

She went inside the house to use the bathroom and by the time she came back out, I pulled out my Jialing red and black motorcycle from the garage. She stopped in her tracks on the doorstep when she saw it.

"Uhh, what's going on?" she asked with a blank expression on her face.

"Let's go for a ride," I smiled as I sat on top of the bike.

"Right now?" she asked with panic in her voice.

"Yeah, why not?"

"I don't like motorcycles, Nate," she told me, crossing her arms over her chest in protest.

"Have you ever been on one?"

"No, but they look dangerous and I..."

"If you've never been on one, how do you know you won't like it?" I countered.

"I'm pretty sure I won't," she said, staring me down.

"Please? I won't go too fast, I promise," I pleaded as I started towards where she stood. When I reached her, I cupped her face in my hands and said, "You never have to be afraid when you're with me, I told you I always got you," and then kissed her full lips.

"What about my hair? The wind will eat it up and you know short hair is harder to maintain..." she began and I shut her up with my mouth.

"I will make some calls and have a hair dresser personally delivered to you, baby. The best of the best, I promise. Come on." I told her and took her hand.

"I'm wearing a skirt," she said, referring to the pen striped one that she'd worn on her first day at King Global.

"Nobody will see any of you; you'll be behind me with your legs wrapped around me," I said with a grin. She gave me a look and hitched her skirt up revealing her luscious, milk-chocolate thighs then climbed on the bike behind me. "Remind me to kiss between those later," I told her and she tapped my shoulder playfully.

We took off and turned out onto the street. At first she was tense and held on to my waist extremely tight, almost taking the wind out of me. But as we cruised, she relaxed and her grip turned into a snug hug. It felt more than good being with Roni and I hadn't realized how comfortable we were with one another.

I turned on to a winding road and we drove past some of the hills in the neighborhood. I hadn't ridden my bike in a while but whenever I did, it always helped me clear my head. In that moment the only thing that was on my mind was the woman that was behind me. Everything about her excited me and when I wasn't with her, I was thinking about her, wanting to be with her, and thinking about how it was the last time that she and I were together. She was changing me and in a good way. From the outside looking in I probably appeared to be okay before meeting Roni, but those that knew me knew better.

We made it back to the house a half hour later and when I turned off the engine she climbed off the bike first and carefully pulled her helmet off.

"Did I go too fast?" I asked her once my helmet was off.

"No. Babe, that was so much fun, I loved it! I felt so...so

free," she exclaimed and I couldn't help but smile. She breathed heavily but I knew it was from the rush of adrenaline.

"I know I feel the same way, it helps me clear my head and not think for a minute, you know?" I told her as I climbed off.

"Did you clear your head just now?" She wanted to know.

"Nah, I couldn't focus with those thighs wrapped around me," I said, coming toward her. When I reached where she stood I pulled her body to mine and kissed her lips hard. "Come on, let's go inside." I told her and held her by the waist with one arm and opened the door with my free hand.

Inside, the entire house was lit by candles that smelled of lavender and chamomile. Peach rose petals covered the floors with a path leading up to the stairs with the beach view from the windows looking luminescent from the glow.

I examined Roni's reaction and she looked as if she walked into her very own fairytale. Her big bright eyes appeared to be brighter and she covered her mouth with her hands in awe. When she turned to me, she put her hands down and the smile on her face tugged at my heart strings.

"So, that's why you insisted we take your motorcycle out," she said looking up at me.

"Maybe," I said lowly, wearing a huge grin.

"Get over here," she said, pulling me by my shirt and kissing me with her full wet lips. She slipped her tongue in my mouth and I returned the favor.

"So, I take that as you are pleased with the ambiance?" I asked her when we both came up for air.

"Yes, Mr. King, I love it," she smiled.

The chocolate covered strawberries and champagne that I had chilling were discarded and I carried her straight upstairs to the master suite. We undressed each other with greedy fingers and once we got in the bed it was like time stood still.

I had one of my favorite Isley Brothers songs "Eternal", playing on the stereo system that was piped into all of the rooms on repeat. When I stared down at her naked body below me, she looked so innocent and beautiful, I couldn't fuck her how I had earlier when we got to Malibu. No, this woman needed to be made love to and I was the only man for the job.

I kissed from her lips down to her full breasts and navel until I reached between her thighs and savored her sweetness. She was already wet for me so I took it upon myself to make her drip with pleasure making her cum almost instantly. She moaned in a hoarse voice and rubbed my head and tugged at my ears when I pushed my tongue inside of her. I groaned with desire; I was glad that I was taking her where she needed to go and filling her body with unbridled passion.

During our brief intermission, I hovered over her and removed the condom that I stuffed under the pillows then ripped the gold wrapper off with my teeth. I slid it down my length and pressed the head at her opening. She looked up at me with pure desire and hunger in her eyes, reflecting exactly what I was feeling in that moment.

That night I felt like I had given her all of me, I went slow and steady and made her come over and over. She kissed my chest and cupped my face, rubbed and scratched my back, and nipped at whatever part of me she could get her mouth on. I reached for the top of the mattress and used it to push all of me into her and she gasped with every stroke. This woman brought the beast out of me and made me want to protect and take care of her, cherish her.

My release came fast and spiraled down my spine like a tornado. I came hard and before the last drop spilled into the condom she whispered, "I love you." I almost didn't hear the words and if I had been a few inches farther away from her face, I probably wouldn't have. But I did. And it was as if she said it loud and clear. She told me she loved me and I was stuck. I wanted to say it back but I couldn't find the words. Afraid of them was more like it.

After I pulled out and kissed her on the nose, I went to the bathroom. As I stared at my reflection in the mirror I felt like a different man. I felt like an idiot. I wanted to tell Roni that I felt the same way and that I loved her, too. In the past I always associated love with my wife and never said that to another woman, had never felt that for another woman… until now.

The smell of Amber Erotic Rush body wash escaping the

bathroom woke me up the next morning. When I climbed out of bed, I found Roni covered in a cotton white towel, staring at herself in the mirror.

"Good morning, beautiful," I said, getting her attention.

"Good morning," she said with a half-smile.

"What's wrong?" I asked with furrowed brows at her blank expression.

"Nothing," she lied.

"Veronica," I said, using my finger to turn her chin toward me. "Hey, talk to me. What's the matter?"

"I haven't told you everything about me." That was the last thing that I expected to hear come out of her mouth.

"What do you mean?"

"You know that I used to dance…but I didn't tell you that the very last time that I did is when I met your brother," she blurted out.

"You met Chase at a strip club?"

"It was back in Atlanta before I ever moved to Houston and before I ever met you," she exclaimed and I couldn't help but laugh a little.

"What's so funny?" she asked, her eyebrows furrowed with confusion.

"I'm not surprised that you and Chase met at a strip club, he practically lives in them," I told her.

"Yea but..."

"Baby listen," I said, cutting her off and pulling her close to me. "I told you that your past is irrelevant. Everyone has one, it helped mold the people that we are today. And the woman that I'm looking at right now is pretty fuckin' phenomenal so whatever happened in your past let's leave it there," I assured her.

"Are you sure?" she asked looking up at me.

"I'm positive," I said and then hugged her tight and kissed the top of her head. "I don't care about what happened before me."

The truth was I didn't want to know. In the back of my mind I knew where that conversation was going and it took everything in me not to allow Roni to finish. That left me with a gnawing feeling in the pit of my stomach though and I numbed it the only way I knew how in that moment and had Roni for breakfast on top of the bathroom sink.

Nathaniel-17

Chase and I sat through a 45 minute meeting with the bootlicking manager we'd hired to run Angela's L.A since it opened a few years back. I could barely stand the sound of his voice but he was smart and knew how to do business. While he talked Chase's ears off, I explored the dining area and checked in with some of the patrons to see how they felt about the service.

Before we got ready to leave I reviewed the numbers and was surprisingly pleased with what they reflected.

"Good work, Jerry," I said, shaking his hand. His palms were disgustingly moist and I wiped mine on the back of my golf shorts after shaking his.

"Thanks Nate, I told you I wouldn't let you down," he replied, his eyes hiding behind the cop-like sunglasses he wore.

"I wouldn't expect anything less. We'll be in touch," I told him with my hands in my pockets now.

"Alright guys, good deal," he told Chase and I and then went back inside the restaurant, bypassing the growing line of customers waiting to get into Angela's.

"So, what else you got going on today?" Chase asked me, glancing at his watch.

"I think I'm clear for the rest of the day until later tonight for our appearance at the club. What about you?" I asked him. His attention was stolen from our conversation to whatever was behind me. With the faint sound of a woman's heels hitting the pavement I turned around to see what Chase was looking at and thought that my eyes were deceiving me for a moment.

"A little help?" she said.

"You bought the whole Chanel store, didn't you?" Chase snickered as he rushed over to the woman.

"Maybe," she giggled. "Oh, hey Nate," she smiled.

"Ashley, I didn't know that you were in L.A., too," I said with a tight smile and then giving Chase a look like I could have strangled him.

"In the flesh. It was kinda last minute, but when I ran into Chase in the elevator we got to talking and catching up," she said, smiling up at my pussy-fiend of a brother and he was wearing a smug grin.

"Yeah, he's full of...surprises isn't he?" I said, glancing in his direction.

"Sweetheart, why don't you take the car back to the hotel while I finish up some business with Nate and I'll meet you there later."

"Okay, don't be too long though," she pouted and then I saw him bend down to kiss her on the mouth and I winced at the sight.

Ashley handed over her shopping bags to Chase's driver and then the SUV disappeared. He and I walked for a few blocks and when we stopped at one of the local pubs in the area I let him have it.

"You gotta be out of your fucking mind, right?" I said once our Jack and Cokes were in front of us.

"What?" he grinned.

"Why in the hell would you bring Ashley to L.A with you? This is supposed to be a business trip, is it not?!"

"So, you can bring Roni, but I can't bring my girl?"

"She's not your girl, she's somebody you started fucking. She's bad news Chase I'm telling you, end it," I warned him.

"Bad news? Nate she's a grown woman and she approached me, by the way."

"Yes bad news, I can feel it. And you mean to tell me you

don't know how to turn a woman down?" I asked before I sipped my drink.

"My only weakness," he gloated and I couldn't help but laugh. Chase downed his drink in one gulp and signaled the bartender for another round. "It's a little early to be getting fucked up, don't you think?"

" Its happy hour somewhere," he told me wiping his mouth and accepting his second drink.

That wasn't like him to drink that heavy so early in the day but aside from business my brother had always lived his life like he was on vacation. I limited myself to one and a half drinks that afternoon but stayed there to keep him company.

I arrived back in Malibu later that evening just as the van from the spa I sent over earlier to the house for Roni was leaving.

When I went inside I saw that she was on the phone talking to Traci so I kissed her cheek and excused myself to go take a shower and get ready for our appearance at the club.

Dressed in dark denim Levis, button down shirt, and Polo loafers I was ready to get this little pop-up at "Lucid" over with. Roni dressed in one of the spare bedrooms because she didn't want the steam from the shower to 'mess with her new flawless hair doo'.

I got downstairs before she did and when I saw the fire engine red dress she was wearing it looked like it was painted on her body. Her face was almost make-up free with an exception of bronze eye shadow and gloss on her luscious lips.

"So, this must be the definition of a fuck-em dress," I said to her with a sly grin, studying her curves from head to toe.

"You think so?" she asked with a hint of seduction in her voice.

"I see I can't let you out of my sight at all tonight."

"Who said I wanted to leave your side?" she flirted. I smiled and downed the rest of my drink before we left.

When we got to Lucid, I held on to Roni's waist as we navigated our way through the crowds. The air was thick with smoke and fog from the machines and the smokers that were in the building. The club was lit by neon lights and at the very top of the spiral staircase, we passed the bouncers and went directly up the VIP lounge. I guided Roni down the balcony until we reached our VIP bungalow. There was a bottle of Armand de Brignac chilling for us and I popped the bottle as she took a seat on the black leather sofa.

We sipped our champagne and stole kisses from each other when Chase conveniently interrupted once he made it to our VIP section.

"A-hem," he said clearing his throat. I reluctantly pulled away from Roni's succulent lips and turned my head to face him.

"It looks like y'all having a damn good time," he looked down at me.

"Uh, we were," I corrected him, wiping away the trace of Roni's gloss that still lingered on my lips.

"Hey, Nate," Ashley said, stepping from behind Chase with a huge grin on her lips.

"Hello again, Ashley," I said with a tight smile. "I don't think you got a chance to meet Veronica the other day," I said and Ashley's smile faded when I introduced Roni who was tucked neatly at my side and crossing her legs.

"Your other assistant, right? Hello," Ashley said in a condescending tone.

"Hello," Roni laughed to herself, looking Ashley in her eyes. Her tone was pleasant but the tension between the two women could have been cut with a machete it was so thick. "Excuse me, I have to go to the ladies room." Roni said, standing and tugging her dress down a little.

"You want me to show you where it is," Ashley asked, but with a raised hand Roni told her,

"No, I can find it," and then walked past Chase and Ashley in the direction of the bathrooms that serviced the VIP area. Chase's phone began to ring and he snickered to himself before answering and walking away, leaving Ashley and me alone.

"So, you and Victoria…are a thing?" she asked as she sat down next to me.

"It's Veronica," I corrected her. "And yes, we're 'a thing'."

"Wow," she said, raising her eyebrows and picking up my glass to finish my champagne. "I had to have a drink after that one."

"Wow, what?" I said, clasping my hands together in front of me.

"Nothing, it's just weird seeing you with another woman. I mean, I've only ever seen you with..."

"With Lauren?"

"Yeah. And then you're dating your assistant of all people? Isn't that against the Nathaniel King code of ethics or something?" she joked.

"Look Ashley, a lot has changed in the past seven years."

"Tell me about it, the last time you saw me I was this scrawny little teenager with glasses and braces."

"I know," I laughed to myself.

"But I'm a woman now, Nate," she clarified, placing her hand on my thigh and I immediately tensed up under her touch. "A woman who knows exactly how to handle a man with power, a man like you," she said, attempting to let her hand drift farther but I stopped her with my own hand and removed it from my leg completely.

"Ashley, you are definitely a woman, but there could and would never be anything between the two of us. You'll always be like a sister to me, Lauren's baby sister, nothing more and nothing less," I explained to her and then poured myself another glass of champagne.

"Lauren wasn't as perfect as you thought she was," she mumbled as she stood and marched off in defeat to the ladies room just as Roni was returning to our bungalow.

I caught a glimpse of Chase on the phone, watching Roni as she walked past him, his eyes lingering on every curve of her body and it all began to make sense to me. He wanted her, and the fact that I now knew they'd met months ago in Atlanta explained a lot. Chase was lusting for Roni from a distance and that shit made my blood boil. Though he was my brother, I didn't completely trust him when it came to Veronica and I felt like he was just waiting for me to slip up or ruin shit so he could move in for the kill.

When she sat back down beside me, Roni and I picked right

back up where we left off with our kisses and touching and ended up leaving Lucid after only being there for about an hour. Once I told Chase I would catch up with him later, we left and he was on his third or fourth shot and Ashley was getting up close and personal with a dark skinned guy on the first level of the club.

In the car, the partition in the SUV was rolled up and Roni was unzipping my jeans. She pulled my dick out and without any warning took it into her mouth and got down on her knees. I was beyond shocked because she had never given me head.

Her mouth was warm and she mimicked a pussy perfectly. She licked from the base to the tip and then sucked me off like it was her mission in life. I gripped the seats behind me for support because she was going crazy on my dick. She used her hand to stroke me up and down in combination with her mouth and I felt like I was high.

"Fuuuck!" was all I could say. She looked up at me, her eyes full of passion. We couldn't get to the house fast enough, and my release was approaching.

I felt my eruption build and I knew it would be a matter of moments before I exploded, so I pulled out of her mouth and came on the floor of the car. She watched as it spilled out from the head with a look of amazement. My forehead was glistening and her lips still looked hungry.

When the car halted to a stop, I rolled the window down to see that we were back at the Malibu house already. I shoved my dick back in my boxers carefully but didn't bother zipping my pants.

Inside the house, it felt like we were on ecstasy and ready for whatever. I pulled her toward me and slammed the door behind us. In one move my mouth was on hers and she was rubbing my head as our tongues did a dance. Her kiss almost made me numb and my only goal was to please her.

We made our way over to the white love seat and I pulled her on top of me. Our kisses continued and I rapidly pulled my pants down to my ankles, and then pushed my dick into her with no warning. She gasped loudly as I filled her and she grinded on me slowly.

"No condom?" she managed to say between kisses.

"We're past that, don't you think?" I asked, breathing heavily.

"I...I guess so," she said as she grinded on me with my hands glued to her ass. We were like a couple of rabbits who couldn't get enough. It wasn't long before we were standing and I had her pressed against a wall, and then me eventually carrying her up the stairs.

We clawed at each other like savages wanting more and more with every second that passed and I gave her everything that I had. With our bodies glistening with sweat and the bedroom echoing with our sex sounds I could've stayed inside of Veronica all night that night.

As she tightened around me, my arousal began to simmer. She was ready too and I knew that this one would leave us both breathless.

"I'm coming!" she panted.

"Come baby," I encouraged her and then quickened my pace so that I could go when she did.

"Shit!" she cried out uncontrollably.

"I love you," I panted. "I love you," I repeated as I thrust deep inside her and her final cry was when we both crashed like waves. My knees grew weak and I collapsed on top of her and kissed her jaw. We had a repeat in the shower and then went to bed close to three that morning.

I found myself restless well after Roni had fallen asleep. I stood on the balcony of the master suite and let the swift gusts of the ocean breeze sweep across my bare chest and feet as I tried to collect my thoughts. Telling Roni that I loved her left me feeling conflicted the moment I'd said it. I did love her and there was no denying it; but in the same breath I couldn't help but think about what Ashley said and how I hadn't thought much about Lauren or Kristina since I'd met Veronica. Was she making me forget them? I grew angrier with myself with every thought of how I had gotten so wrapped up with another woman that I was beginning to lose sight of two of the most important people to me.

That night I found myself tossing and turning after I

eventually found sleep; and my dream or nightmare was more like it, came in the form of a flashback.

The night of Lauren and Kristina's accident played over and over in my head and for some reason, I couldn't seem to wake up. Night terrors had become a big part of my life and started right after I lost my family in that fatal car crash. Every night at the same time faithfully, I battled with the vivid depiction of how everything happened and it took me almost a year to seek help. Whenever this happened, it always got the best of me and left me in shambles the following day. Work normally kept me focused but being with Roni had me on an emotional rollercoaster.

Lauren and I had been having problems for a while around that time, and King Global was still a work in progress; which meant that majority of my time was spent there and traveling for business. On that evening in particular I had promised her that I would be home for dinner.

"Nate, where are you?" she said as impatiently as she paced the kitchen floor back and forth. I was already an hour and half late and was still working on a model for a private school I was supposed to break ground on in two weeks.

"I'm just finishing up a few things at the office baby," I told her.

"You're still at work when you promised me that we would have dinner as a family at least once this week?!" she shouted.

"I know, I'm sorry. I promise I'll be home in time to put Krissy to bed, I just have to finish this model-."

"No, don't give me anymore of those empty ass promises of yours Nathaniel-."

"Lauren please don't start, I'm working," I said before she ended the call.

I headed home about an hour later and by the time I got there, there was no sign of my wife or my daughter. She hadn't left a note and she had barely packed anything except for a few clothes for her and Kristina. I had to collect my thoughts before I went to look for them as this wasn't the first time that Lauren had called herself leaving, but it was the first time that she had packed any clothes for herself. After I finished my glass of Jack Daniels, I grabbed my car keys.

When I got outside to the driveway I noticed it had started to rain. I called Lauren's phone a few times as I drove to the few places I figured she would be. I drove for almost an hour and as I passed the exit to get to our house on the freeway, I saw what looked like a huge accident on the other side of the road. Normally, I wouldn't have paid it any mind but the car looked identical to the silver Mercedes SUV that I had bought Lauren as a 3rd anniversary present the year before. Other drivers honked at me because I had slowed my speed so I could try and make out the license plate on the now almost crushed vehicle.

When I saw "LKING3" from the bumper, I almost caused an accident myself as I cut other people off on the freeway to get off and get around to the other side.

When I made it to the other side of the road where the police, fire department, and now ambulance were I couldn't even see straight. My heart had stopped beating when I saw the car and all the crushed and twisted metal that surrounded the two most important people in my life and my sole reasons for living.

The semi that had hit them was off in a ditch on the side of the road, but I could see the paramedic giving the driver medical attention. I wasn't able to get close enough to see Lauren because the firemen had the jaws-of-life going to try and get them out. I was able to see my baby Kristina from the back seat who looked like she was asleep, but I knew she wasn't.

She was gone and I would never hear her say "Daddy" again, or follow me around the house in my shoes, or wake me up with wet kisses. I knew that Lauren and I wouldn't get to fix our problems, or she wouldn't get another chance to cuss me out again, or even make love. They were gone before we got to the hospital, gone before I made it over to the other side of the road.

I woke up in a cold sweat and my heart and lungs felt like they were on fire, just as I felt the night of the accident. My breathing was staggered and my chest and back was drenched with sweat along with the sheets that I was wrapped in. When I looked to my left, Roni was still sleeping peacefully. In that moment I hated myself for letting things go as far as I had with her knowing I still struggled with my own demons. A pained expression covered my face as I tried to control my breathing, and I closed my eyes tight as I kissed Roni's forehead and then climbed out of bed, careful not wake her. I ran my hands over my head and when I looked at the screen on my phone, the time was 5:12 a.m.

I went for a run on the beach and then took out my motorcycle for a spin to try and clear my head. Neither worked. Aside from being slightly hung-over, Roni could tell that I unintentionally put up a wall so she gave me my space and I sent her on a shopping spree.

Sunday when we landed in Houston, I had the crew load up a town car with all of Roni's things.

"Okay, Nate, what's going on? Ever since yesterday you've been really quiet and…distant. Did I do something?" she asked, looking up at me and squinting at the sun.

"No, no you didn't do anything." I told her.

"Then what is it?" she pleaded.

"We need to talk." Roni was confused and hurt. I could tell by the sour look on her face.

Nathaniel-18

"I need some space. I need some time to figure some shit out, everything seems to be moving too fast," I told her as she and I squinted at the setting sun. She swallowed hard before she said, "Oh."

"It's not you-," I began and she interrupted.

"It's not me, it's you right?" she said finishing my sentence.

"Veronica please, don't make me sound like a cliché. Last night I did a lot of thinking and I realize that I still have come unresolved issues I need to deal with. I feel like I'm losing focus when I'm with you sometimes. Lauren and Kristina…they were and will always be a big part of my life and with you around it's like they never existed. My head is fucked up right now and I'm just so sorry that I let things go as far as I did before I got my mind right. I just need some time," I said all at once. Her head was down as she nodded. Taking some space away from Roni was the last thing that I wanted to do but I had to have clear head before I made my next move.

"Tony is gonna take you home," I told her and she remained silent. I kissed her forehead and ushered her into the backseat of the car then shut the door.

"Sir, we'll be ready for takeoff in about 45 minutes."

"Alright, thanks, Hank," I told my pilot and then walked back up the stairs of the jet and prepared for my next departure.

Flying solo was even lonelier than I imagined it would be. I hated to put space between Roni and me but in actuality I couldn't think straight with her around. I almost felt like being with her had been clouding my judgment in some way. She made me fall in love with her and had me breaking all my rules.

Ashley prancing around didn't help. She was a constant reminder of Lauren and her presence made me feel guilty just thinking about Roni; almost as if Ashley was a sign that things were definitely moving too fast with her and I didn't need to just pump my breaks, the car needed to swerve and go into park before I wrecked some shit.

I managed to get a few hours of sleep during the flight which I was grateful for because I hadn't gotten much in the past 48 hours. Roni was still in my thoughts and even though I felt guilty for the distance that I had sprung on her, I needed to collect my thoughts sooner rather than later.

As I stepped off the plane, my phone rang and the caller I.D. displayed a number that wasn't programmed into my contacts but I answered anyway.

"Nate King."

"Long time, no hear, King Tut," the husky voice on the other end of the phone said and I knew who it was right away.

"Tell me about it," I said as I walked over to the Jeep Wrangler that was waiting for me when I landed at the San Jose, Los Cabos airport.

"Yeah, I'm back in the states and I need to talk to you about some shit."

"I'm at the Villa."

"I'll be there tomorrow at noon," The person on the other end of the phone said and then the call ended.

Julian McNeil, better known as "Mac", and I were always as thick as thieves. He and I met when I was about 16 years old after my mother and Robert moved our family from Inglewood, California to Houston, Texas. Mac was about ten years older than me and I looked up to him like an older brother. He was this suave, dark-skinned nigga that never played about his money and kept a pretty woman on his arm. Mac was made of money and we couldn't have met at a more opportune time.

Our first encounter was actually an ironic one and was right after I started doing some teen modeling so that I could save for college. I was coming from downtown after spending all the money I had on headshots and took a wrong turn in a not-so safe neighborhood. I went to the nearest gas station to ask for directions and when I came out, two guys from around the way thought that they could try me because I wasn't dressed like a thug and was driving a $50,000 car that my mother insisted I accept to get around the huge new city we lived in.

They took jabs at me by calling me a "pretty boy" to get me riled up because if there was anything that I hated, it was being called a "pretty boy". The first one pushed me and I instantly swung, getting a good hit on him right at his jaw. The other one came up behind me, like most bitch- ass- niggas do, and wrestled me down to the ground so that his friend could get a few good hits on me. The guy that had gotten me down on the ground was wearing what had to be the oldest looking pair of Timberland boots I had ever seen and attempted to bury my face underneath them but I stopped him by punching him in the shin of his other leg causing him to almost lose his balance.

From the ground I could hear a car's tires screech and a deep husky voice say "What the fuck you lil niggas think y'all doing?" The other one that was still hovered over me was suddenly knocked on his ass and I got up off the ground. My back-up took care of him and I finished off his friend that attempted to run the minute he saw me coming for his ass. They both got stomped into the cement at that gas station that night and the only mark on me was a few swollen knuckles.

Mac introduced himself to me and asked me 'what was a guy like me that drove a BMW, doing on that side of town'. I told him about how I got turned around but didn't divulge that I was a teen model. Somehow, we did however start talking about how I was saving money for college and that was when he first propositioned me to make a few thousand dollars in one day.

For the next couple years, I made drug runs for Mac throughout the entire state of Texas and still did my modeling on the side until I was about 18. By the time I graduated high school I had enough money saved to pay off my tuition at UCLA for all four years if I wanted to.

When I went off to college is when I started moving big weight and Mac helped me develop my own little operation. I recruited my own crew of hitters and had so much cocaine distributed on campus and the surrounding areas, the white kids couldn't get enough of it and bought it up like Girl Scout cookies.

It wasn't until I met Lauren and things got serious with her that I thought about quitting. I promised her once I graduated and had enough money to start my own company that I would leave the drug game alone and on my 27th birthday and the day I started King Global, I turned over all of my connects and remaining product to Mac.

I arrived to my house in Cabo at sunset and decided to get some work done to try and keep my mind off of the weekend I had just had. My housekeeper loaded me up on coffee and I worked on my laptop outside while I watched the waves of the ocean crash onto the rocks and moisten the sand. I couldn't help but let my mind drift off to what it would have been like had I brought Roni there with me. Even though I escaped to Mexico to try and detox from her, she was planted in my thoughts and seemed to be embedded in my head somehow.

At noon, sharp, the next day just as I was about to start on what felt like my third pot of coffee since I'd arrived to my villa, my housekeeper Marisol alerted me that I had a visitor. I walked back into the house from the lanai to see Mac's six foot five frame standing in the middle of my living room dressed in a white linen pants suit and his now long dreads pulled back in a neat ponytail.

"King Tut in the flesh, baby!" he grinned as I walked in his direction, calling me the nickname that he had given me over a decade ago.

"Mac, what's going on man?" I said, shaking his hand and then hugging him.

"Not a whole lot," he smiled, revealing his white teeth and that signature gold one in the right corner. "You look like shit, man, what's going on with you?"

"Been up working all night since I got here, haven't been to sleep yet," I told him. "Bullshit, those bags under your eyes aren't from working all night, my nigga. What's going on?" he asked, reading me like a book.

Over lunch I spilled my guts and kept it one hundred with Mac about what had been going on. It actually felt good to let it out since that was something I rarely did. I didn't get into too much detail but I did share with him how conflicted I was about Roni, Lauren's memory, Ashley resurfacing, and moving forward.

We chopped it up that afternoon but I told him I needed to get back to work, and he needed to get back to his lady that was waiting for him at his beach house.

By the end of the week, I had more work done than I would have if I was in my office for eight hours a day, in a five day week.

By the end of the week, my disappearing act finally caught up with me and after so many text messages my mother decided to sick Alaina on me.

"Nate, what hell are you doing in Mexico?" she yelled through the phone.

"I needed a break Alaina, damn," I said, rubbing my face as I packed my clothes.

"A break from what?!" she wanted to know. "You were just in L.A for four days with Roni. How many breaks does one man need?"

"I just have a lot on my mind, that's all."

"Don't get evasive with me, Nathaniel. What happened? And what did you do to Roni?"

"I didn't do anything."

"Liar. She was more quiet than usual when I invited her up to my office for lunch but she did tell me that you said you had 'some things to figure out'."

"Ugh." I sighed as my heart silently ached for the unintentional hurt I inflicted on Roni. She didn't deserve it.

"Whatever is going on you need to fix it," she demanded.

Veronica-19

Nate had been M.I.A for a solid week from King Global after we got back from L.A. and I couldn't help but feel hollow inside. The only thing that was able to momentarily shake me out of my 'Nathaniel King' withdrawals was a call from my girl Frankie back in Atlanta.

She had called a few times earlier in the week but because I was stationed in my feelings, I ignored her calls until that Friday when I got off work.

"Hey girl, I'm sorry I haven't returned your calls, I been super busy with work and stuff-," I lied as I adjusted my wireless earpiece that was connected to my phone.

"Girl, what the fuck?!I've been trying to get in touch with you to let you know what's going on," Frankie answered in a shaky voice and sounded short of breath.

"What? What is it? What's wrong?!"

I asked all at once.

"Girl Chico is out, he was released from Fulton County a few weeks ago, but I just got word the other day when I tried to call you," she informed me and my heart skipped a beat as she spoke.

"After all that evidence, he got out with no prison time or nothing?!" I panicked, gripping the steering wheel tight with both hands.

"He had been sitting in there for a year remember? And I knew once I heard he hired Ericka Lucas that he was gon get out. My home girl said he got two years' probation and some fines, that's it."

"How does she know?"

"She friends with some chick named Ashley that he supposed to be fuckin' with now."

"This is fucked up,"

"That ain't it, though, he came to Emerald City, he was asking about you, Roni."

"He was?" I asked, swallowing hard as Frankie continued.

"Girl yeah, asking me had I talked to you n' shit, I told him naw," she said. I sighed with premature relief. "He musta knew I was lying because he choked me up and everything, calling me a lyin' ass bitch. Girl you need to watch your back, he knows that your sister lives in Texas so he probably assumed that's where you went," she told me which was code for 'I told him you moved to Houston with your sister'.

"You think he might try and come here?" I asked her as I pulled into the parking lot of our apartment complex.

"I wouldn't put it past him girl, just watch your back and remember you didn't hear from me," Frankie told me and ended the call.

I sat in my car with the engine running for what seemed like forever. I didn't know what to think, didn't know what to do. My biggest fears had become reality and Chico was out of jail and was a free man. Back when Frankie had told me about who he'd gotten as his defense attorney, I knew that there was a good chance, but I also knew that there was a lot of evidence to support the case that the state of Georgia had against him. Frankie was right about him knowing that Traci lived in Houston and if he got word from anyone in Atlanta who knew me, it would be a matter of time before we crossed each other's paths whether I wanted us to or not.

I didn't mention anything to Traci about it when I finally made it in the house after sitting in my car for over a half hour. I didn't want to talk, I didn't even wanna think but I couldn't help it. If there was one thing that I knew about Chico, he was a persistent and determined man and if wanted me, he would stop at nothing to find me.

There was only one person that I wanted to talk to about what was going on and that same person seemed to be avoiding me like the plague. Nate was who I felt the closest to since I moved to Houston and we became…whatever it was that we were, and now I was in trouble and he was nowhere to be found.

Work had even been…shitty, to say the least. There was no sign of him around the office by the time Monday rolled around again, Roxy had this permanent side-eye made just for me and I wasn't sure why.

If it wasn't Chico's release consuming my thoughts, then I was replaying the entire four day weekend in Malibu in my head and tried to figure out what transpired that caused Nate to become so cold and conflicted. Was it Ashley? Had she said something to him that sent him down memory lane and was that why he needed a break away from me?

When I got back from lunch one afternoon (and still no sign of Mr. King), or picking over a salad was more accurate; I saw Ashley sitting on the corner of Roxy's desk holding a plastic spoon up to her mouth giggling hysterically.

"Okay, I guess I should get back to work, girl. I'll see you later," Ashley said, pulling her skirt down once she was standing.

"Alright, I'll text you when I get off," Roxy told her and when Ashley passed my desk she giggled to herself and then headed toward the elevators to return to her floor. When I looked at Roxy, she was wearing this stank look on her face like I had wronged her in some way.

"Is there a problem?" I asked, looking at her from across the room. She offered a fake laugh and then answered with,

"What are you talking about, Veronica?" batting her false lashes in my direction.

"For the past week you've been giving me this…look like I've done something to you and I'm pretty sure I haven't," I responded.

"Me? No you haven't done anything to me but I just find it interesting that all of a sudden Mr. King hasn't been here in what, over a week since the two of you got back from that so-called business trip?"

"And what exactly does that have to do with me?" I asked, raising an eyebrow.

"Funny you should ask. The hotel where you reserved your little room sent an email that indicated you never checked in and refunded the money to Mr. King's business account," she informed me and I wasn't sure what to say.

"There was a lot of work to be done and Mr. King let me stay in the guest house," I lied.

"Hmph. I bet he did," she said sarcastically and rolled her eyes then returned to her work.

I shrugged Roxy off. I was not about to allow her noseyness get me all stirred up. And I wasn't the only liar in that room and knew for a fact that the hotel never sent an email. She had gotten her information from her new BFF. My mind was way too occupied with Nate than it should have been and I was starting to become a little obsessive.

Internally I had become an emotional and nervous wreck. I found myself looking over my shoulder whenever I went somewhere, or jumping at the sound of doors slamming too hard, wondering if Chico was nearby. In the same breath, I missed Nate and it took everything in me not to contact him, but I couldn't help but feel rejected by him. I almost began to regret telling him that I loved him. Maybe if I had kept it to myself, he wouldn't have felt pressured to say it back.

Later on after work that night, Traci and I decided to have movie night and she was waiting for me in the living room watching the previews from the "Sex and the City" DVD while I washed my face.

I stared into the bathroom mirror at myself and just broke down. I couldn't help myself. I missed Nate and I wasn't sure what I was supposed to think at that point. Was our so-called relationship or whatever, over?

On the other side of the door, Traci had been on her way to

her bedroom to grab a blanket when she heard me crying and sniffling in the bathroom. It angered her that I was so upset and hurt by Nate's distance. Opening the door to check on me, she furrowed her brows with anger and when I came out with no trace of tears, we started the movie.

That night we pigged out on chocolate chip cookies that Traci baked, popcorn, chips, and we ordered pizza. It was the ultimate sister sleepover.

"Has Roxy's stank ass said anything else to you?" she asked me as she stuffed her face with a handful of popcorn.

"Not really. It's actually been really quiet this week. I know she swears that there is something going on between us though," I told her as I nibbled on a cookie.

"Snake ass."

"Yeah. I'm not worried about her or Ashley. There's nothing neither one of them can do to make me feel worse than I already do."

"What's her deal anyway? She seems to be everywhere since she came into town, lil busy body ain't she?" she spat with her nose turned up.

"I don't know, she's was in cahoots with Chase in L.A., now I'm pretty sure she's probably dancing around in Nate's head, stirring up memories and what-not. How do you compete with someone's dead wife?

"Roni, you gotta stop this," Traci told me, reaching over and rubbing my shoulder. "You don't compete and you need to stop putting yourself down. There's nothing that you've done wrong here. He is struggling with his own issues and I'm sure it has nothing to do with you. You were honest and that should count for something. Maybe it's better that this happened now before you both got in too deep." Traci concluded.

"Too late for that," I said and clutched the pillow that I was laying on, a lump forming in my throat with tears I refused to let out.

My newly inflicted self-doubt had me in a tailspin and I didn't know which way was up anymore. Everywhere I went, I was paranoid about Chico finding me, or sulking over Nate and my situationship. I began to question whether or not King Global was the place for me. I liked my job, but the fact of the matter was I had opened myself up to Nate completely and he had cast me to the side. Now I was in limbo and he was nowhere in sight especially when I felt like I needed him the most.

Chico's release from jail made everything that much more complicated and made me feel like leaving King Global wouldn't have been the worst thing.

On my drive home that afternoon, I thought my eyes were playing tricks on me. I had been sitting at a red light for what seemed like an eternity and when I looked to my left I could have sworn I saw Chico standing in front of a sandwich shop on the corner. He was wearing a white V-neck shirt that hugged his bulging muscles and Nike joggers. I gasped at the mere thought that it was really Chico and when I blinked, the light turned green and there was no sight of him.

I ran a stop sign trying to get home as fast as I could. When I got out of the car I did a quick scan of the apartment complex and kept my head down until I got into the building. As I checked the mailbox, I took out my phone and tried calling Frankie to see if she'd heard anything else or if she knew Chico's whereabouts.

"We're sorry, your call can not be completed at this time, please hang up and dial again," the phone said on the other end which told me that that number was no good anymore.

I was confused, why had Frankie changed her number and didn't give it to me? Chico must've really shaken her up when he came to Emerald City inquiring about me and Frankie clearly wanted no parts in the mess that was us. If she was scared enough to change her number, then there was a good chance that Frankie was probably laying low or had disappeared altogether.

I took a deep breath as I clutched the mail in my hand and climbed the stairs to the second floor. When I got inside the apartment I locked both locks and put the chain on the door to try and ease my mind. I thumbed through the mail and saw that there was a small envelope addressed to Traci and I and when I opened it, inside was a formal invitation to Alaina and Ricky's wedding. I silently began to dread the idea. Of course I wanted to go, but my thoughts got the best of me and I remembered that if I didn't see Nate for the rest of the week at work, I would definitely see him at the wedding because he was Ricky's best man and Alaina's brother. He wouldn't miss it. I wasn't ready to see all of his family, and due to the space that he had put in between us; I wasn't sure if I was ready to see him. I was still hurt and with every day that passed it only became more difficult to be away from him.

The rest of the mail was junk, a pre-approval for a credit card, and something addressed to that 'Yasmin Bishop' again. I made a mental note to add it to the growing pile of her mail that needed to be returned to the sender.

I thumbed through the Houston classifieds after my shower and came across an Ad for a Human Resources Assistant at Capital One Bank not far from King Global. There was an immediate opening and the pay was competitive so I applied. I didn't think that I would get it but I figured it wouldn't hurt to apply.

For the remainder of that day I stayed in my room and became a prisoner of my own thoughts. Had I really seen Chico at that stop light? Or was he a figment of my paranoid imagination? I wasn't sure, but the fear I heard in Frankie's voice that day was terrifying enough to know that Chico still held onto the notion that I was the one that set him up and almost sent him to prison.

That night, our last encounter replayed in my head so vividly I could still feel his fists pounding into my face. Him dragging me across the cold hardwood floors of our apartment, and the anger in his stare when he drilled inside me against my will. He'd left me battered and trapped with a baby made from what only could be described as the pure hatred he must've felt when he thought I'd betrayed him.

Those same angry tears that I'd felt over a year ago slid down the apples of my cheeks as I stared up at the ceilings above me. I felt more helpless than ever before. Chico was on a mission and now I was sure that he would stop at nothing to find me and finish me off and; I couldn't have felt more alone. I was a sitting duck and was starting to regret setting him up in the first place.

FIT for a KING–P. Sharee

Veronica-20

Wednesday the Vice President of King Global needed someone to fill in for his assistant that had come down with the flu. Courtney from HR asked one of us to take her place for the rest of the week and because I saw that as an opportunity to get away from Roxy, I volunteered.

Coincidentally, that was the same morning Mr. King returned to work. As I was walking out of the ladies room, I took a few steps back and peered around the corner as Roxy greeted him before I departed to the 19th floor.

"Good morning, Roxanne," he said as he approached her desk.

"Good morning, Mr. King, welcome back," Roxy smiled.

"Thank you," he said as his eyes moved over to my empty desk. She read his thoughts from his facial expression, rolled her eyes and said, "Veronica is helping one of the VPs today; his assistant is out sick," she told him.

"Oh, okay," he said, masking his disappointment. "I'll be in my office if anyone needs me."

"Yes Sir," she smiled and he disappeared. Seeing him again for the first time after almost two weeks still made my knees week. The look on his face when he saw that I wasn't on the 20th floor where I belonged tugged at my heart strings a little and made me want to go to him, but I wouldn't let myself.

My day on the 19th floor hadn't gone so well, it sucked to put it more bluntly. After Ashley "accidentally" spilled coffee all over my cream blouse, I ended up wearing a black and gold 'King Global' t-shirt that I found in one of the storage closets which was almost too small.

As if that wasn't enough, the pervert of a Vice President stared at my ass pretty much every chance he got and had no real work for me to do other than go out and get his lunch and respond to some emails and help cover the phones.

I left at 5:30pm and took the elevator to the parking garage. As I quickly walked to my car, I made sure I looked around for anyone that may have been lurking. When I was close enough, I peeked in my backseat to make sure that there was no one inside. I heard footsteps and quickened my pace through the garage. Though I wasn't sure who it was, I rushed over to my car, started it up, and then locked the doors. I peeled out of the garage like a bat out of hell and didn't bother to look back, taking the long way home that afternoon.

When I checked my phone, I noticed I missed a call from an unknown number and there was a voice message as well.

"Hello Ms. Banks, this is Jenny Horowitz from Capital One. We received your resume and application and wanted to see if you were still interested in the HR Assistant position? I've left the office for today so this is my cell number. Please give me a call back whenever you get this message. I look forward to hearing from you, talk to you soon. Bye." The message said.

"That was quick." I said as I drove home. I definitely didn't expect to hear from Capital One, especially that soon. It made me really think about my options and before I could bat my eyes, I was returning Jenny's phone call and agreeing to an interview during my lunch hour the next day.

I needed to stand on my own two and make a life for myself, which was the reason behind my madness. I had been in Houston for about three months and still didn't feel like I was independent. My sister who I was living with had gotten me and job, and who also was having a baby. Then I started a relationship with my boss. At that point, my future with Nate was uncertain and even if by some miracle we made our way back to each other; I wanted to be my own woman and not be known as his assistant that he started sleeping with.

I ended up working on the 19th floor again the following day and didn't mind it actually. I didn't have to see Nate and pretend to do my work with him in the very next room; and I didn't have to endure Roxy's constant glances in my direction or her snarky little comments. I was actually able to do the minimal assignments that were asked of me by the VP and once those were done I was able to surf the Internet for jobs and even started looking at apartment listings downtown, uptown, and near the galleria area.

For lunch Jenny and I decided to meet at Arista, the same place that Alaina and I had had lunch at a couple weeks before. It was a nice restaurant and was close to King Global which made it an ideal location for a quick lunch interview.

"Yes, I'm supposed to be meeting Jennifer Horowitz." I said when I approached the hostess.

"Yes, of course Ms. Banks, Mrs. Horowitz is expecting you. Right this way, please," the young lady said and led me through the main dining room to the rear of the restaurant to a more private table. When we reached the table, an average sized white woman sat at the table. Her thick blonde hair rested on her shoulders in a sleek inverted bob but her roots were graying. She was dressed in a gray Dior pant suit and her lips were painted with crimson lipstick.

"Veronica Banks?" her raspy yet husky voice said when she looked up at me.

"Yes, Mrs. Horowitz."

"Please, call me Jenny," she stood up from her seat with a smile revealing the creases at the corners of her eyes. "I'm glad you could make it on such short notice dear, please have a seat." She said after she shook my hand and then we both sat down.

"So, Veronica, let's get right down to business because I know this is your lunch hour. Why don't you tell me a little bit about yourself?" she told me diving right into her questions.

"Well, I'm currently an Executive Administrative Assistant for the owner and CEO of King Global; I've been there for almost three months."

"And why do you want to leave? Are you unhappy?" she interrupted.

"To be honest Jenny, my sister got me the job and I kinda would like to start off on my own and actually use my degree. I've always been interested in HR and I think that a position like this would give me a chance to work more with people, which I love," I embellished.

"I see," she grinned a little and then took a sip of her coffee. I went on to tell her what my job entailed and then she gave me a more detailed description of the job that was available. After we ordered our food, we ended up spending the remainder of the interview just laughing and talking about whatever. I liked Jenny a lot and I could tell she liked me. She was really down to earth and didn't make me feel uncomfortable for a second like a lot of interviewers were known for.

"I have to ask, what is it like working for that delicious specimen, Nathaniel King?" she blurted out and I almost spit out my drink at her candidness. "You can't tell me you haven't fantasized about the...package he must have on him," she continued and I almost lost it.

"Um," I started to say but could not find words.

"I mean, how do you ladies get any work done around that place?"

"Believe me, it's not without difficulty," I assured her, trying not to smile.

"I like you, Veronica," Jenny told me with honest eyes.

"I like you too," I told her truthfully

"Well, as far as I'm concerned honey, the job is yours."

"Really?" I said, unable to hide the excitement in my voice.

"Yes ma'am. When can you start?" she asked, opening her leather portfolio that she had brought with her but hadn't touched except for then. She removed the fountain pen that was wedged neatly in the center of the binder and was about to write down my tentative start date. "Two weeks?"

"Can I let you know Monday?" I asked.

"That's fine with me," she smiled over the table at me.

"Thank you so much, Jenny," I smiled back at her.

"No problem. Thank you for taking time out of your day to meet with me," she said as we both stood at the same time. I reached inside my purse and pulled out my wallet.

"Put that thing away, it's on me. Well, actually it's on them. Expense it," she said playfully and we both giggled.

"Thanks again. I'll talk to you on Monday," I told her.

"Okay honey, you have a good weekend."

"You too." I told her and left.

On my way back to King Global, I couldn't help but feel a little conflicted. My interview with Jenny had gone exceptionally well and she offered me the job on the spot. That was something that I didn't expect and something that I certainly hadn't prepared myself for. I was quickly gaining that independence I wanted or at least that I thought I wanted.

FIT for a KING - P. Sharee

Nathaniel–21

Friday was even more awful than Wednesday and Thursday. I still hadn't gotten up the courage to call Roni. She was filling in for Peter's sick assistant for the past two days since I'd returned to work so I hadn't been able to see her. Instead, I had to deal with Roxanne and her brazen antics to get me to notice her. She seemed to have more confidence than usual and I knew that had everything to do with Veronica's absence.

Friday she was supposed to return to the 20th floor, to her own position. I gave myself a pep talk in the elevator and that morning I would break the ice once and for all.

"Roxanne, could you have Veronica come into my office as soon as she gets in this morning, please?" I asked Roxanne as I passed her desk when I got into the office that morning.

"Veronica won't be in today, Mr. King," she informed me.

"She won't?" I said as casual as I possibly could.

"No, she has the day off today, remember?" she reminded me.

"Oh right, it must have slipped my mind."

"Is there something that I can help you with?" she said with a hint of seduction.

"No, no thank you."

"Are you sure?"

"Yes, it wasn't important," I lied and then went into my office. "Ugh." I sighed and set my suitcase on my desk with frustration. I took off my jacket to my suit and tossed it on the loveseat. I was beside myself and could not focus. Roni and I hadn't spoken in about two weeks and even though I knew it was because of me, I couldn't help but feel like she was slipping through my fingers.

I loosened the tie around my neck and when I sat down in my wingback I tapped the spacebar on my keyboard, typed in my password, and a picture of Veronica popped up on the screen once it was unlocked. I changed it the day before we left to go to L.A and the picture was of her asleep in my bed peacefully after one of our long nights of love making. I couldn't help but grin a little and think about how good things had been between us until I abruptly brought them to a screeching halt. I forced myself to shrug it off and opened up the King Global database to work.

My entire day was a blur. I amped myself up on caffeine and got to work to try and keep her off my mind. During the morning I was drowned with conference calls and looking over designs for up and coming projects. The afternoon was filled with meeting after meeting and signing what felt like a manual worth of contracts, releases, and God knows what else.

I finally got to check my emails at around 4pm that afternoon and noticed that there was something from Roni. I ignored the subject line and opened the message immediately. It wasn't very long and I noticed that she had copied it to Courtney in Human Resources. When I reached the end of the message I sat back in my chair and sighed.

"You gotta be fuckin' kidding me!" I yelled, slamming my fist down on to my desk. She had emailed me her two weeks' notice and I felt all sorts of fucked up.

My thoughts spun out of control and I fumed with anger. I speculated on why would she be leaving her job but in the same breath I was sure it was because of me. My biggest fears of her feeling rejected were confirmed; and because of what transpired between us she probably felt like she couldn't work for me anymore. That was the last thing I wanted and was never my intention to hurt her or want her to quit her job. Aside from our personal relationship, Veronica did her job damn well and was a hard worker. Now I was driving her away because of my hang-ups and inability to stop living in the past.

When I left work for the day, I tried to mentally switch gears and prepare myself for my sister's weekend of wedding festivities. The first item on the agenda was dinner at The Capital Grille Uptown for the bridal party only. Alaina bugged me about showing up for the past three days so I couldn't skip it or any event being the best man and all. I tried calling Roni on the way because I was done with being in my feelings and we needed to talk. She didn't answer of course which definitely pricked at my pride.

When I arrived at the restaurant, the host showed me to where everyone was in one of the private dining rooms. That evening was intended only for the bridal party so the attendees included me, Chase (who hadn't arrived yet), Ricky and Alaina of course, Savannah, Alaina's friend Christy, Kyle who was late as well, our cousin Rachel, and Vince with his girlfriend Nikki.

When I snuck off to the bar, from inside I could see Chase was pulling up to the valet line in his brand new all white Audi SUV. The last time that he and I had spoken, he informed me had he had gone to the doctor due to a burning sensation he had whenever he peed. Now if Chase was a betting man which he was from time to time; he would have bet a small fortune that his little gift was from none other than Ashley.

During dinner I picked at my food and constantly checked my phones to see if Roni called back and of course she hadn't. I wondered what she had been doing and why she hadn't returned my call. My pride wouldn't let me blow her phone up like I wanted to, and a text message was too impersonal especially because of how we'd left things the last time that we spoke.

The night was pretty much a waste and I spent it half listening to the idle chatter and Chase telling me how he hadn't realized that Ashley had somewhat of a promiscuous personality after the little gift she'd left him with.

Afterward he and the rest of the bridal party decided to head to Matrix for drinks and I passed but assured them that they would be well taken care of and would get the full VIP experience.

I took a deep breath and sighed as I waited for the valet to pull up in my Mercedes. Before I climbed inside, I declined my family's final offer to join them and tried to call Roni again as I headed home but got no answer.

Instead of parking in the garage, I left my car out in front of the house in the circular driveway and dragged myself inside. I wasn't quite ready to call it a night being that it was barely nine o'clock on a Friday. Instead, I went into my home office, poured me a tall drink and sat down at my drafting desk.

As I sat and thought about the mess that I had made with Roni and me, I began to sketch a blueprint. It had been a while since I'd designed anything by hand but it felt good. It felt familiar. I stayed up until about one that morning and ended up sleeping in one of the downstairs guest rooms.

The next morning started off with an intense workout that was much needed. Not only was I lonely and had been missing the shit out of Veronica, I was also horny as hell and needed to relieve some pent up frustration. I took out my anger on the punching bag, then doubled up on the treadmill, push-ups, and crunches.

The pessimist in me allowed my thoughts to be tainted with the idea of her rejecting me when I did find words and told her that I wanted her and that I wanted us back. What if she didn't want that anymore? What if the space between us was enough time for her to decide that she didn't want to be in a relationship with a man who ran from his feelings? Or a man that she thought was still hung up on his dead wife? I hadn't given that much thought until that moment. After all, she had put in her two weeks' notice and was making plans to leave King Global, maybe that was her way of leaving me, too.

As Ricky's best man, I was in charge of the bachelor party but almost dreaded attending it. My thoughts were consumed with the day ahead and when I would get to see Roni. I didn't drop the ball though. I arranged for 'The Men's Club' to be reserved strictly for the bachelor party and had plenty of private dancers for the attendees.

Vince and Chase seemed to be having the most fun of all of us and everyone else was just drinking and chilling.

I kept myself busy on the phone handling business calls and checking emails. I could have cared less about the dancers because the only woman that I wanted to strip for me wasn't too happy with me at the moment. Watching my friends and brother enjoy themselves was enough for me, but being in the club did give me an idea and I had to make another phone call while the thought was fresh in my head.

The strip club was supposed to be followed by a few drinks at the bar of the Four Seasons Houston, and then we would call it a night at the penthouse suit where the groom, his best man, and groomsman would be staying.

After piling my drunk brother and friends into the two Escalades that we took to 'The Men's Club', I went back in to the club to settle the bill and as I came out I saw that Kyle was jogging across the street to an unfamiliar black Camaro with a female driver…and Traci drove a silver-blue Dodge Avenger.

FIT for a KING- *P. Sharee*

Nathaniel-22

The next day I was up before the sun. My insomnia got the best of me and I needed to make peace with the decision that I had already made in my mind. After making a quick stop, I headed to Forest Park East Cemetery while the rest of the penthouse was still snoring and scratching themselves.

I arrived close to seven that morning and parked on the opposite side of the road. As I held on tight to the lilies that I brought with me, Lauren's favorite flower, I took a deep breath as I approached her and Kristina's headstones.

"I know it's been a few months since I've been out here, but it's something that's been weighing heavy on my heart, Lauren," I began and then kneeled down onto the moist grass.

"I miss you and Kristina every day and sometimes I still can't believe that you're gone but I've convinced myself that you're in a better place now and I'm learning to live with that," I said and gently placed a bouquet in front of each headstone, then continued to talk.   "Krissy, daddy misses you so much. I can still hear your little laugh sometimes, or the way you use to give me raspberries on my cheeks to wake me up in the morning. I know you're in a better place and I love you to pieces." I said getting choked up on my words. "L, I've been having dreams again, and I can't help but think that they have everything to do with the fact that I met someone and I told her that I love her. Ever since then I've been feeling like telling her that, I was being unfaithful to you." I confessed as I let go of the lump in my throat and allowed my tears to fall.

"Other than you, I've never felt love for another woman and it actually scared the fuck out of me. I know that she could never replace you in my heart, but she is an addition that I feel like I can't live without." I sobbed and wiped my nose with the back of my hand.

"I couldn't completely let her in until now, until I told you about how I'd been feeling. I can only pray that I'm making the right decision and hope that I have you and Krissy's blessing. I miss you all more than you'll ever know and will always love you," I said and continued to kneel on the moist soil for a moment and just think. I ran my hand over my face to wipe away my tears. Only God knew how much I missed my family and how I would have given up every dime I had to get them back. But the fact was I couldn't and they were gone and after almost seven years of grieving, I was finally ready to move on and allow myself a chance at happiness.

The wedding was supposed to start promptly at two o'clock so I made it back to the hotel just before nine. As I approached the front entrance, I saw Kyle getting out the black Camaro from the night before, and so did the driver who turned out to be none other than Ashley. I decided to hang back a little and let Kyle finish whatever it was that he was doing before I made my presence known. I watched him kiss Ashley on the mouth, just as Chase had when we were in L.A. and then give her a pat on the ass before she climbed back into the car and sped off.

"Nate, what's up?" he asked as we made it to the door at the same time. "You're up early."

"Looks like you are, too." I said.

"Yeah, I am. I had a few things to handle last night. I texted Rick."

"A few things like what? Handling Ashley?" I said and he rubbed the back of his head and chuckled.

"Something like that," was his response.

"What the fuck are you doing, Kyle? I thought you were working things out with Traci."

"I am," he sighed.

"How are you when you still fucking around with other females? And Ashley of all people, who's fucking Chase by the way." I informed him and judging by the expression on his face he was not aware of that little detail.

"It was just one time, you know how I feel about Traci, man."

"I know how you say you feel, but your actions are saying something different." I said as I pressed the button for the elevator.

"I know, I keep fucking up but she dropped a bomb on me a few days ago and I haven't been right since," he said as I entered the code on the elevator for the penthouse.

"What bomb?" I was curious.

"She's pregnant," he said, which wasn't all that shocking.

"All the more reason to do right by her, man. She loves your dumb ass, man the fuck up."

"I know. What's with this profound loyalty you have for Traci anyway? I'm your family. Or is it because she's Roni's sister?"

"I like Traci and she deserves a good dude and since she chose you, I'm gon' call you on your bullshit whenever I see you fucking up. And also because she's Veronica's sister." I added.

"Yeah, I already know," he grinned.

⚛

I was as anxious as a kid on Christmas day to see Roni again. Being away from her for all those days was supposed to help me clear my head, but in actuality it made me think about her that much more. I missed her smile, her laugh, her voice, even the way she smelled...

Our first encounter was when I saw her at the church during the actual wedding ceremony. She looked beautiful as always and was dressed in a pale pink dress that was tight at the top and

179

flared at the bottom, stopping just above the knee. Her hair was in twist braids and in a flawless bun on top of her head, with just a touch of make up on her face.

At the reception after meeting and greeting what seemed like my entire family and friends, I finally got my chance to talk to Roni when I cut in on a dance with her and one of the male guests that was there.

"Hey, you," I said lowly as we began to sway to the music.

"Hey, you," she said quietly.

"You look beautiful," I told her.

"Thank you," she said avoiding eye contact.

"I tried calling you, a few times," I said, trying to sound casual.

"I know," she answered, looking everywhere but at me.

"Roni, I know I should've called way before now but I just..."

"Had a lot on your mind, right? I know. You don't owe me an explanation, Nate," she told me and finally looked me in my eyes with her glossy ones.

"Yes I do. I wasn't trying to shut you out, but before we left L.A. I started to feel things that I hadn't felt in years and it just got complicated."

"Complicated?" she repeated.

"Yes. Falling in love with you made me feel like…like I was cheating on Lauren or something. I know that sounds crazy, but it's true. When I met you, I stopped having nightmares about Lauren and Kristina's death and felt like I was…happy again and I didn't feel like I deserved to be. When I told you I loved you is when the nightmares returned and I felt like you were making me forget them," I said and she furrowed her thin eyebrows.

"You know I would never try to erase their memories, ever."

"I know. And I'm not blaming you for anything; it's just something I've been struggling with."

"I can't compete with Lauren, Nate, and I won't," she told me with a grim expression.

"I don't want you to. I've finally made peace with all of

that," I told her and we were both quiet for a moment. "How have you been?" I said into her ear. She looked up at me, eyes still glossy and said, "Not good." And shook her head. "Me either. I wanted to toss my computer out of the window when I came across your two weeks' notice. I don't want you to leave King Global. I need you there. I need you with me, Roni. I've been so fuckin miserable without you, baby. I miss you." I confessed. "The words to this song are how I feel about you." I said as Charlie Wilson sang his ballad 'You Are'. She broke our eye contact and was silent.

"Veronica, look at me," I pleaded and she turned her head to face me. Her big, bright eyes welled up with tears.

"I miss you, too," she said almost in a whisper. I bent down and kissed her lips softly then pulled away and pressed my forehead against hers.

"I am so in love with you." I told her with a pained expression and her tears fell.

"I'm in love with you, too," she cried and I wiped away her tears with the pad of my thumb.

"I promise I won't ever shut you out again, you have my heart. I'm not going anywhere unless you're right here by my side, you hear me? At work, outside of work, I don't care who knows about us. I don't want to keep it a secret anymore, okay?" I told her as I ran my hands up and down her sides.

"Okay," she giggled through tears. "I love you so much," she smiled.

"I love you more. Come here," I said, cupping her face and kissing her passionately. My hands left her face and I wrapped my arms around her waist and deepened the kiss as our tongues slipped into each other's mouths. I pulled away long enough to take her by the hand and whisk her out onto the terrace for a little more privacy.

"Did I tell you how much I missed you?" I asked from behind her as we leaned up against the cement balcony that overlooked the pool.

"Once or twice," she joked and giggled a little.

"I missed that laugh," I told her.

"You did?"

"Mmhm. I missed everything, hearing your voice. This neck. These ears," I said as I kissed those respective parts of her.

"Is that so?"

"Yes ma'am. These thighs, whoo, let me stop," I said into her ear before I let my hand move under her dress.

"Yes, let you before I take you somewhere and make you fuck me at your sister's wedding," she said and I felt my dick twitch and begin to harden from her words alone.

"You already know you never have to twist arm for any activity that involves seeing you naked, Ms. Banks."

"Oh, I know, Mr. King," she grinned.

"I wanna take you somewhere, special."

"When?"

"Tonight, right after the reception."

"Where?" she asked, turning to face me.

"It's a surprise, you have to trust me. Can you do that?" I asked, looking into her eyes.

"Yea but..."

"No buts, just trust me." I told her, placing my finger to her lips.

"Okay," she smiled and I kissed her softly.

"I love you," I told her.

"Say it again," she demanded.

"I love you," I obliged.

"I love you, too," she said and pressed her lips against mine.

I needed 48 hours alone with Roni so that we could reconnect without all of my friends and family around. I wanted it to be just the two of us with no interruptions.

As we walked back inside to rejoin the wedding guests, I caught a glimpse of what looked like some sort of dispute between Traci, Kyle, and Ashley whom I didn't even see at the wedding but had managed to weasel her way into Alaina and Ricky's reception.

Roni and I exchanged looks, and I held onto her had tighter as we made our way out into the hall to try and smother the flames.

"I knew it, I knew you couldn't be faithful! You are such a fuckin liar and a creep! I can't believe I tried to give you another chance," Traci cried as Roni and I got to where the three of them stood. Kyle had that infamous dumbass look on his face as Traci read him the riot act.

"Tray what happened?" Roni asked, rushing to her sister's side. Traci embraced Roni in a warm hug and sobbed uncontrollably on her shoulder.

"Kyle, man, what the fuck happened?" I asked. Ashley stood in silence for a moment and seemed to be stifling her amusement. Kyle glared at her but didn't say anything.

"Don't look at me like that, I didn't know she was in the bathroom stall while I was on the phone," Ashley lied with a shrug of her shoulders.

"I'm sure you didn't," Traci added when she lifted her head from Roni's shoulder and wiped her eyes. "All you've been doing since you got here is stir up shit-"

"Don't throw stones when you live in a glass house boo," Ashley began, placing her hands on her hips. Traci laughed to herself and Roni stepped in front of the two women. When I looked past them, I saw Chase coming from the men's room. He squinted his eyes at the group of us that were clustered outside of the reception banquet room.

"Ashley," Kyle began but she cut him off.

"Naw she wants to point the finger at you, but she's fucking Chase!" she blurted out and Kyle's jaw dropped at Ashley's confession.

"Bitch-." Traci said and tried to charge at Ashley but Roni held her back.

"Tray it's not worth it, come on let's just go." Roni told her. The sisters linked hands and went down the hall in the direction of the restrooms.

"You should go, Ashley," I advised her. She squinted her eyes at me and then marched off, practically stomping her feet resembling a toddler.

"It isn't enough that you want Nate's girl, you had to have mine too huh?" Kyle asked Chase with his hands in his pocket.

"Kyle I didn't know man, I swear," Chase said honestly with his hands up in surrender.

"Whatever man, fuck you," Kyle said and walked past Chase, bumping him in the shoulder. I just looked at Chase, shook my head and walked away to make a phone call. I wasn't the least bit surprised that he had gotten himself in the middle of someone else's drama. I did however find it interesting that even Kyle noticed Chase's obvious infatuation with Roni. He wasn't even trying to hide it anymore.

Once everything was in place for mine and Veronica's little getaway, I went looking for her. She was nowhere to be seen in the banquet room where the reception was dwindling down, so I headed towards the ladies' room to see if she and Traci were still in there.

Just as I was about to tap on the door, I paused at the yelling that I heard from the other side of the door.

"He's taking you on a trip and you two are back together just like that huh?" Traci bellowed to Roni.

"Yea, I guess we are. Why are you so upset?" she asked, raising her voice with her last sentence.

"Wow," Traci said sarcastically.

"Wow what?"

"You, you're so gullible Roni. He practically threw you away not even two weeks ago and now he's so in love with you? Girl wake up," Traci spat.

"Are you serious right now? Weren't you the one who encouraged me to give it a chance and said that Nate was a good dude? And now that Kyle has shown his ass yet again, I'm the idiot? That's not fair Traci," Roni said defending herself and I cheered her on inside.

"This has nothing to do with Kyle and everything to do with you not being someone's fuckin lap-dog Roni-." Traci shouted.

"You know what, I'm done with this conversation. I can't believe you said that. I'm glad I know what you really think of me," Roni yelled back.

"Right, run away like you always do when I need you," Traci said and then the bathroom door flung open.

At 7 o'clock sharp my phone rang just as Alaina and Ricky were getting into their 'Just Married' limo.

"Yeah...uh huh...okay." I said and then ended the call. My plan was going smoothly behind the scenes. I couldn't wait for Roni to see what I had in store for her.

"We love you all!" Alaina waved from the window of the limo and then it sped off out of the circular drive. Once they were gone, the valet pulled up in my Aston Martin.

"You ready?" I said, leading Roni over to the car.

"Yes," she pleaded with me as I opened the door for her.

"Damn, Nate, that's how we do it, huh?" Vince called to me from the crowd of wedding guests.

"You already know." I called back to him with a big grin.

"Yeah, I see you." he smiled.

I caught Roni watching Traci storm off from the large crowd of people and climb into the backseat of a taxi. The look on Roni's face was almost as if she wanted to cry but was too pissed to do so. My mission was to get us to the airport and away from the drama as fast as I could.

FIT for a KING — P. Sharee

Veronica-23

By the time we landed, I had given Nate a rundown on how Traci turned on me while I was trying to do the sisterly-thing and comfort her after the blow-up with Kyle and Ashley. He in-turn comforted me, mostly using his tongue to do so. He had also convinced me to let him blindfold me until we reached our destination before we got off the plane. I thought it was a little silly, but went along with it anyway. I also felt a sense of relief to know that if I was with Nate and we were no longer in Houston, there was no chance that Chico knew where I was.

The wind hit my face hard when we took off and even the air tasted different. Like it was salty and maybe we were near a beach or something. I wondered if we were back in Malibu but then remembered that the flight there was a bit longer.

Though California was a beautiful place and I enjoyed the time we spent there together; there was also a part of me where L.A. left a bad taste in my mouth. That was where Nate became distant and where we reached a turning point in our relationship. I hoped wherever we were on our way to would solidify our new commitment to each other and bring us closer so that L.A. would just be a bump in the road for the two of us.

When the car came to a stop, I could hear loud music from a beating drum accompanying other instruments. There were no recognizable words to the tunes but I could hear voices from what sounded like a crowd of people.

The driver door slammed and then Nate opened the passenger door for me and helped me out. I could hear the crash of ocean waves nearby, which told me that I had been right about the beach.

Nate's hands reached up behind my braids and untied the blindfold as I was pressed up against the car door and slowly removed it from my eyes. I blinked a couple times and then when I opened my eyes I couldn't believe it. Before us stood this amazing beachfront home that looked like something from a travel brochure. I was speechless as I took in everything. This spur of the moment trip was exactly what I needed.

He gauged my reaction for a moment before he took my hand and led me up the walkway to the entrance. The inside was even more breathtaking with the arched doorways in the foyer and throughout the rest of the house. There was a huge, open living room area with a wicker sectional for seating that opened right into the large kitchen. There was Spanish tiled floors and floor-to-ceiling windows throughout.

"Babe this is…amazing. Where are we?" I uttered when I turned around to look at Nate.

"We are," he said coming up behind me and wrapping his arms around my waist "In Cabo San Lucas."

"Mexico?"

"Yes, and right over here is the Sea of Cortez." He said as we walked right out onto the lanai where we could see and smell the ocean.

"It's so pretty." I told him. "What made you wanna come here, with me?" I asked quietly. He turned me around so that I faced him.

"Because this is where I was when we came back from L.A. I came here to try and get my head together but all I could think about was you. And out of all the places I've been to in the world, this has to be one of my favorites. So I told myself if I got another chance with you, this would be the first place I would bring you, the first place I wanted to make love to you again after our little hiatus," he confessed. I leaned up and kissed him on the mouth with wet lips. When I pulled away, he snatched me back and deepened the kiss by pushing his tongue in my mouth almost effortlessly and all I could taste was champagne and him. I missed Nate so much while we were apart. Those two weeks felt like two years to me. But once we were with each other again, all the bullshit went out the window and we belonged to each other again. This time we were in love and not afraid to say it. I loved this man so much I wanted to shout it from the rooftops. Being with him was like finally feeling like I was home. He was home.

"Señor King! Estás de vuelta?" I heard a Mexican man say from the house next door. Nate and I looked up in unison

"Paco, como estás?" Nate said back to him with a grin.

"Únete a nosotros spara una fiesta de esta noche, por favor?"

"You feel like going to party," he asked looking down at me.

"I don't care as long as I'm with you," I smiled up at him.

"Un momento, por favor?" he called to Paco.

"Si, si," Paco nodded and then he went back into what I assumed was his home.

Nate led me into the master bedroom that was decorated in all white with a king four-poster bed and crisp white sheets with a matching canopy. It had the same tile as the rest of the floors in the house and an enormous en suite bathroom with a tub and huge picture window overlooking the beach.

On the bed, there was a bag from one of the local boutiques and when I looked inside there were three bikinis in my size with matching cover-ups and sandals.

"So, this is a pool fiesta I'm assuming?" I said as I held up the two piece black bathing suit that I was contemplating on wearing.

"Every fiesta in Mexico requires pool attire." He grinned at me. "So, let's hurry up and make an appearance so I can get you back here and feast on this body of yours." He told me with a look that made me want to jump his bones right then and there.

Once we were changed, we walked hand in hand next door

to who Nate referred to as the Morales familia. He greeted them in their native tongue and I just smiled and tried to remember any Spanish that I possibly retained in high school but failed miserably. Their home was similar to Nate's except for it was two levels and their pool wasn't as big. They fed us a Mexican dish that resembled enchiladas and then we went out onto the beach for a bonfire and drinks. That was actually the last thing that I remembered because after that Paco's wife, Louisa, gave me this drink that had a hint of cinnamon and tasted delicious. I think I had about five or six of the shots and Nate had quite a few as well. We stayed up and partied with the Morales' almost until the sun came up and somehow ended back at his villa and had a drunken quickie before we collapsed in bed.

The next morning I was awakened by the sound of a phone vibrating from the night stand to my right. My body was so sore, it hurt to open my eyes. I felt like I could feel my heart beat in my head and my mouth was drier than the Sahara desert. I raised my head slightly and as I tried to turn it to the left, I realized that it was stiff. I got a glimpse of Nate who was lying beside me completely naked with the sheets bunched in between us.

I managed to roll over so that I was lying on my back and covered up my naked breasts with the discarded white sheet between the two of us.

"Ohh," I moaned in agony. My head was killing me and it was torture to keep my eyes open. Nate must've awoken from the sound of my moan and popped his head up and squinted at the sun that shined in from the large window and shear drapes. He opened one eye and left the other one closed as he looked at me.

"What happened last night?" I said and realized that my voice was hoarse.

"All I remember is we went next door," he replied.

"To a fiesta," I added.

"With Paco and his new wife."

"What was her name?" I asked.

"Lisa, no it was Luisa." he told me.

"Babe, I feel like shit."

"Me too baby. What time is it?" he asked and I shrugged my

shoulders. He reached over to his nightstand to look at his phone and then said, "Damn, it's almost one."

"In the afternoon?"

"Yea. We had to have a good time if you lost your voice," he grinned.

"I guess so. My entire body is aching," I confessed.

"I just have a headache. I'll go and get us some aspirin," he told me and slowly peeled his perfect body up from the bed. He went into the walk-in closet and retrieved his and her cotton bathrobes and tossed one on the bed for me and put the other one on and opened the bedroom door.

I laid there and stared up at the canopy before me. I did know that I was in Mexico and that was still exciting, but what had happened the night before was definitely a blur. I must have blacked out because I wasn't usually a heavy drinker, and even when I'd been drunk in the past, I always remembered a majority of what happened. This time I could come up with nothing.

Nate came back into the bedroom and shut the door behind him. He was carrying a silver tray with two glasses of what looked like orange juice and a bottle of Bayer headache medicine. He came around to my side of the bed and set the tray on the nightstand next to me.

"Sit up," he ordered and I tried my best. "Is that the best that you can do?" He stifled a grin when he saw that I was barely sitting up.

"Yes, I'm in pain," I said as my voice cracked and he couldn't help but laugh. "I'm hurting, don't laugh at me," I pouted.

"I'm sorry; your voice just sounds so cute like that," he grinned. "I'm sorry, baby," he told me and kissed my forehead. "Take these," he said and handed me four of the Bayer tablets. "And drink the entire glass. This is a hangover remedy me and Ricky came up with in college. It works every time if you drink the entire glass, I promise."

"Uh oh," I said before I popped all four of the pills in my mouth and took a sip of the concoction. It didn't taste bad at all and it was cold so it somewhat quenched my thirst for the cotton mouth that I had woken up with. Nate squinted his eyes at my hand as I drank from my glass.

"What?" I asked, my voice still cracking.

"Your finger is red, let me see," he said reaching for my left hand and when we both stared at it, we saw the initials "NK" tattooed on my ring finger.

"What the-?"

"You got a tattoo with my initials last night huh?"

"I guess I did," I said with wide eyes. Next I examined both of his hands and noticed that he too had a tattoo with "VB" tattooed on his ring finger. "Looks like we both did." I told him.

"What the hell happened last night?" he grinned.

"I have no clue."

"We need some answers." Nate said as we exchanged looks.

After our much needed bubble bath, I dressed in another bikini per Nate's request; and it seemed like I didn't have any other options. This one was lime green and had white polka dots. The bottoms were panties and the top tied at my neck and back. The cover up was white see-through fishnet material and stopped at the knee.

"Buenos tardes, Señora King, Señor King," the housekeeper said to Nate and me as we entered the living room. Now I knew my Spanish was awful, but I also knew that "Señora" meant "Mrs." and that was something that I was not. Nate and I exchanged looks and laughed a little then he said with a polite smile, "No Marisol, Señorita Banks." She looked confused and just nodded to him. "Come on baby, I invited Paco and Luisa over for lunch. Maybe they can tell us what happened last night." He told me as he took my hand and led me out onto the lanai.

The Morales' were waiting for us at the patio table and speaking in Spanish about something that was obviously hilarious to the two of them. Nate and Paco started talking in Spanish since his and his wife's English was limited. I watched the two men converse back and forth but my junior high Spanish failed me miserably so I sat an nibbled on a bagel while Nate got down to the bottom of what went on the night before.

"We got married?!" I heard him say in English and I

dropped the butter knife that I had on my plate.

"Sì," Paco said and continued his explanation in Spanish. When he finished the story he clapped his hands and was wearing a huge smile

"Oh my God." I said, holding my hand over my forehead.

"That explains the tattoos," Nate said and then let out a hearty laugh.

"Nate what did he say? We got married?! This is not funny, not even a little bit," I said all at once with panic.

"Yes, it is, this can't be legal. We were drunk as hell and there's no marriage certificate or anything," he said with a slight grin. I relaxed my shoulders for a moment and hoped that he was right.

Luisa looked at the both of us and then handed us a white envelope that she pulled out of her beach bag. Nate reached for it and then removed the piece of paper that was inside. There it was in black and white, our marriage certificate. It was notarized and an actual legitimate document with both Nate and my signatures.

"I can't believe this," I said as my breathing quickened.

"Baby, calm down. Here, drink some water," Nate told me as he handed me my glass. I took it with shaky hands and took a long sip. I closed my eyes for a second but didn't feel any better.

"Please excuse me," I said to the table and then practically ran back inside the house and into the master bedroom.

I couldn't get my breathing under control so I sat down on the now freshly made bed and put my head between my knees. Almost a minute later I heard the bedroom door open and then shut softly.

"Roni, are you alright?" Nate asked as he came around to where I sat. I lifted my head up with tears in my eyes and looked at him. "Baby, why are you crying?"

"Aren't you the least bit concerned about what happened last night?"

"I mean, I am, but I don't think that it's the end of the world," he told me as he kneeled on one knee in front of me.

"What are we gonna do? This is…a big deal, Nate, and it's serious. Why aren't you freaking out?"

"Because it's not the end of the world, Veronica," he said again. "And is it the worst thing in the world to be married to me?" he asked, taking offense at my reaction.

"You know that's not what I meant."

"Then what did you mean?"

"We just fixed things and we've only known each other for like three months."

"Do you love me?" he asked.

"Of course."

"And I'm crazy in love with you."

"What does that mean? That we're ready to be married?"

"We obviously thought that we were last night."

"Yeah, while we were drunk off our asses."

"All I'm saying is, let's think about this. Seriously think about it and if we decide together that this isn't something we want, I'll call my lawyer and have it annulled and it'll be as if it never happened. Okay?"

"I love how you're the calm one of the two of us," I said, looking down at him. He looked up at me with those enticing eyes and a smile that I couldn't resist.

"One of us has to be," he told me with a smile as he rubbed my bare thighs.

"I bet the Morales family thinks I'm crazy, huh?" I asked him.

"No, they understand. I guess they didn't realize how drunk we were and that we're still trying to process all of this."

"Did they leave?" I asked and he nodded.

"Come here," he said, pulling me to my feet.

We looked into each other's eyes and our lips locked like magnets. Every thought that filled my head temporarily subsided under Nate's intense kisses. He ran his hands underneath my bathing suit cover-up and then lifted it over my head and let it fall to the floor. I tugged his white t-shirt over his head and then he pulled the strings of my bikini top and freed my breasts.

"I missed you so much," he whispered as his lips brushed up against mine.

"I missed you, too." I responded and pushed his shorts

194

down until they pooled at his feet. The last article of clothing that was removed was my bikini bottoms and then he turned me around and laid me back on the bed and used his dick as a sedative for me.

At sunset we had a candlelit dinner on the lanai.

"Babe, this is beautiful," I said, staring at Nate from across the table.

"I'm glad you like it. I wish we didn't have to leave at the crack of dawn." He told me as he sat his wine glass down on the table.

"I know, me, too." I replied and then took a bite of my tilapia. We both were silent for a moment and then he spoke again.

"Are you still upset; about us getting married, I mean?" He asked before he took in a forkful of mixed vegetables.

"To be honest, I haven't thought about it since we found out. You've managed to keep me distracted," I said with a seductive grin.

"I have?" he asked knowingly with this intense stare that sent a chill down my spine.

"Yes, Mr. King, you have," I flirted.

Nate had cleared my mind of all the marriage talk earlier by occupying me in the bedroom so I hadn't given it much thought. I was more focused on being with him and happy that we were finally getting back to us. I wasn't worried about anything, not even the fear of Chico that had been embedded in me since I learned of his release from jail. I was still conflicted on whether or not to tell Nate, and I knew Mexico was not the time.

After dinner we went for a stroll on the beach and the marriage talk picked up again.

"So, let's go through the pros and cons of staying married," Nate said as he held my hand and we walked barefoot with the white sand squishing between our toes.

"You wanna put a business spin on this, Mr. King?"

"I mean, I wouldn't say that, but let's weigh our options here."

"Okay." I said, shrugging my shoulders.

"Good. Pro: We're in love."

"Con: We haven't known each other very long so we don't

know that much about each other." I rebutted.

"Not true. We just got over a very large hurdle in our relationship and know even more than we knew before. You basically met all of my crazy family and I met the only family that you really have in Houston." He countered. "Pro: We have amazing sex and are very compatible. We're both business driven and we make each other laugh."

"I like that one." I smiled.

"Which one?" he asked, looking over at me. "The amazing sex?"

"No, but that's a given." I said and he threw his head back with laughter.

"Yes, it is," he told me.

"No, I was talking about the one about us both being business driven and making each other laugh. That's a good one, and an important one." I told him.

"It is. Any more cons?" He asked me.

"What about all your hang-ups about Lauren and everything?"

"I'm past all that and I know that she would want me to move on and be happy. I realize that now. And you make me happy. I can't imagine not having you in my life," he said, stopping us both in our tracks and looking down at me and holding my hands.

"Isn't there a part of you that thinks that it's ridiculous to marry someone that you haven't known for very long?"

"Ridiculous?" he repeated and dropped my hands.

"I mean, what would your family say? There was no pre-nup, nothing. Nate, you are a very wealthy man and I wouldn't want anyone to think that...."

"First of all, my family adores you, even you and Alaina are close and she hates everybody. All my friends were on your side while I was being a fool and putting space between us. And even if they didn't approve, I wouldn't care. I'm my own man, always have been, always will be. I don't need the world's approval for any of the decisions that I make. You need to stop thinking and worrying about what everyone else thinks and focus on your own happiness for a change, Veronica. We make each other happy and I believe that you were meant for me, I just wish you could see that," he told me and then walked back in the direction of the house.

I obviously offended Nate and hurt his feelings. I felt like a complete fool. I was head over heels in love with this man and whether we were drunk or not, we decided that we wanted to spend the rest of our lives together. That didn't happen every day. Drunken mistakes consisted of sleeping with someone due to being under the influence or flashing people at a bar, or even girls kissing girls. Not deciding that you want to spend the rest of your life with a person. And to top it off with something as permanent as tattoos? There was more to it than just alcohol. Our drunken actions did indeed speak our sober minds and I let logic and fear blind me of that.

When I made it back to the house, I found Nate in the living room with the fireplace going and an untouched glass of Jack on the coffee table. He had a fixed frown on his face when he looked up at me but didn't say anything.

"Nate." I said in almost a whisper.

"Yeah?"he said in a ghost like voice and then rubbed his hands over his face and I caught a glimpse of the tattoo of my initials on his finger and closed my eyes for a moment.

"I'm sorry if I offended you, it's just..."

"Don't apologize. It's fine. I'll call my lawyer in the morning and have him draw up the annulment papers; it'll be done by close of business." He told me and then got up and walked past me towards the master bedroom.

"Nate." I called after him but he ignored me.

He was really upset and I wasn't sure what to say. Part of me was willing to take a chance while the rest of me was terrified. The last thing I wanted was for him to feel like I loved him less than he loved me; because the truth was I would have done anything for Nathaniel King. He was a king in my eyes, my king now and I would have done whatever to make him happy, but in that moment I felt like I couldn't reach him.

I went into the bedroom and heard the shower running. The

steam was so thick; I could only see the shape of Nate's body from behind the glass door when I went inside of the bathroom. Without thinking, I started to peel off the sundress that I was wearing and tossed it onto the tile floor. I wasn't wearing a bra so once my underwear was off, I tiptoed over to the shower and then pulled the glass door open and stepped inside. His back was to me and when I pressed my chest up against him, I felt him tense up which was something he had never done with me before. I kissed his back and ran my hands down his torso. He stood still and shut his eyes tight as I touched him. My hand slowly grazed his wet skin further down until I reached where his pubic hair began and I grabbed his dick. As I started to stroke it, it grew hard and rigid under my touch and I felt him relax up against my skin.

"Nate," I said in almost a whisper. "Look at me," And he slowly turned around to face me with a pained expression. I pressed my chest up against his chiseled frame and looked up at him. "I don't want you to think that you're more invested in us than I am, or that I love you less than you love me. Because the truth is I never thought a love like this was even possible, and all of this is…scary." I began. His erection was pressed up against my stomach but his hands rested at his sides.

"I've never met anyone like you and sometimes I feel like it's all too good to be true. Like how could somebody like you who has everything and could have any woman that you want; want someone like me? Like what did I do to deserve you?" I said as a lump formed in my throat.

"Is that what you think? That you're not worthy of me?" he said finally, with his eyebrows knitted together.

I looked down but didn't respond. He pushed my chin up with his fingertip. "Do you know how amazing you are? How kind and sweet you are? How pure your heart is? When I first saw you I was ruined. Everything about you had me hooked and I was playing myself when I thought that I could just shrug you off and keep it professional between the two of us. Roni, you knocked down the wall I put up years ago; made me break all my rules. And now, after all this time I finally feel complete, so if anyone isn't worthy, it's me," he confessed and my tears fell when I blinked.

His words were like a song that I knew came straight from his heart. This man loved me with all of him, with every fiber of his being. I had never known that kind of love and it was more than I could have ever hoped for.

He cupped my face and brushed his lips over mine sweetly. Tears continued to fall and I closed my eyes to try and hold them back but failed.

"I love you and I don't wanna spend another moment without you," he said when he pulled away.

"Don't break me," I whispered as I looked up at him.

"Never. You are my heartbeat," he whispered then kissed me deeply. Without parting our lips, he picked me up and pressed me up against the wall of the shower and pushed himself inside of me. With our bodies we made promises to each other and showed the other that we were committed. And I wasn't certain, but I could have sworn I saw tears in Nate's eyes. They never fell but I thought that his eyes had a gloss to them as he made love to me. It was like he was surrendering to me and giving me all of him, giving me his heart completely.

Veronica-24

Once our Labor Day weekend came to an end, my new husband and I reluctantly returned to Houston. Half of me felt like the luckiest woman alive. I finally had a man that loved me and cherished me and treated me how I deserved to be treated. The other half of me was still indignant about mine and Traci's argument and wanted more than anything for my sister to share the happiest news of my life with me, but I couldn't. She was battling the mess with Kyle, the paternity of her unborn child and the best thing I could do for the both of us was to give her some space.

The return to Houston also brought Chico back to life. We weren't in Mexico anymore and I no longer felt safe back in Texas, even if Nate and I were married now. I knew I needed to tell him about the whole mess with Chico, I just wasn't sure how.

That Tuesday morning, Nate and I stepped onto the 20th floor still holding hands as we walked past the reception area. Both receptionists were on the phone but their facial expressions did not go without notice. We continued on to where mine and Roxy's desks were. I saw her and Ashley before they saw me and when the two of them looked up and saw our hands linked together, you could've knocked them over with a feather.

"Good morning…Mr. King," Roxy said slightly confused.

"Morning Roxanne, morning Ashley," Nate said as we stopped at my desk. "I'll see you in a few," he said giving me a peck on the lips. I nodded and he disappeared into his office. When I sat down at my desk and powered on my computer, I could feel Roxy's eyes on me and Ashley walked away in a hurry like her underwear was on fire. Roxy's facial expression when Nate kissed me was priceless and I couldn't help but feel a little uncomfortable.

When I looked over at her I said, "Good morning," And she just looked at me like I had called her everything but her name.

"I knew it," Was the first thing that came out of her mouth.

"You knew what?" I asked.

"I knew that you two were fuckin' around. Ever since you started working here he's been different. And then, the night at Matrix when you disappeared and I saw him outside after the riot, I knew better," she said in a cold and angry tone.

"You..."

"And then the trip to L.A. when you never checked into the hotel..."

"You're saying all of this to say what?"

"That you're a lying ass bitch who's trying to sleep her way up the corporate ladder, that's what I'm getting at!"

"You can't be serious. And, I am not about to have this conversation with you about what I do in my personal life. We're not BFF's so why would I confide in you about anything when everybody around here knows how messy you are." I told her.

"Don't try to turn this on me; you're the one that's a liar. You're seducing your boss to get ahead, how pathetic," she spat.

"I have an education, can you say the same? I don't need to sleep my way up anything. And you're one to talk, you said it yourself how you've been 'throwing' it at Nate since you started and how much you wanted to fuck him. Now you're pointing the finger at me because we're together?"

"Together? Honey, please, this little extended booty call won't last. He's not going to commit to any woman because he's still hung up on his dead wife so..."

"You don't know what you're talking about."

"Oh, sweetie, but I do. You'll be done and he'll be looking for another assistant and I'll still be here," she said smugly. We both turned around when we heard the door open that led to Nate's office.

"Can I see you two in my office, please?" he said in a stern voice.

"Yes, Mr. King," Roxy said, popping up from her seat first. He held the door open for the both of us and then followed us inside.

"Veronica," he said, motioning for me to stand beside him. "Roxanne, please have a seat." And then the smug grin faded away.

"I couldn't help but overhear the conversation that the two of you were having outside there and the first thing I want to say is that I don't appreciate it. It was very unprofessional and not the time nor the place to discuss such matters." he said looking at us both. I felt my shoulders slump a little but I remained quiet.

"Second of all Roxanne, there are a few things that you need to be aware of so that we don't have to have this conversation again," he said, turning to Roxy. "Veronica and I are very much-so together. We got married over the weekend. That's as far as I will go concerning my personal life but I felt the need to inform you because as of right now the two of you work together. The conversation that you were just having was, like I said, inappropriate as co-workers and absolutely unacceptable for you to speak to my WIFE in that way and it will not be tolerated under any circumstances."

"I apologize, Mr. King," she spoke up immediately.

"Your apology should be directed to my wife."

"Veronica, I'm…sorry."

"Look, Roxy, I'm not taking over or anything and I don't want to be your enemy. I know that all of this may seem like a lot, it's a lot for us, too," I spoke up.

"Exactly," Nate said, backing me up. "Try not to let this affect your work and everything will work itself out. In the meantime, Roxanne, if you could rearrange my morning schedule, Veronica and I have a few things that we need to go over. Hold all my calls unless they are of high priority, please," he instructed her.

"Yes, Mr. King."

"Thank you. That'll be all," he said as she retreated back to her desk.

"Nate, I'm sorry about all that bickering but she was really pushing my buttons."

"You don't have to explain. I know Roxanne can be a hellcat that's why I called you two in here."

"Oh. What do you and I need to go over? Should I grab the iPad?" I asked.

"No, this is husband and wife business."

"Ohh," I said. He took my hand and pulled me onto his lap once he was seated in his chair. He stroked my cheek with the pad of his thumb and kissed me on the mouth. "This couldn't wait until later, Mr. King?" I smiled at him.

"I rather do it now, Mrs. King."

"Do what?"

"Do you think we should take Traci to lunch and tell her that we got married?"

"I'm not sure that's a good idea. We need a break from each other. She was so nasty at the reception and I don't understand why. What about telling your family?"

"I wanted to wait to tell them all together when Alaina and Ricky got back from their mini- honeymoon. They'll be back Thursday. We can have everybody over for dinner then. I just thought that we'd tell Traci now so that she won't think it's odd that you're moving in with me."

"Ugh, I have to move now?" I whined.

"You're not serious, are you? There's no way that my wife is spending a single night away from me."

"I know that. I don't want to be away from you I just hate packing and unpacking." I told him.

"We can have someone do that for you," he grinned.

"Really? It wouldn't be too much trouble?"

"Not at all. Minor detail."

"Thank you, baby," I said, kissing his cheek.

"I love that you're so easy to please," he smiled at me and kissed my lips again. Nate spent the morning on the phone with his accountants and lawyers creating a personal bank account for me and whatever else he felt the new "Mrs. King" needed while I worked on some things for him and declined the job offer at

Capital One Bank.

At lunch I decided to go to Traci's apartment and grab a few things. I didn't want to run the risk of running into her and wasn't sure that she wanted to see me yet either, so my lunch break was a safe bet that we wouldn't cross paths.

I drove Nate's car, which made me a little less paranoid about my Chico-complex. The dark tint on the windows hid me from the outside and when I got to the apartment, I looked around quickly before I went inside.

I checked the mail like usual and I stopped on something addressed to that 'Yasmin Bishop' that had yet to forward her mail. It was a letter from the IRS and I was beyond annoyed. When I got inside, I locked the door behind me and searched for the "return-to-sender" pile that Traci and I had. It wasn't in its usual spot on the table and I wondered if Traci had already taken it to the post office.

Suddenly, I heard a loud buzzing sound and it almost made me jump out of my skin.

"Shit," I said to myself, placing my hand over my heart. Realizing that the sound was Traci's alarm clock coming from her bedroom, I rushed to the very back of the house and found the alarm and silenced the damn thing. As I turned on my heels to exit the room, I accidently knocked over a Manolo Blahnik shoebox and its contents that sat on Traci's dresser. Dozens and dozens of white envelops spilled out on the carpet and when I looked down, they all were addressed to 'Yasmin Bishop'. I furrowed my brows with confusion and wondered why my sister was saving all of this random person's mail.

I began picking up the envelopes and noticed that they were all opened. Skimming through the documents, I saw that Yasmin was in debt up to her ears and owed some of everyone. She had credit card bills a mile long and was using one card to pay off the other. I couldn't help but wonder why Traci had all of this stuff and if she knew that opening someone else's mail was a felony.

When I got up off the floor and tried to pile everything back in the shoebox the way I'd found it, I stopped on what looked like an old newspaper clipping.

"Oh my God," I said to myself as I covered my mouth with

my hand. It was an article about teenage shoplifters from 15 years ago and there were three girls' mugshots. Two I didn't recognize, but the third was unmistakable. It was Traci and underneath her picture read the name Yasmin Bishop.

The front door unlocking startled me and I dropped Nate's car keys on the bedroom floor. Traci was home unexpectedly and I felt like I was looking at a ghost.

"Back from your little vacay?" she said sarcastically as she walked down the hall after shutting the front door. "What are you doing?" she asked once she got closer.

"Is this you?" I asked holding up the newspaper clipping.

"What are you doing in here Roni?"

"Don't Roni me! Is this you?!" I yelled.

"First of all, calm down," she said uncomfortably calm herself.

"Calm down?! Who are you? You're this Yasmin Bishop whose mail has been coming here since before I moved in here?! Who you said was a former tenant, but it's you! You're her-."

"Roni," she said but I wouldn't let her get a word in.

"Don't say my name! You are a fraud! You've been lying to me all this time, telling me that you were my sister but you're not! I trusted you; I came here to live with you!" I screamed. I was furious and crying uncontrollably by then. I didn't even know who I was looking at. Her eyes were filled with tears now and her fists were clenched at her sides.

"I gotta get out of here," I said bending down to pick up the car keys off of the floor.

"Wait, let me explain," she pleaded.

"There's nothing to explain," I sniffled. I let the piece of paper fall to the floor and then shuffled past her to the front door.

"Roni please! I'm just like you! I lost my family too-."

"Stay away from me!" I yelled and then slammed the door behind me.

Nathaniel-25

Thursday came faster than we anticipated. I was working like a Hebrew slave every day in the office and up to my nose in meetings with the board, conference calls with companies overseas, and looking over job bids for the month.

Meanwhile, my new wife wasn't quite herself. She was more quiet than usual and whenever were out or leaving the office, I would catch her looking over her shoulder or jumping at the sound of a door closing. When I asked her what was bothering her, she offered evasive and empty answers or distracted me with sex. She had however been keeping herself busy with working on making sure that everything would be perfect for dinner with her new in-laws. She'd even gone so far as to take off a half day of work so that she could get home and start the necessary preparations for that evening. On my way home, I couldn't stop thinking about the night before.

Roni decided to take her lunch break to go and change her name down at the social security office and the DMV on her driver's license. I offered to come with her but she declined and went alone. It was raining cats and dogs all day but she insisted that it wouldn't take her long and a little rain never hurt anyone. With a stream of bad luck which included a flat tire and locking her keys in the car, she surrendered and called me.

FIT *for a* KING- *P. Sharee*

A couple days before, I stashed a little blue box from Tiffany in the drawer of my nightstand when Roni wasn't around. When I came out of the shower that evening wearing only a white towel around my waist, I looked at Roni who couldn't have looked more sexy to me in that moment. She had a make-up free face which I loved; and she was sitting up in bed reading a book on her iPad with my reading glasses on her face. Her braids were up on top of her head as usual and she just looked amazing to me. She looked up when she saw me and had a sweet smile on her face.

"You look so sexy sitting there reading quietly." I told her.

"I do?" she asked surprised.

"Mmhm." I grinned and then let my towel fall to the floor, revealing my hard throbbing dick. "See." I said and her eyes trailed from my face down to my dick that was eye level with her from where she sat on the king size bed.

"I see," she said licking her lips and still not making eye contact with me.

I picked up the iPad and sat it on the nightstand then climbed on top of her. She willingly laid back and allowed me to undress her which wasn't hard since she was only wearing boy shorts and a tank top.

Once we were in the middle of the bed, I reached over and turned out the lights and kissed her lips passionately as I spread her legs. I continued to kiss her and reached my hand down between us and found that she was already slick for me. I lifted up just a little and then slid inside of her and she fit me like a glove now. Her pussy was so warm and greedy, her muscles gripped me instantly and I knew I wouldn't last very long if she kept this up.

"God, baby, I love you so much." I confessed.

"Ooohh baby, I love you, too. You're too good to me," she told me.

"I could never give you enough, never." I whispered in her ear as I stroked her deep.

"You already do," she said and nibbled on my neck which drove me crazy and she knew it. I pushed deeper inside of her and reached over to my nightstand and opened the drawer. "What are you doing?" She asked short of breath.

208

I took the blue box and laid it next to her head and opened it. I removed the 5- carat princess, cushion cut diamond ring. She looked at me and then saw the ring in my hand.

"This is just a small token of my appreciation and how much I love you. I figured you should have a proper diamond." I told her and then slid it onto her ring finger over her still tender tattoo that displayed my initials.

"Nate, oh my God!" she gasped and wrapped her legs around me.

"And," I said, reaching into the box and pulling out the matching platinum wedding band with diamonds all around it, then sliding it on the same finger. "This is so you remember you are my queen now and there's no living without you." A single tear rolled down her cheek and she pulled my face closer to hers and kissed me hard and caressed my head. I continued to thrust inside her until we both exploded and came undone together.

I made it home a little after six and my family was told to arrive promptly at seven that evening. The sound system was playing some soft instrumental jazz music throughout the house and the aroma of food complimented it all.

I found Roni in the kitchen putting the finishing touches on what looked like some hors d'oeuvres. Her braids were in a neat bun, like she had worn to Alaina's wedding and she was wearing a white pencil dress that had a black pattern at the front of the waist and that wrapped around and down the sides. She had on a pair of black Christian Louboutin's that had white and black straps all over and the only jewelry she was wearing was her engagement, wedding rings and some white pearls in her ears. A newly stocked closet was one of my wedding gifts to her and that dress alone had paid for whatever I'd spent. Her multi-carat diamond ring was blinding and she didn't even flaunt it, for fear of showing off.

When she looked up at me, her face relaxed from the focused look she was wearing as she put the finishing touches on what she was making.

"My baby is always working hard even outside of the office," I said, setting my briefcase down in one of the kitchen chairs then going over to where she stood. When I reached her I rested my hand on her hip and kissed behind her ear. "Hello, my wife."

"Hello, my husband," she responded and then turned to put the tin tray of hors d'oeuvres in the top half of the double oven. When she turned around she gave me a peck on the lips and attempted to walk away until I stopped her.

"I haven't seen you since noon and that's all I get?" I objected. I wrapped my arms around her tiny waist and kissed her to show her how much I missed her. It started off hard with extra wet lips then quickly turned into slow and sensual. I could have undressed her right there in the kitchen and made love to her on the countertop.

"Mmm," she said, pulling away then wiping both of our mouths and returning back to what she was doing.

I tried to convince her. I knew that it bothered Roni that her only real family member wouldn't be there when we told my family that we had gotten married. It was apparent that Traci seemed less than thrilled and even though she hadn't verbalized it, I knew that it bothered Roni that she didn't seem to have the support of her sister. I almost thought that it bothered me more than it bothered her that she had no relationship with her mother and never knew her father. I was beginning to realize that my wife was stronger that I gave her credit for.

When I went into the living room and made myself a drink, I noticed that there were three bottles of wine chilling at the bar. Earlier in the week, she asked about my mother's likes and dislikes and made a list so that she wouldn't forget. She picked up a couple bouquets of white tulips and placed them strategically all over the house along with a few other of her subtle little touches.

Just as I was adding ice to my Jack and Coke, the doorbell rang. I glanced at my watch again and saw that it was about 6:30 pm.

"How come you're never this early for work?" I teased Alaina when I saw her and Ricky on my door step.

"I make my own schedule, smart ass." Alaina said, unable to hold back a laugh at my remark. She playfully pushed my shoulder and then walked past me, her heels clacking on the marble floors as she headed into the kitchen.

"That's the woman you decided to spend the rest of your life with, huh?" I said to Ricky as he came inside.

"Aww, you got jokes?" He smiled.

"Whasup bro, how was the honeymoon?" I chuckled as we shook hands and half hugged each other.

"Not long enough." He said with raised brows. "Y'all got it smelling good in here."

"That's Roni, she's been hiding her cooking talents from me until now I guess."

"Well, tell her to share the wealth and give Alaina a couple of lessons." He joked and I threw my head back with laughter.

"I'm going to tell her you said that." I teased as we entered the living room. "Ay, man, you want a drink?"

"Yeah, I'll take whatever you sipping." Ricky told me and I used the tongs in the ice bucket to put a couple of cubes in a glass identical to mine and made him a drink. I allowed Ricky to give me the PG version of him and Alaina's honeymoon and told him how I had whisked Roni off to my villa in Cabo over the weekend.

"How'd she like that? I bet she was surprised?"

"Aww, man, she loved it. We had a great time, neither one of us wanted to leave." I said with a huge grin.

"That's whasup. I'm glad y'all worked it out. I like Roni; I think she's good for you, Nate, man. I can tell she makes you happy."

"Yeah, she does. I can't imagine life without her." I told him.

"I know the feeling."

"I wasn't going to say anything until everybody got here but..."

"What's going on?" Ricky asked, intrigued in what I was about to say next.

"When we were in Mexico…we got married." I said low so that only the two of us could hear. He damn near dropped his glass and cleared his throat before he spoke again.

"No bullshit?"

"No bullshit." I told him and showed him my ring finger that displayed my tattoo with "VB" initials.

211

"Damn, that's…that's great! Congrats," he said, hugging me.

"Thanks. I know it's probably up there on the list of craziest shit that I've ever done but…it feels so right with Roni and I love her so much. I'm talking about think-about-her-every-day-all-day-can't-stand-for-her-to-be-away-too-long-give-up-everything-I-own-to-be-with-her-die-for-her kinda in love."

"Whaat?"

"The-best-pussy-I-ever-had-in-my-life-so-fuckin'-good-we-should-name-it type shit do you hear me bro?" I said and we both chuckled.

"Preeach! Damn nigga, I never thought I'd see this day again." Ricky told me.

"Me either." I admitted.

"What y'all in here talking about?" Alaina asked, coming into the living room with Roni.

"Guy stuff." I lied horribly.

"Mmhm," she said suspiciously. "I'm about to say the hell with Mama and Daddy and say let's eat now. It's smelling too good in here." Alaina told us just as the doorbell rang. I followed close behind Roni as she strutted to the front door. It looked like the cast of a dysfunctional black family sitcom on my doorstep when we opened the door. There stood my mother, Robert off to the side with both hands in his pants pocket, and Savy and Chase standing behind them.

"Hello, hello everyone," my mother said, greeting the entire room once she was inside the house.

"Hey, Ma," Alaina said, hugging our mother. "Hey, dad," she said to our step-father. We all exchanged casual hellos and then mingled until it was time to eat. Chase and Ricky talked amongst themselves over a drink while Savy and Alaina looked at some of Alaina's honeymoon pictures on her iPhone. Roni drafted me to help her finish dinner, and my mother migrated toward the powder room

Dinner was served promptly at 7:00 p.m. and Roni had the table set perfectly with the silverware and the square shaped plates that she found somewhere in the kitchen that she absolutely had to serve dinner on. There was a bouquet of tulips as the centerpiece and she made plenty of the chicken breasts, asparagus, and red skinned potatoes for everyone to have seconds or even thirds. The chilled bottles of wine were added to the table and after I said grace, everyone dug in.

"Veronica, this is delicious, did you make this yourself, honey?" Mama asked as she wiped her mouth with a napkin.

"Yes ma'am." Roni smiled shyly as she took a sip of her wine.

"Wow beauty, brains, and she can cook? Nate, it looks like you hit the jackpot, bro." Chase said to me while stealing a glance at Roni. She smiled politely in his direction.

"Don't I know it?" I said with a smug grin.

"It is really good." Ricky added and everyone agreed. I looked down at the opposite end of the table and gave Roni an 'I-told-you-so-smile' and she grinned at me and shook her head. We snapped out of our little daze when we heard a fork drop heavily on one of the glass plates. Everyone's eyes shot in Savy's direction.

"Roni, what is that flawless ROCK doing on your ring finger?!" She asked in a high pitched voice. She caught a glimpse of it just as Roni was setting her wine glass down on the table.

"Um," Roni began and then she looked at me with panic.

"What the..." Alaina said and got up from where she sat and rushed over to examine Roni's hand. Idle chatter began to fill the room and I took a sip from my own glass before I spoke up.

"Actually," I said loudly so that my voice overpowered the room. "That's why we had all of you over tonight." I said, getting up from my seat and going to where Roni was surrounded by my two dramatic sisters as they practically appraised the diamond on her finger. "Will you two go back to your seats, please? Thank you." I said, shooing them away. "Roni and I…got married in Mexico over the weekend." I finished.

"Married?" My mother said, raising her eyebrows.

"You did what?" Robert asked.

"We got married." I repeated.

"Get the fuck outta here." Chase said with a grin.

"Chase!" Mama said in reference to his choice of words.

"I'm sorry, Ma," he said like he used to when we were kids. She gave him a look and then returned her eyes to where Roni and I stood.

"Would you two care to explain?" Robert said and I gave him a look that sent a chill over the entire room.

"What is there to explain? We got married in Cabo and that's that."

"No need to get defensive honey, we just want to know what made you decide to get married so soon?" My mother asked sweetly.

"And how much alcohol was involved?" Chase added with furrowed brows.

"Chase, shut up." Savy told him.

"We were…under the influence but that didn't impact our decision. I'm head over heels in love with this woman." I explained.

"That's reason enough if you ask me. Congratulations, baby." Mama said and was the first one to hug Roni and me.

"Thank you." Roni said to her.

"Thanks, Ma." I said and kissed her cheek.

"You're welcome, baby. I'm happy for you both," she told us with a genuine smile.

"Sooo, let me get this straight; you two eloped after my wedding?" Alaina finally spoke up.

"Something like that." I said with a half grin.

"Leave it to you to try and hijack my wedding date Nathaniel." She joked.

"Technically it was after midnight so it was the day after." I said with a wink.

"Are you two sure it's legal? I mean, after all, it is Mexico." Savannah asked.

"Of course, I had my lawyers check everything out. We have a marriage certificate," I answered.

"So, it's official then?" Alaina asked.

"Yes." I said.

"Well, in that case," she began and walked back over to us,

"Congratulations," she said and hugged me first. "I'm so happy for you," she told me in my ear near tears. "I love you."

"Thanks, I love you too, now stop being a punk." I said with a smile. When I released her she hugged Roni next.

"Welcome to the family, girl," she told her.

"Thank you," Roni smiled.

"You stuck with us now," Alaina joked. "I'm really happy for you two and I know my brother loves you. And deep inside he's a big softy so don't break his heart, okay?" she told her.

"I won't," Roni assured her.

When I looked around the room, the rest of the table wore puzzled expressions. Chase downed his drink and then slammed it on the table before he stood.

"I want to propose a toast to my brother- in-law Nate and my new sister- in-law, Roni…," Ricky began and everyone reached for their glasses.

"Nah Rick, let me say something to my little brother and new sister-in-law." Chase interjected. "First of all, I don't see how any of you can praise this…this 'marriage' when these two were just broken up. Now, they're married after a drunken weekend in Cabo?"

"You're one to talk about being drunk all the damn time," Alaina snapped at Chase with squinted eyes.

"Oh, you going there with me? Or you want to tell everyone how your new husband been around town robbing Peter to pay Paul and how you've been paying all the bills?" Chase shot back. He looked over at Ricky with a smug grin who looked like he could've jumped over the table and kicked his ass on sight.

"Wow," Savy said, shaking her head and raising her wine glass to her lips. Chase decided he was on a roll that evening and decided to keep up with his little rant.

"Chase you need to calm the hell down, that was uncalled for." I told him as I stood with Roni at my side.

"Savannah, Savannah, you don't wanna go there with your big brother now do you?" he smiled smugly like he had some dirt on her too. She didn't respond, just glared at him through squinted eyes.

"Let's go!" I said finally pushing him out of the dining room and outside to the patio poolside while my mother and Robert started in on Savy and whatever she was or wasn't hiding while Alaina and Ricky left abruptly in the midst of everything else.

"Whasup? What the fuck is going on with you?" I asked him.

"Nothing bro, I'm good." He lied as he rubbed his hand over his face and shoved his other one in his pants pocket with a grin.

"Bullshit. You come in here two shades to the wind and the minute I say that we got married, you start gunning for the whole fuckin' family! What's up with that?!" I wanted to know. He chuckled to himself and then looked over at me with a frown.

"I just think it's interesting how you and Roni weren't even speaking last week and now this week you're married." He told me in serious tone.

"Wow, so that's how you feel? Weren't you the one who said that Roni was a good woman and all that?"

"She is. And for the life of me I can't understand how I met her first, but you're the one she ended up with. That shit is crazy." He said shaking his head.

"Am I hearing you right or is it the liquor talking? You got something you want to tell me, bruh? Are you in love with Veronica or something?!" I said raising my voice.

"What if I am?!" he shouted back. "What if I am and it was my fuckin' bad luck that my little brother stole the one female that I ever thought twice about away from me."

"Stole her? Y'all met once at a fucking strip club and never saw her again until you showed up at King Global, but I stole her? I didn't even know you knew each other until a few weeks ago but I stole her? Get the fuck outta here." I told him.

"You don't deserve her. You won't be able to give her the time that she needs or any of that. She's going to be unhappy just like Lauren was." He said and took another sip from his bottle.

"What?" I said and before I knew it I was charging at him and punching him in the jaw. Robert had obviously heard our argument and charged outside to pull me and Chase off of each other. Everyone else heard the yelling and came rushing outside.

"What's going on?" Mama asked. Robert was still holding on to me and Chase was wiping blood away from his mouth.

"Oh my God." My mother said, rushing over to him.

"You need to calm down, Nathaniel." Robert said in my ear.

"What happened?" my mother asked me.

"Man, let me go." I said, snatching away from Robert, my blood boiling at 250 degrees. "Ask him." I said, referring to Chase and then walked back into the house.

"I can still see where your heart really is lil brother!" Chase called to me with a chuckle. Roni was standing near Robert while he was restraining me and when I pulled away she followed me back into the house.

"Nate!" she called after me as I walked up the stairs. I didn't turn around and didn't respond.

I went into the bedroom and into my walk-in closet and started unbuttoning my shirt.

"So, you're just going to ignore me, is that it?" She asked walking into the closet.

"Did you fuck Chase?" I blurted out.

FIT for a KING– *P. Sharee*

Nathaniel-26

"What?!" She shouted back at me.

"Answer the question, Veronica." I roared.

"Where is all this coming from?" she asked confused.

"He says he's in love with you."

"What?" She chuckled to herself.

"I'm serious."

"That's ridiculous." She laughed nervously.

"Is it?" I asked and then turned away from her and removed my shirt.

"Yes, it is." She said, forcing me to turn back around. "I don't think its love that he feels, maybe lust. I'm with you. I love you." She explained and I felt my heart rate slow down with every word of her explanation and my breathing slowed.

"Hey, I'm all yours. Until the day I leave this earth, my heart will never belong to another man." She said taking off her wedding and engagement rings to show me her healing tattoo with my initials. "I mean, I may not remember doing this, but now I wouldn't change it for anything in the world," she said with a smile that melted the anger away from my heart. I closed my eyes and inhaled, then exhaled when I opened them.

"I love you, Mrs. King." I said with a serious expression.

"And I love you, Mr. King." She smiled up at me and I leaned down until our lips touched.

"Nathaniel?" a voice said that sounded like they were in the doorway of our bedroom. When we emerged from the closet, we saw that it was my mother.

"Hey Mama, I'm sorry about all that downstairs." I said immediately apologizing to my mother.

"Nathaniel, you know how I feel about violence, especially between my sons." She said with disappointment on her face. "And I know what your brother said about Lauren was unacceptable but you two are adults and should be able to settle your differences without putting your hands on each other."

"I know, Ma."

"We're gonna go, I just wanted to say goodbye to you and Roni and thank you for having us over. Baby, dinner was lovely and I will be taking me a to-go plate. I had to put me some food in some Tupperware so I can finish my dinner in peace," she said, turning to Roni with a sweet smile.

"Oh, you're more than welcome, Angie. I hope next time we have you over things will be a little more civil." She told her and then looked over at me with a tight smile.

"I'm sure it will." She said hugging her. "We'll see ourselves out," she told me and I kissed her cheek then she left.

I reached for Roni's hand but she stepped back so that my hand dangled and didn't touch hers and looked up at me with a look of despair.

"What? What's wrong?" I asked confused.

"So, you punched Chase because he said something about Lauren?" She said, recapping the discussion that we had just had.

"Yes, but it was more than what he said about Lauren."

"When did you hit him? When he said that he was in love with me or when he said whatever it was he said about Lauren?" She asked and I was silent for a moment. "That's what I figured." She told me and then stormed past me.

By the time she made it downstairs, everyone was gone and the heavy door was slamming behind them.

"Roni!" I said, now chasing her.

"Leave me alone, Nate," she told me as she marched into the dining room. She immediately started clearing the table and

220

emptying the plates when she went in the kitchen. I grabbed the rest of the plates and glasses from the table that she'd missed and took them into the kitchen.

"No. We need to talk about this." I told her.

"Talk about what? Talk about how you punched your brother out, not for what he said about being in love with your wife, but for whatever he said about your late wife? Is that what you wanna talk about?!" she shouted.

"Will you at least let me explain?" I yelled.

"Explain," she said, sitting the stack of plates in the sink and then folding her arms.

"Chase, he is a fuckin' idiot and he said that I didn't deserve you and that I wouldn't be able to give you the time that you deserved and…"

"And what?" she asked impatiently.

"And that you were gonna be unhappy just like Lauren was," I finished.

"What is that supposed to mean?" She asked, raising her eyebrow, arms still folded.

"When Lauren and Kristina were still alive, I had just started King Global and I worked a lot, way more than now. I was still trying to establish my company and didn't spend as much time with them as I should have. That was one of the main reasons that I took their deaths as hard as I did. I felt like I never got to do some of the things that I wanted to do with them, things that I never got to say. So when he said that, it made me think about if I ever lost you, I would have those same regrets." I told her. I leaned on the counter for support because I felt like a ton had dropped on top of me just explaining my feelings to her.

Her expression softened and she unfolded her arms.

"You never answered my question," I said, getting back to the original task at hand after I saw her visibly relax. "Did you fuck Chase?" I repeated. She looked down at her shoes and her shoulders slumped with shame. "Veronica, answer the question." I said with my arms now folded across my chest. I knew what the answer was before she whispered the word 'yes'. Hell, I knew when she tried to tell me back in Malibu but I didn't let her finish.

I didn't want to hear it then and I sure as hell didn't want to hear it now but I needed to. After her confession, the silence seeped in again and neither of us could find words to say to the other.

We went to bed without making love, which we had done every night since she moved in and pretty much every night that we spent together. Dinner with my family was a complete disaster and I wasn't sure what to do from there. Roni and I both had obviously been harboring some ill feelings about different things in our relationship that were still unresolved.

My fight with Chase wasn't much of a surprise either. Part of me knew that he had feelings for Roni since the day he met her, or at least the day I thought they met. And for him to actually admit that he was in love with her ignited an anger in me that I tried to bury years ago. I could have beaten the shit out of him if Robert hadn't pulled me off of him. It was obvious he had been dishonest about how he really felt and wasn't the least bit sincere about him being happy for us and wanting us to work things out. That wouldn't be the end of our little disagreement; he had some explaining to do.

By Saturday the silence was killing me. Roni returned home a little after noon that day from brunch with my mother and sisters, and I was in my office working at my drawing desk on the blueprint that I had started.

When she walked past she was surprised to see the door to my office open.

"Roni!" I called to her. She stopped in her tracks and I got up from where I was sitting and rushed over to her. She didn't say anything, just looked down at the floor. "Can we talk, please?" I asked lowly, my breath grazing the back of her neck. She still didn't say anything, just gave me a silent nod. I carefully took her hand and led her into my office. She took a seat in one of the chairs in front of my desk and I sat in the one next to it and took her hands in mine.

"I can't take this, us not speaking. It's driving me fucking crazy. I don't want things to be this way, I don't want you to be angry with me or feel like you have to compete with Lauren or any other woman. You're the only one I love and..."

"Nate," she said, interrupting me but I had to finish my thought.

"I will do whatever it takes to fix this between us and if that means selling the house, I will do it. I was only holding onto it for sentimental reasons and memories but I realize now that I don't need to do that because I will always have memories of my daughter's first steps and the day we brought her home. I have pictures and..."

"Wait, is that why you haven't sold it? Because it was Kristina's first home?" She asked with her brows knitted together.

"For the most part. I always felt like I never really got to be her Daddy and I just…," I said and then my voice trailed off.

"Baby, I never wanted to try and erase your memories of Kristina or Lauren. I understand that they were your family and I believe that you only worked as hard as you did so that you could provide and give them the best life possible. I just don't want to feel like I'm living in someone's shadow, or like I'll never be good enough..."

"I don't ever want you to feel like that. I love you more than anything, you brought me back to life and I am so thankful for that. I'm thankful for you every day. I don't want us to fight and I just wanna be your husband, a good husband," I confessed and got down on both knees in front of her.

"You are a good husband and a good man," she said, touching my cheek. I turned my face so that my lips were to her palm and planted a soft kiss there. She smiled down at me and I smiled at her.

"I'm sorry if I made you feel inadequate baby, you are perfect and were made just for me."

"I'm sorry, too; I know I was being a little unreasonable with the silent treatment and everything," she admitted.

"Pssh, you turned it into an art form." I told her and she giggled a little. "I missed that sound. I missed you." I said, wedging myself between her thighs.

"I missed you, too," she said as we leaned in and kissed each other passionately. When she broke the kiss she said, "Can we have make-up sex now? I've been missing him," she told me, looking down between us. I grinned and told her,

"You never EVER have to ask that question. He has been harder than Chinese arithmetic waiting to get to her again," and she burst out into a hysterical giggle. I quickly stood and reached down and tossed her over my shoulder.

"Nate!" she squealed.

"Don't try and have second thoughts now," I told her as we headed for the stairs.

We made love all that Saturday afternoon. It felt so good to be close to Roni again and show her that my feelings were sincere and how much I loved her with my body. From that point on I would make sure that she always knew that and that nothing and no one would ever have the chance to make her feel like she wasn't good enough or that there was any competition, because there wasn't. I had never met anybody like Roni and that was the reason why I was so crazy about her. The shyness mixed with the raw and natural sex appeal, and the bit of edge and feisty attitude that she had about her made the perfect combination.

I woke her up Sunday morning with swift licks from my tongue as I savored each drop of her arousal. Aside from how beautiful she was to me, especially in the morning; I wasn't sure what had gotten into me. There was just something about tasting this woman first thing when I woke up that made my dick harder than usual when I was in her presence.

"Mmm," she moaned when I finished but not before she came twice back to back.

"Good morning," I said licking my lips as she removed the satin sheet from my head when I came up for air.

"Good morning, Mr. King," she smiled. "You know how to wake me up on the right side of the bed I see," she joked.

"I can't help myself, you know…cunnilingus is my favorite breakfast," I said resting my chin on her stomach.

"I see," she giggled and raised up and we switched positions so that she was on top of me. "How about a little…fellatio?" she asked as she hovered over me. Before I could say yes, my blackberry rang on the night stand next my iPhone and the caller I.D. read "Courtney Miller King Global".

"It's Courtney, babe" Roni told me. She reached over and grabbed the phone and I answered while she planted soft moist kisses on my neck and chest.

"Courtney, this better be important," I said into the phone.

"Hey Nate I'm sorry to call on a Sunday but I have some information for you." Courtney's raspy voice said on the other end of the phone.

"I'm listening." I said as I palmed Roni's ass, anxious for whatever her next move would be.

"It's about Roxanne, your suspicions were confirmed. She's been making personal purchases on the company expense account that she has access to and I was just informed that she hired a P.I for some 'special project' which I'm not sure what all that is about."

"Interesting. Forward me all the documentation and have hard copies for me in the morning. I'll need you in my office at 9am sharp."

"Will do. I'll let you get back to your morning. Tell Roni I said hello."

"Alright Courtney. Thanks," I said and ended the call.

"Is everything okay?" Roni asked, nibbling on my earlobe.

"Not exactly." I said sitting the phone on the bed next to us.

"What's wrong?" she asked looking me in the eye.

"Tomorrow, I have to terminate Roxanne," I told her.

"What? Why?" she asked, wearing a shocked expression.

"Aside from being the known trouble maker that she is; she's also been making personal purchases on one of the company expense accounts which is completely unacceptable."

"Are you serious?" she asked in disbelief.

"Very." I told her.

FIT for a KING – P. Sharee

Veronica-27

When we got to work on Monday, I was less than thrilled about what was on the agenda for the day. Even though Roxy wasn't the most pleasant person to me lately, I still didn't want to see anyone lose their job. She was on board with Nate for a while and was good at what she did.

I convinced Nate to let me go to the Starbucks on the corner before we got to King Global to grab breakfast and coffees for everyone on our floor while he and Courtney dealt with Roxy. When the elevator stopped on the 20th floor, I had a drink caddy full of small coffees and in the other hand a box containing cinnamon bagels and scones. The receptionists looked relieved to see coffee and helped me with the box of scones.

"Thanks, Roni," one of them called to me.

"You're welcome; let me get this banana nut scone to Nate before he starts calling my phone," I joked with her and then walked around the corner to where my desk was. Just as I was setting the coffee and scones down, Roxy was storming out of Nate's office. When she looked at me, fury was all over her face and she looked like she could have spit nails at me.

"Huh, I figured yo conniving ass would be off somewhere hiding while your 'husband' did ya dirty work," she said, her voice icy to match the glacial expression that was on her face.

"Excuse me?" I said, turning around completely to face her.

"You heard me, I did not stutter," she said, shoving her personal belongings into a box that once held reams of copy paper. "Me getting fired has yo shady ass written all over it. But be clear, we are far from done. You may have won the battle but the war has just begun." She told me.

"War? What are you talking about? I'm sorry you lost your job but don't try and act like it has anything to do with me, Roxy, I've never done anything to you."

"Save it..."

"Roxanne, that's enough, please just get your things and go before I have to call security," Courtney said, stepping out of Nate's office.

"I'm going, I'm getting my stuff," she yelled at Courtney and she and I exchanged looks.

"Roni, let me borrow your phone for a sec." Courtney told me and I stepped aside so that I wasn't in her way. Roxy was still glaring at me like she wanted to shove me down a flight of stairs or something.

"Yes, can I have security on the 20th floor to escort a former employee off of the premises, please? Thank you." Courtney said and then hung up the phone.

In less than a minute, one of the guards that worked downstairs was stepping off of the service elevator onto our floor, as Roxy placed the last of her things into the tiny box and grabbed her purse from the drawer of her former desk.

"Ma'am." The security officer said to her with one hand on his glock and the other reaching for her.

"I'm going; I don't need your help." She told him as she picked her up box. That was when she realized that it was heavier than she thought and she would need his assistance. He smiled and showed the gold tooth that was a few teeth away from the front and bent down to pick up her box. He walked ahead of her and she swung her purse on her shoulder and walked behind him.

"Later...Raven," she said so only she and I could hear and then they stepped onto the gold elevators and left.

She had just called me by one of my old aliases I used back in Atlanta when I used to strip. How could she have possibly known such a thing because it was something I never discussed, least of all with someone like her? My appetite suddenly faded away and I was speechless. What did Roxy even mean by 'Later, Raven'? Whatever it was, it couldn't have been good and with everything that Nate had going on I wasn't about to bother him with Roxy's little ploy to make me squirm just because she was pissed about losing her job.

Courtney left and went back to her office to grab the files that she needed for the morning of interviews that were ahead of us; and I took the coffee and scones into Nate's office once I shook my look of panic.

Veronica-28

Nate and I left King Global together a little after 5:30 that evening and headed to Arista to meet his mother, Robert, Alaina, and Ricky for dinner.

"What's the matter, you've been awfully quiet today, Love?" Nate asked me as we linked hands and walked into the restaurant.

"I'm fine, just a little tired, that's all," I said which was partially true.

"Well, we don't have to stay long if you don't want to..."

"No, babe, it's fine, really," I assured him.

"Are you sure? I'm worried about you baby, you haven't been yourself for the past week. Talk to me," he asked with concern.

"I'm sure," I said with a half smile. "I'm okay I promise," and then I stopped in my tracks and touched his cheek then kissed him on the mouth with moist lips.

"Mm, gimme another one," he demanded. I gave him a warm smile then kissed his lips again. Inside I felt terrible that I was keeping so much from Nate. He was my husband now and he deserved to know the truth about Chico possibly being after me not to mention the Yasmin/Traci debacle. I told myself that I had to stop hiding things from him and I would come clean about everything that night when we got home.

While the hostess checked where our table was, I looked around the restaurant cautiously. A black Camaro that was parked across the street outside caught my attention and I squinted as the driver rolled the window down and flicked what looked like a cigarette out onto the ground.

The hostess escorted us to one of the best tables in the restaurant which was a large booth up on the second level. Angie and Robert were already seated and in deep discussion about someone or something when we approached the table and Ricky was stealing a kiss from Alaina.

"Hey Mama, you look beautiful," Nate said, hugging his mother.

"Thank you, Son," she said, hugging him tight and then kissing his cheek.

"Hello, Mrs. H…I mean Angie," I smiled, remembering her ordering me to call her by her first name.

"Hey honey, how are you?" she said, embracing me in the same motherly hug that she had given the ones before me.

"I'm fine and you?" I asked her.

"I'm fine," she told me.

"Hello, again, young lady," Robert said, greeting me as he always had with a kiss on my hand and a kiss on the cheek. I would have been lying if I said that he didn't make me feel a little uneasy. That was another thing that I wouldn't tell Nate because he already wasn't too fond of his step-father and that would only add fuel to the smothered flames.

"Hello, Mr. Hathaway." I said with a tight smile and then took my seat next to Nate.

"Thank you all for coming on short notice, I know you all are busy with your careers and lives and everything; but I had to pull the Mama-card today." Angie told us and the whole table laughed.

"Nonsense Ma, you don't have to do that we were glad to come right everybody?" Alaina said giving me, Ricky, and Nate a look.

"Right." I said.

"Of course," Nate and Ricky said.

"I took the liberty of ordering a bottle of Armand de Brignac for the table." Robert informed us.

"Are we celebrating something, Dad?" Alaina asked.

"Of course, we're celebrating two of my children and their new spouses." Angie informed us with a warm smile.

"Aww, Ma, that's sweet," Alaina told her mother.

"It is," Nate added.

"Kinda a do-over for last week," Robert said with a chuckle and Nate shot him a glare that could kill.

"I need a drink, I'll be right back." Nate said and got up from the table abruptly. I furrowed my eyebrows with confusion but then realized he probably just needed a moment and he wasn't always in the best mood when he got off work. Dinner with his family had kinda robbed him of his cool-down period so he probably was little bit on edge; not to mention that Robert Hathaway wasn't exactly his favorite person.

"Darling, I'll be right back." Robert told Angie and then stood up on his long legs and took a few strides over to the bar where Nate stood.

"Jack and Coke, please," Nate told the bartender.

"Yes Sir, Mr. King," the bartender said and got started on his drink.

"Make that two." Robert told the bartender and slid a $50 dollar bill on the bar. "Nathaniel, did I say something to piss you off?"

"When aren't you saying something to piss someone off, Robert?" Nate said smugly.

"That didn't answer my question."

"Is there a reason that you followed me over here? Perhaps to make yourself seem like the concerned and loving step-father that you aren't?" Nate asked with sarcasm and accepted his drink then removed the tiny black straw and took a long sip.

"I came over here because I am concerned, about you."

"For what?"

"This…this 'marriage' that you've gotten yourself into. You're going to have it annulled aren't you? I mean you couldn't possibly be serious about staying married to your assistant that you married in Mexico without a prenuptial agreement, might I add, could you?" Robert said to him.

"You have a lot of nerve coming over here acting as if you're concerned about anything. What I do and who I choose to do it with is none of yo fuckin' business so you better watch how you speak about my WIFE." Nate said, stepping closer to Robert who was a few inches taller than he was. "And second of all, there will be no annulment, no pre-nup, no post-nup, none of that. I trust my wife which is lot more than I can say about you."

"Your wife, you've know her for what? Five minutes?" Robert chuckled.

"I know her well enough to know that I don't need a pre-nup." *I'm glad she can't hear this conversation*, Nate thought. "So this conversation is over and read my lips when I say don't you EVER step to me about me and mine. And I better not ever hear you say anything out of place about Veronica or you and I will have a problem," Nate said and took another long sip from his glass then set it back down on the bar with nothing but ice inside. "Thanks for the drink," he said and walked away.

Robert had a smug grin on his face and took a sip of his untouched drink, then took his phone out of the inside pocket of his suit jacket.

When Nate returned to the table we all were talking about Angie and Alaina putting together a small wedding ceremony and reception for him and I.

My phone vibrated from my black Chanel bag that was seated beside me on the white leather seat. Nate's hand rested on my thigh under the table and I reluctantly reached for the phone. It was a missed call from an unknown number and I wanted to see who it was and what they wanted.

"Please excuse me for a minute," I announced to the table.

All the men that were seated stood when I did and I practically rushed in the direction of the bathroom. Once I was inside and knew I was alone, I redialed the one number from but got no answer. I set my purse down on the sink and tried to catch my breath because my nerves were starting to get the best of me.

Mine and Frankie's phone call still lingered in the back of my mind and I knew I needed to tell Nate what was going on.

Before I left the bathroom, I splashed some water on my face and took another deep breath. When I opened my eyes, Ashley was coming out of one of the bathroom stalls.

"Well, if it isn't the new Mrs. King," she said smugly. "I gotta give it to you girl, you are good, damn good," she smiled crookedly and tucked her sapphire colored clutch under her arm and began to clap her hands. I didn't respond, just watched her reflection in the mirror.

"It's amazing how you can go from hoeing in the strip club, to marrying a fuckin millionaire. That pussy of yours must drip gold or something," she said and then laughed to herself a little. It didn't surprise me that she knew of my days as a stripper, especially since Roxy had called me by my old alias only the day before.

I glared at her in the mirror but still remained quiet.

"You don't deserve a man like Nathaniel King. He's perfection, and you, you're like yesterday's trash compared to him," she declared, taking one step in my direction. "You will never be able to keep him, you'll never be enough for him. You'll never be Lauren," she added.

"And neither will you, so you can save your little monologue for someone who doesn't know any better," I said, surprising myself with my own rebuttal. "I may not deserve him, but the fact still remains that he is my husband, he chose me and he loves me, flaws and all. You think about that the next time you address the new Mrs. King, sweetie," I told her. I snatched up my ivory Birkin bag off of the counter and strutted towards the bathroom door. When I opened it, I gasped at the sight that stood before me. There was Chico, in the flesh. Not the ghost of him, not someone that resembled him, but the man himself.

My stomach churned with anxiety and my heart raced with rapid palpations. I felt short of breath and my palms grew moist under his intense gaze.

He didn't say a word, just gave Ashley a nod. In one blink, I felt her frail arms grab me from behind by the neck. Without thinking, my reflexes kicked in and I was able to free myself from her grasp and push her off of me on to the tile floor of the bathroom.

"Bitch, I'm gonna-," she attempted to say but Chico silenced her with his intense stare. While he seemed to be silent but still momentarily distracted by his puppet, I tried to make a break for it but failed. His large and heavy arms were around my body so tight that it he gripped me any tighter, he would have crushed me. When I opened my mouth to scream, he pushed what looked like a white washcloth up to my mouth so I couldn't. The last thing I remember was how disgusting whatever was on the washcloth tasted and being carried out of the ladies room before I lost consciousness.

The end...of the beginning

The DIRTY Divorce SERIES

www.lifechangingbooks.net

HOT NOVELS BY AZAREL

LCB BOOK TITLES

See More Titles At
www.lifechangingbooks.net

ORDER FORM

MAIL TO:
PO Box 423
Brandywine, MD 20613
301-362-6508

Ship to:	
Address:	

Date: _____ Phone: _____

Email: _____

City & State:	Zip:

Make all money orders and cashiers checks payable to: Life Changing Books

Qty.	ISBN	Title	Release Date	Price
	0-9741394-2-4	Bruised by Azarel	Jul-05	$ 15.00
	0-9741394-7-5	Bruised 2: The Ultimate Revenge by Azarel	Oct-06	$ 15.00
	0-9741394-3-2	Secrets of a Housewife by J. Tremble	Feb-06	$ 15.00
	0-9741394-6-7	The Millionaire Mistress by Tiphani	Nov-06	$ 15.00
	1-934230-99-5	More Secrets More Lies by J. Tremble	Feb-07	$ 15.00
	1-934230-95-2	A Private Affair by Mike Warren	May-07	$ 15.00
	1-934230-96-0	Flexin & Sexin Volume 1	Jun-07	$ 15.00
	1-934230-89-8	Still a Mistress by Tiphani	Nov-07	$ 15.00
	1-934230-91-X	Daddy's House by Azarel	Nov-07	$ 15.00
	1-934230-88-X	Naughty Little Angel by J. Tremble	Feb-08	$ 15.00
	1-934230820	Rich Girls by Kendall Banks	Oct-08	$ 15.00
	1-934230839	Expensive Taste by Tiphani	Nov-08	$ 15.00
	1-934230782	Brooklyn Brothel by C. Stecko	Jan-09	$ 15.00
	1-934230669	Good Girl Gone bad by Danette Majette	Mar-09	$ 15.00
	1-934230707	Sweet Swagger by Mike Warren	Jun-09	$ 15.00
	1-934230677	Carbon Copy by Azarel	Jul-09	$ 15.00
	1-934230723	Millionaire Mistress 3 by Tiphani	Nov-09	$ 15.00
	1-934230715	A Woman Scorned by Ericka Williams	Nov-09	$ 15.00
	1-934230685	My Man Her Son by J. Tremble	Feb-10	$ 15.00
	1-924230731	Love Heist by Jackie D.	Mar-10	$ 15.00
	1-934230812	Flexin & Sexin Volume 2	Apr-10	$ 15.00
	1-934230748	The Dirty Divorce by Miss KP	May-10	$ 15.00
	1-934230758	Chedda Boyz by CJ Hudson	Jul-10	$ 15.00
	1-934230766	Snitch by VegasClarke	Oct-10	$ 15.00
	1-934230693	Money Maker by Tonya Ridley	Oct-10	$ 15.00
	1-934230774	The Dirty Divorce Part 2 by Miss KP	Nov-10	$ 15.00
	1-934230170	The Available Wife by Carla Pennington	Jan-11	$ 15.00
	1-934230774	One Night Stand by Kendall Banks	Feb-11	$ 15.00
	1-934230278	Bitter by Danette Majette	Feb-11	$ 15.00
	1-934230299	Married to a Balla by Jackie D.	May-11	$ 15.00
	1-934230308	The Dirty Divorce Part 3 by Miss KP	Jun-11	$ 15.00
	1-934230316	Next Door Nympho By CJ Hudson	Jun-11	$ 15.00
	1-934230286	Bedroom Gangsta by J. Tremble	Sep-11	$ 15.00
	1-934230340	Another One Night Stand by Kendall Banks	Oct-11	$ 15.00
	1-934230359	The Available Wife Part 2 by Carla Pennington	Nov-11	$ 15.00
	1-934230332	Wealthy & Wicked by Chris Renee	Jan-12	$ 15.00
	1-934230375	Life After a Balla by Jackie D.	Mar-12	$ 15.00
	1-934230251	V.I.P. by Azarel	Apr-12	$ 15.00
	1-934230383	Welfare Grind by Kendall Banks	May-12	$ 15.00
	1-934230413	Still Grindin' by Kendall Banks	Sep-12	$ 15.00
	1-934230391	Paparazzi by Miss KP	Oct-13	$ 15.00
	1-93423043X	Cashin' Out by Jai Nicole	Nov-12	$ 15.00
	1-934230634	Welfare Grind Part 3 by Kendall Banks	Mar-13	$15.00
	1-934230642	Game Over by Winter Ramos	Apr-13	$15.99
	1-934230618	My Counterfeit Husband by Carla Pennington	Aug-14	$ 15.00
	1-93423060X	Mistress Loose by Kendall Banks	Oct-13	$ 15.00
	1-934230626	Dirty Divorce Part 4	Jan-14	$ 15.00
	1-934230596	Left for Dead by Ebony Canion	Feb-14	$ 15.00
	1-934230456	Charm City by C. Flores	Mar-14	$ 15.00
	1-934230499	Pillow Princess by Avery Goode	Aug-14	$ 15.00
			Total for Books	$
		Shipping Charges (add $4.95 for 1-4 books*)		$
		Total Enclosed (add lines)		$

* Prison Orders- Please allow up to three (3) weeks for delivery.

Please Note: We are not held responsible for returned prison orders. Make sure the facility will receive books before ordering.

*Shipping and Handling of 5-10 books is $6.95, please contact us if your order is more than 10 books.
(301)362-6508